Cyndii
Thank you for everything
you do and have done
for me; including encouraging
me to write and publish this
book. Hope you enjoy it.

THE STREETLIGHT

By Matt Dever

TABLE OF CONTENTS

ACKNOWLEDGEMENTS

I would like to thank my close, personal friend, Andy Leclerc (Aerialflyboyz@gmail.com), for his photographic expertise with the front cover of this book. He came to my aid when I needed his expert assistance with pictorially capturing the essence of this book.

I would also like to thank my new friend, Sam, for vividly portraying the disturbing eeriness of the main character, Jasper, on the front cover of this book.

Finally, I would like to give thanks for everyone who supported and encouraged me throughout the writing and editing of this book. If it wasn't for their positive motivation and cheer, this novel may never have been published.

INTRODUCTION

When we were children, my brothers, sisters, and I didn't visit our family in Pennsylvania, that often, due to the distance between our homes. Our dad was born and raised in Pennsylvania while my mom was born and raised in New Hampshire. As we lived closer to New Hampshire and Maine, we made frequent visits with my mom's side of the family.

In May of 2016, my brother, niece, and I were in Pennsylvania to attend my grandmother's funeral. We stayed at our late aunt's house on Berry Avenue in Clarksville, Pennsylvania. We were all raised in an urban environment, so travelling the unlit, back roads of southwestern Pennsylvania was a little foreign to us. Even though my brother and I had our experiences driving down dimly lit country roads up in New Hampshire and Maine, the country roads in that part of Pennsylvania seemed eerie.

One night, as we were heading back to where we were staying, my niece was remarking about how dark it was as she was not used to there being an absence of streetlights illuminating the roads. After miles of driving down the road, we came upon a single streetlight. I remarked at how an isolated, country-road streetlight might make for an interesting ghost story. My brother spoke up and said, "Matt, you should write a book about it."

I didn't think much more about it until we returned home from Pennsylvania. I remembered a story I had made up, in 1993, at the summer camp we attended in New Hampshire. The story revolved around a converted sanitarium in Hartford, Connecticut and the mysterious disappearance of some of its residents when it closed. Seeing as how most of the people at that camp were from the New Hampshire area, the story was made so believable, that the creepiness ripped through all the teens in the cabin, who had huddled together to comfort each other's horror. I began to piece together a concept which combined the story of the asylum in Hartford, Connecticut, and the strangeness of that lonely streetlight on the dark Pennsylvania road.

My grandfather was a naval signalman aboard the U.S.S. Holly. As a child, I fondly remember sitting at the kitchen table with him on Blossom Street in Portsmouth, New Hampshire, while he reminisced about the days he was in the service. In one hand, he held an unfiltered cigarette, in the other, a ceramic coffee mug. I would listen intently of the stories he would recall from his days aboard that ship, while my siblings and cousins were outside galivanting around the neighborhood and frequenting Marconi's Market, on South Street, to spend their allowance on penny candies and soda. I would sit at the round wooden table, across from my grandfather, with both of my forearms resting on the table and marvel at the tales he would share. My grandfather would try to teach me Morse code, but I was never able to commit it to memory as I did

not put it to daily use. As they say, practice makes perfect and I was more

inclined to watch Saturday morning cartoons, play touch football in the street,

or partake in the neighborhood hide-and-seek rituals over practicing Morse

code.

I began writing this story using HTML, purchased a web domain, and posted the

evolving chapters on that site; sharing updated statuses with my friends and

family on social media. This was a huge test for me as I have been writing short

stories most of my life, but never shared them with anyone other than

schoolteachers who assigned composition papers for homework. I took a

massive leap of faith and jumped well beyond my comfort zone just to see if

anyone would find my writing entertaining enough to read further. I was

shocked at the success that my maturing manuscript received from those who

read it, so I decided to continue writing, fueled by the feedback I was receiving.

I had never intended to publish the story, but through consistent

encouragement, I found myself pressing on and eventually began the process

of publishing.

The story you are about to read is a work of fiction. Though most of the

locations and landmarks are real, any characters resembling actual persons,

living or dead, is purely coincidental.

No animals were harmed during the making of this book.

CHAPTER 1: WELCOME TO CLARKSVILLE

Narrow streets. Open pastures with bales of hay the size of monster truck tires. Towering maples and oaks. Roller coaster hills and roads. Quaint houses. Farms. Grain silos. Livestock. These are just some of the things you'll see in the charming town of Clarksville, Pennsylvania. A quiet, rural setting, plush with laid-back, country lifestyles and neighborly relationships. You will see people sitting out on their front porch, leisurely rocking back and forth in an antique rocking chair, holding a cup of coffee, just watching the effervescent behavior of familiar faces and out-of-towners passing by, and a dog sitting obediently beside their owner.

The educational structures in the neighboring towns are smaller than inner-city schools, and their population is made up of neighboring towns' schoolchildren who are bused in to satisfy their scholastic needs. The elementary school also serves as the junior high school. The high school is a scaled-down version of its urban counterparts. Stories are told to younger generations by their elders of how getting to school was so much more difficult in their day: the proverbial old tale of walking miles up steep hills through five feet of snow, while only wearing hand-knitted mittens, hat, and a scarf that, when unraveled, was the length of a bride's wedding dress train.

In Clarksville, you will see younger kids roaring through the main roads and wooded terrain on 4-wheelers or dirt bikes in the scruffiest jeans, FASTCAR shirts bearing their favorite driver's name, and boots that could be used for both heavy construction labor and marching through the woods to find that perfect prize game when hunting.

Clarksville's main grocery store is the length of half a football field, but has just the right number of amenities necessary to sustain a family's daily living. The parking lot consisted of three rows of white-painted squares wide and long enough to fit a pickup truck. Generic sale signs were plastered on the storefront's windows, and special seasonal items were placed outside in front of the store; lining both sides of the entryway. On the far right of the storefront was a mechanical rocking horse mounted on a faded yellow-painted box that had a coin-slot on the front. There were wooden shelves reserved for baked goods provided by local residents.

As you travel through the sidewinder roads, you are met with the all too familiar farm fragrances that are a potpourri of animal manure, dried hay, kicked-up dust and dirt, a tractor's diesel fumes, and whatever meat was sizzling on the barbecue for that evening's dinner.

During the morning, the amber sun casts an artistic glow on the pastures and trees presenting an element of pure peace. At dusk, the reddish-orange setting sun paints a slumbering calmness over the land. Clarksville only has one or two streetlights as you venture through winding and hilly roads, so if you were a visitor, you'd have to drive extra cautiously to avoid driving off the narrow roads. Locals are very familiar with these roads and are keenly aware of the locations the town's few police officers like to set up their speed traps; and wave humorously as speeders slow down.

Everyone is intimately familiar with each other's lifestyles and business. This was made evident by local gossiping women's knitting clubs and huddles of old men with their beer bottles in one hand, and cigarettes in the other.

Doug Miller (also referred to by the townspeople as "Old Man Miller") was making his way west down Chartiers Road. He was wearing faded blue denim overalls with a red-and-white plaid button-up, collared shirt (with the top button left unfastened) and a bright-white cowboy hat resting snuggly on his head. His cottony, white chest hair poked through the opened top of his plaid shirt like a dandelion in its reproductive stage. His face, wrinkled with age, and a pair of thin, squinty eyes looked from under an umbrella of fine, white/gray

8

hair that protruded out from his hat. He wore an overgrown mustache that swayed up and down when he talked; like leaves would do when there was a light breeze flowing through them. He had a strong, southern drawl accompanied by a distinguishable intonation when he spoke; it made his voice crack like a pubescent boy's. Doug Miller was a slender man that a strong gust of wind could knock over on his backside. He was the epitome of a southern farmer, through and through.

"Evening, Chief. Looks like there's a storm a-brewing," Old Man Miller greeted.

"Evening, Doug. What's the good word?" Ralph responded.

"Well, I reckon we're going to get dumped on by that cloud over there," Miller replied as he raised his right index finger up to the dusky sky.

"Sure does. You get your barn all closed up? Just in case the rain blows sideways?"

"Sure did, Chief. I could smell that storm an hour before those clouds arrived. Say, Chief, what's a night owl, like you, doing up so early?"

"Had to run up to Cherry Road to pick up one of Betsy Daley's fresh pecan pies before she went to bed. I couldn't wait until morning to go to the store. I just had the craving for some good, old-fashioned, home-baked pecan pie. And no one does that better than Mrs. Daley."

"You can say that again, Chief."

"Say, Doug, what are you doing out here, so far from the farm, when you know that cloud is going to burst open any time soon?"

"You know me, Chief. I can't pass up an opportunity to walk outside in the fresh, cool summer air while a storm's rolling in over the hills."

"True, but this one doesn't look like it's going to be very forgiving to walkers. You're going to get soaked."

"Still have that naval master chief worry, don't ya?"

"You know what they say: you can take the man out of the navy, but you can't take the navy out of the man, know what I mean?"

"Yes, Chief, that's for sure. It always makes me chuckle when you paraphrase that old saying." Old Man Miller moved his focus from Ralph's face down to the large Golden Retriever lying next to Ralph's wooden rocking chair on the porch. "And how is little Max this evening?"

Max sat up and let out a couple of barks in response to Old Man Miller's greeting. "You keeping that old Chief safe, Maxi?" Miller continued.

Max let out a couple friendlier barks, then flinched as if he wanted to run over and meet up with Miller in the middle of the street. Max paused and looked up at his master, who was seated in the rocking chair right next to him, and began panting. Max's tail was wagging back and forth, creating a sweeping pattern on the dirt-dusted floor planks of the porch. "All right, Max, go ahead," Ralph allowed.

Max bolted from the front porch, across the multicolored lawn of both dead grass and flourishingly rich green grass, then broke out onto the pavement and met Miller by jumping up and planting his two front paws on Miller's left side.

"Thatta boy, Maxi. Who's my best friend?" Miller greeted as he began to bend down slightly to meet Max's eager face. Max began to lap Miller all over his face, slicking down his puffy mustache and cleaning some of the dust off his face. Miller laughed amusedly. He set Max back down on his front paws and began to pet Max on the top of his head. While still bent down, Miller turned his head to the left, returning his attention to Ralph, continued to rub his hand around Max's head. He asked, "You got any big trips planned? I can keep this fella on my farm while you're gone."

Ralph snickered and answered, "Only if you pay for my plane ticket with all that money you have."

"'Fraid I can't help ya there, Chief," Miller replied jovially. "Are you going to join me down at the farm for my annual Fourth of July neighborhood barbecue and fireworks this year? I keep asking you every year, and every year you have some reason not to come."

"That's just not my thing, Doug. I've told you how fireworks remind me of some of the night enemy encounters we had when I was at my post on the ship. They don't scare me, but it doesn't bring back very fond memories. I watched as one of those bombs tore through one of our allied ships, creating a massive explosion, filling the night sky with bright-orange and white light. I saw some brave young men resort to plunging into the cold water from the deck as the boat buckled in the middle."

"Yessir, I can only imagine how horrible that must've been for you. I understand if you don't want to be right under those fireworks when they're going off. Does it bother you even being a mile down the road from fireworks?"

"Not as much as it would if I was right there. But as always, I do appreciate the invitation. Maybe one day."

"It's been almost 40 years that I've been asking now, Chief," Miller responded with a hearty laugh.

"Maybe," Ralph replied.

Old Man Miller stopped petting Max's head and said, "Go on, boy, go back to your daddy." Then he looked back up at Ralph and said, "Well, I'd better get moving along. She's blowing in here pretty fast now."

"That's a good idea, Doug. Get back home as quick as those old legs can carry you."

Max ran back towards the front porch, turned, and sat down right next to the rocking chair. Miller raised his right arm in the air and waved his open-palmed hand back and forth at Ralph. "You'd better get inside too, Chief."

"I'll be all right here; the wind is blowing in from the south. Good night, Doug."

"G'night, Chief."

Ralph Dubain was a retired naval signalman responsible for communicating with allied vessels using a powerful lamp equipped with shutters that would open and close with a small handle on the side. Having this position on the ship, he was well-versed in Morse code, as this was the main form of stealth communication with the neighboring friendly ships. Holding this title, he didn't have a great deal of people to talk to when he was stationed to his post, and he worked through the night to keep communication open with the other ships.

As a result, he became a night owl. His sleeping patterns found him resting through the day and up at night behind that shuttering device, all alone.

Ralph often had conversations with other signalmen on nearby ships to reduce the anxious emotions and squelch the boredom that often accompanied men who held this station in that branch of the military. Ralph was also responsible for communicating with ships from foreign countries who were fighting the Germans alongside the United States. For this, he needed to be fluent in the languages of our foreign allies. Those flickering discussions often included what they had for dinner that night, girlfriends and wives back home, humorous anecdotes, and family. Ralph himself was raised by his single mom who was once married to the local doctor, but her husband decided it was a better life to be with a popular cover girl.

On the evening of January 16, 1945, Ralph was having a conversation with a Russian signalman, Vladimir Petrov, on the Soviet destroyer *Diejatielnyj*, 1,000 yards from his ship. Vlad told him of his upbringing as the son of a goat rancher and whose education consisted of reading many books and the local newspapers. Vlad's family didn't have a lot of money, but they were happy and content with their lifestyle and were a strong Catholic family who gave thanks for any blessing bestowed upon them.

15

Like Vlad, Ralph was not a member of a financially thriving household, but what his mom made at the local salon was just enough to get them through their day-to-day lives. Ralph and Vlad shared memories of how they kept entertained in all the different seasons, which included riding second-hand bicycles through the streets and meandering through the woods and open fields to enjoy the quiet sounds of Mother Nature and her animal inhabitants. Even though these two men were chatting by way of flickering light, they were both keenly aware of their responsibilities and never let their discussions distract them from their watchful duties; a luxury neither could afford.

Utilizing the shuttering lamp each one had on their respective ship, they engaged in informal discussion. Ralph never heard Vlad speak, but could imagine a Russian accent he had heard from other Russian sailors in the past.

"Dobryy vecher, Seaman Dubain," Vlad signaled.

"Dobryy vecher, Seaman Petrov," Ralph signaled in response.

"How was chow?" Vlad asked.

"What do you think? Soggy, warm, and salty. Typical cuisine for us American subordinates. What about yourself?"

"Beef Stroganoff, rice, and bread. But I wouldn't really call the meat 'beef'; there are not too many cows out here in the ocean."

"That's hilarious. You're probably used to a lot better food back home."

"I wish you could experience what a real homemade beef stroganoff tastes like. Fresh mushrooms from the garden, real goat milk cream, moist chunks of fresh cow beef, and newly harvested brown rice. Mmmm, it makes my stomach feel such loss when I think about that compared to what we're served."

"Well, you haven't tried anything as scrumptious as honey barbecued ribs cooked over cedar briquettes and roasted corn on the cob smothered in butter produced that morning from cows on the same farm. That food is especially better when Betty Mae is cooking in the hot summer weather with as little clothes on as she can get away with."

17

"Why did you have to tell me that? Now I not only want barbecue ribs, but the female companionship of Betty Mae."

"Yeah, that 'cuisine' is just as tasty. But I'm sure that you have some very beautiful women in Russia, too, comrade."

"This is true, but they're nothing like—"

A bright flash blew up from the port hull followed by a loud boom, and a large cloud of orange and red sparks formed in the air. The battleship buckled in the middle where the torpedo, from the unseen German U-997 submarine, had hit. An alarm went off on the Soviet battleship and Ralph heard the screams and yelling coming from Vlad's boat. Deep black/gray smoke began to rise from the massive hole that was created in the side of the ship. Ralph grabbed his binoculars, raised them to his eyes, and surveyed the chaos coming from the Russian ship. He first looked at the location where Vlad was stationed, but didn't see him there. Ralph continued to slowly move the binoculars around the different parts of the deck. To his horror, he saw some Russian naval men jumping over the side of the boat, falling 30 feet into the cold water, hoping that the impact would kill them before the fires that broke out on their ship would. As Ralph moved the binoculars scanning more of the water, he noticed a submarine periscope circling towards his boat. Ralph reached down and pulled a lever that immediately engaged a roaring, deafening alarm accompanied by a strobe of flashing red-and-yellow lights all around the ship. Sailors scurried along the deck of the ship, yelling orders with frantic tones, and large deck guns began to target the German U-boat. There were 6 popping sounds, 6 smoke trails, and then a burst of red lights in the sky, created by an explosion of sparks from the massive flares deployed.

Ralph noticed that the wake behind the periscope was increasing, indicating that the U-boat was picking up speed with every passing second as it neared his ship. From over his left shoulder, about 50 yards away came a thunderous boom, nearly knocking him off his post. The colossal 16-inch deck gun launched its destructive projectile towards the U-boat. In a few short seconds, there was a geyser-like eruption of water and a very distinct sound of metal being slammed. Within a split-second later, the water over the U-boat sank in for a moment, followed by a towering upsurge of salt water that filled the air and created a swooshing sound. The battleship's 16-inch deck gun's shell had hit the U-boat dead center, causing an instant implosion into the main engine compartment, igniting all the fuel, and instantaneously destroying the submarine.

Regaining composure from the earthquake effect that the deck gun had issued

on him, Ralph brought the binoculars back up to his eyes and returned to his

surveying of the Soviet destroyer *Diejatielnyj*. His heart sank with a plunging

force when he spotted Vlad floating lifelessly face down in the water, with a

small flame burning the back of his uniform. He lowered the binoculars and

bowed his head. He had watched as his ally confidant met his fate in such a

brutish manner. Ralph would never forget that experience for as long as he

lived.

As a child, Ralph and his mother, Georgina, would sometimes take a train and

head over to Boston, Massachusetts, and then catch a bus from there to

Middleton, Massachusetts, where his Aunt Claire lived. That is, when Georgina

could save up enough money to cover the travel expenses. They would stay

with Claire in her 2-bedroom Cape where Ralph would sleep on the couch while

his mom had the spare bedroom. Claire Dubain was the head nurse at the

Danvers Psychiatric State Hospital, one of the board of directors, as well as

Ralph Dubain's aunt on his dad's side. Even though Ralph's father had

abandoned them, Claire remained in contact with Ralph and his mother when

Ralph was growing up. Claire did as much as she possibly could, but even

though she held a respectable position, she wasn't wealthy, as some might

expect. Claire had a close connection with all the patients in that hospital

before it began to become overcrowded with the flood of patients being admitted there from either the court system or general hospitals who believed that the patients could not live independently without harm to themselves or others. Claire was a frail-looking young lady, but her physique was deceptive. She was, in fact, a very strong individual. Claire ran three miles every morning before getting ready for work. She had the muscle tone comparable to a bodybuilder, but didn't have the skeletal makeup to be a contestant in Ms. Universe competitions. As a head nurse in a psychiatric institution, she often had to restrain patients who were twice her size, who also mistook her physique as weak and off balance. But they were quickly corrected with her strength and ability to secure violent patients from causing physical harm to the staff and other patients.

When Ralph and Georgina stayed with Claire, they would often go to Danvers Hospital and volunteer. They would partake in everything from reading to patients, talking to them about anything the patients wished to discuss, and helping with meals and cleanup. The hospital fed them for their efforts and generosity as the staff tended to the more intense situations. There were times when Ralph and Georgina would work late into the night, after Claire had gone home, and the hospital allowed them to stay in the staff residence dormitory and provide them all the linens and hygiene products they would require for the night and morning. The senior directors made it impossible for Ralph and his mom to be in harm's way by placing them in parts of the facility that would not risk their safety.

In the spring of 1927, the visits with Aunt Claire began to take on an unsettling and haunting atmosphere. Claire would arrive home somber, exhausted, and had no interest in discussing the day's events as she had always done. She would be very jumpy and easily startled, which was not her personality at all. Each time Ralph closed a cabinet door, the bathroom door, a closet door, or a bedroom door, Claire would gasp and flinch in her chair. Her eyes would constantly be surveying the house as if she was looking for an intruder. If Ralph or Georgina tried to go into a room without the lights on, she would spring up from wherever she was seated, grab one of the flashlights she had strategically placed around the house, race up to them, and give them the flashlight. She would always say the same line as she handed the flashlight to Ralph or Georgina: "You never know when you'll need it."

Something was definitely spooking Claire, but she never said what it was. Her new seemingly irrational behavior caused Georgina to have some very unsettling concerns about Claire's state of mind. She wondered if her job had finally infused its stress into her ability to maintain a calm and relaxed composure. They saw this strong woman, one who had never shown any signs of fear or dread, slowly erode into a panicky individual who was keenly attuned to every movement that was taking place in her home. If the wind picked up outside and shook one of the windows' exterior shutters she would gasp,

become temporarily frozen in place, and if she was in the middle of a sentence,

she would instantly cease what she was saying and yell out, "GO AWAY!!!"

This very disconcerting behavior found Georgina and Ralph visiting less and less

frequently. Claire was never violent or physically dangerous, but it was her

mental state that Georgina didn't want Ralph exposed to, as this wasn't the

same woman Ralph had come to know all his prior years. Additionally, while

visiting Claire, Georgina would often wake up in cold sweats during the night,

following dreams and sensations of being grabbed and restrained against her

bed. She never told Ralph of these horrifying nightmares, but was always very

concerned that Ralph might experience the same thing, and she wouldn't know

how to explain the violating phenomenon.

CHAPTER 2: "TIME TO COME INSIDE!"

Regardless of what era your generation is from, as long as there have been streetlamps, there has been the lasting rule of "when the streetlights come on, it's time for you to come inside." How many times have some of us been in the middle of a fun game of four-square, or hide-and-seek, or touch football, or kickball, and you hear the infamous line all kids dread hearing from their parents screaming out the front window, "The streetlight's on!!!! Time to come inside!" And how often has the, "I'll be there in a few minutes, I just want to finish this round!" been successfully honored by the beckoning parent? I will venture a guess that in Ralph's era of growing up, as well as his mom's, those words would probably only be uttered once, and then you would learn that they should never be repeated again.

Ralph learned of his mother's passing when he was en route back to the States. As an only child, he knew that he was now responsible for continuing the family name. However, Ralph never settled down with a wife. He was honorably discharged from the military and took possession of the house he grew up in. Because of his length of service in the navy and the nocturnal position he'd held, he became more of a recluse than a socialite and spent his days sleeping, and his evenings sitting on the front porch in one of those antique rocking chairs, with his furry companion and best friend, Max. He could always be seen with a cup of coffee in his hand and a cigar smoldering in between his fingers; that is, for those who happened to be awake at night and very early mornings. Ralph wasn't a grumpy man, neither was he temperamental, but rather just a quiet soul who would allow his creative mind to entertain his brain. He would have a newspaper on a small end table next to his rocking chair, and would pick it up to read a single article, then put it back down and listen to the silence. Even though there were no melodic sounds of ocean waves filling the air, he often felt like he was back on that battleship.

One of the town's four streetlights was on the corner of Chartiers Road and Summit Street, diagonally across the street from where he sat on his rocking chair. Sometimes, Ralph would put his hand up close to his face, close one eye, and use his thumb and pointer finger to create a makeshift shutter, using the streetlight as a signal lamp, and would have conversations (using Morse code) with his old pal, Vlad, who was there only in spirit and, as a result, Ralph never received any response back. But on a very hot and humid summer evening on July 4, 1985, where the thermometer was stuck on 87° Fahrenheit, all that would change.

Jasper Callahan was a local boy who lived on the upper east bend of Summit Street, which was just up the road from Ralph Dubain's house. In 1985, Jasper wasn't tainted with cell phones, text messaging, e-mail, Internet, or kinds of gaming devices; his entertainment was left to his own imagination. Jasper, a 10-year-old, blonde-haired boy with ocean-blue eyes and standing no more than 4'8" was considered to be the "doll" of the neighborhood. You know these kinds of boys, the ones where old ladies chase them down the road in hopes of squeezing their puffy, hamster-like cheeks. To try and provide a visual, imagine a miniaturized blonde-hair rock star with a Blind Cheetah "Hysterical" shirt on, ripped jean shorts, denim sneakers, and a Judas Cradle ball cap with a bandana hanging down from the back of the hat.

Ralph remembered Jasper, specifically. Not because the town's population was less than 200 people, but because Jasper always had this look of intrigue painted on his face. He was a very curious lad and would often stop and stare at structures for no reason at all. He was very much fascinated with the grain silos that were a few miles down the road from where he and his family lived. Jasper was the next-to-youngest of the four Callahan kids. His oldest brother, Noah, was a junior in high school. His older sister, Bekah, was a freshman in high school, and Holly was in third grade.

Noah was your typical older sibling who took his position in the lineage a little too seriously. Even though their parents, Steve and Doris, were in the same house, Noah would take it upon himself to be the disciplinarian of his younger kin.

Naturally this upset the other kids, but Steve had a successful contracting company and Doris was an emergency room nurse over at Brownsville General Hospital, which was approximately 20 miles from where they lived. Doris held the second-shift rotation for a greater percentage of the time, so she wouldn't walk into the house until closer to 1:00 a.m.

Steve's job found him travelling all around southwestern Pennsylvania and sometimes very long overnights to Philadelphia. So at times, it **WOULD** be Noah who was the key disciplinarian when Steve and Doris weren't home. However, in those few moments of time when the whole family was awake and together, Noah never dropped the whole parenting act.

On the evening of July 4, 1985, there was a huge fireworks show that Old Man Miller was hosting at his farm. It just so happened that this was the farm that had two massive grain silos that had some strange, hypnotic draw to Jasper Callahan. As the fireworks show was going to be happening when it was dark outside (which only makes sense), Noah had the responsibility of taking all the kids down, because Steve was going to be in Ohio for the week and Doris had to fill someone's second-shift rotation while she was on vacation for the July 4 holiday. Naturally, Bekah, Jasper, and Holly were emphatically overjoyed with that decision.

So Noah shepherded his siblings a couple miles down the road and arrived at Old Man Miller's farm. They were met with the aromatic ambiance of freshly mowed fields, cow manure, and hamburgers/hot dogs grilling over a huge fire pit. On that same grill iron were huge steaks, luscious-sized chicken breasts, corn on the cob, potatoes, and some vegetable kebabs. There was a small kiddie pool filled with ice and bottled water, and loaded with cans of soda (pop, as it is called in Clarksville); beer, juice, and a myriad of cold drinks for all different palates and ages.

Jasper wasted no time in running up to the serving table, grabbing a hamburger, a hot dog, some potato salad, a hot ear of corn from the grill, and reaching into the well of ice-cold drinks, he produced a Pepsi for himself. Although a very considerate young boy, he was usually a little selfish when it came to "waiting" on any of his siblings. After all, wasn't it his mom and dad who had told **NOAH** he had to be the parent tonight?

Old Man Miller had the pyrotechnics coordinators and technicians begin the show at 9:00 p.m., which was dark enough to enjoy every little spark that lit up the country sky. Naturally, the streetlights had been on for some time now, but tonight was a special occasion. Ralph did not attend the festivities because he would rather enjoy them from the comforts of his own yard. This was also very indicative of his social connection with the rest of the town: seclusion.

It was around 10:30 p.m. when Ralph was sitting on the porch and saw

something flickering. The streetlight seemed to be malfunctioning and kept

casting light and dark flickers against the night road. But Ralph couldn't turn his

gaze away from it. The rhythm of the flashes seemed to be orchestrated, and

not random at all. So Ralph continued to stare at it until he realized, or thought

he realized, it was a message. A message from whom? Was someone really

listening all those years that Ralph had created conversations using his

makeshift signaling lamp and shutters? Were they just now responding?

Ralph then began to think, *That is just ludicrous, sir. Your eyes are playing tricks*

on you. Old Man Miller's fireworks are probably causing some kind of

atmospheric disruption that is having an effect on the streetlights. But

something was a little too choreographed and not so random about these

flickers. Ralph decided to entertain his delusion about a response from a

phantom signalman and began taking note of the pattern of the flickers: dash-

dot-dot-dot, dash-dot-dash-dash, dot, dash-dot-dot-dot, dash-dot-dash-dash,

dot, dash-dot, dash-dash-dash, dot-dash, dot-dot-dot-dot. When Ralph figured

out the message being sent, he cringed in horror and watched as the flickers

repeated their cycle. Again, it was the same message: dash-dot-dot-dot, dash-

dot-dash-dash, dot, dash-dot-dot-dot, dash-dot-dash-dash, dot, dash-dot, dash-

dash-dash, dot-dash, dot-dot-dot-dot.

Ralph's heart began to race. His head began to swell with that kind of fear you feel when you're about to open a closet door in a dark room. His elderly hands began to tremble. Each time the message completed its cycle, it would start over again and go through faster and faster after each cycle. Dash-dot-dot-dot, dash-dot-dash-dash, dot, dash-dot-dot-dot, dash-dot-dash-dash, dot, dash-dot, dash-dash-dash, dot-dash, dot-dot-dot-dot. When the flickering reached the speeds equal to that of a strobe light, Ralph finally leapt up and screamed out into the darkness, "**LEAVE HIM ALONE!!!!!**"

Directly after he finished saying *alone*, there was a blinding burst of light and Ralph was knocked back to the ground. With Max barking out into the night in the direction of the streetlight, Ralph began to shake off his bout with something foreign. He reached for the armrest of his rocking chair and steadied himself back up to a seated position in the chair. He grabbed a hold of Max's collar and rubbed Max's neck to calm him down. Ralph began thinking, *I am* **truly** *going mad. I am making up some very horrible concepts in my head and they have to stop. I need to get another cup of coffee.* Ralph got up and made his way through the screen door and into the kitchen. He turned the burner on and placed a teakettle on it, grabbed his instant coffee container, and prepared a small cup with a scoop of coffee crystals, a couple spoons of sugar, and some non-dairy creamer. Then he waited for the water to boil. As he waited, he couldn't shake that very ghostly phenomenon that had happened with the streetlight. "I am letting the horrors of the military poison my rational mind."

As Ralph began pouring the boiling water from the kettle into his cup, he heard the faint sounds of kids' voices getting louder as they neared the house from the direction of Old Man Miller's farm. Jasper had a very unmistakable laugh, where it started as a high-pitched shriek and then would plateau with a chuckling vibrato accompanied by some gasping sounds. Now, it was not the dangerous kind of gasping commonly associated with asthma or some other type of respiratory disorder, but more like a dance of sound to show his amusement over something he found entertaining. It was that laugh, mixed with off-key singing from a couple girls, that made Ralph keenly aware of who was coming up the road. He was paranoid. He was trembling. "Was that light really saying what I think it was saying? Or am I just having severely vivid flashbacks to the war?" He listened as the voices grew louder the closer they got.

Ralph made his way out to the porch and stood leaning on one of the front porch supports. He watched as the kids slowly came into view. The streetlight began to cast some light on them, but they were still mostly cloaked by the midnight sky. Then the streetlight began its pattern again: dash-dot-dot-dot, dash-dot-dash-dash, dot, dash-dot-dot-dot, dash-dot-dash-dash, dot, dash-dot, dash-dash-dash, dot-dash, dot-dot-dot-dot. This was no longer a delusion. This was something that was clearly happening, proved because Bekah said,

"WHOA. Did you guys see **THAT**????"

Now that there was confirmation that this flickering wasn't some kind of

massive tumor taking over Ralph's brain but had been validated by Bekah's

acknowledgement, it was clear that something quite ominous was happening.

The kids were almost directly under the streetlight when Ralph cried out,

"**HEY!!!! CALLAHANS!!!! COME OVER HERE FOR A MOMENT!!!**" Noah and the

kids were very aware of who Ralph was and that their parents told them **NOT**

to be afraid of Mr. Dubain, as he was not one who would do anything violent or

criminal. In fact, Steve and Doris told the kids if they ever had the chance to

meet Mr. Dubain to say thank you for his service to this country.

When Ralph called the kids over, they were not cautiously suspicious at all. As

Bekah, Jasper, and Holly began making their way to the front porch, Noah

stood there underneath the streetlight. When Ralph realized this he called out

to Noah, "**You too, young man.**" Oh boy, someone called Noah a "young man."

Now the attitude had to kick in.

"Why do I have to listen to what you tell me, Mr. Dubain?" Noah snapped. "I'm

responsible for these kids, and Mom and Dad left **me** in charge. They can go

over and say hi, but I'm going to stand right here under this streetlight, if you don't mind."

"But, Noah," Ralph continued, "I want to hear what you thought of tonight's festivities over at Old Man—err, I mean—Mr. Miller's farm."

Noah stood under that streetlight with his arms folded and standing as straight as a Boy Scout saluting the American flag. As the other kids made it up to the edge of the porch, Ralph asked them, "So tell me, Callahans, what was your favorite part of tonight's party?" He was somewhat listening to what they were answering with, but for the most part, his eyes were fixed on Noah and that streetlight. The streetlight began to flicker again, but this time it was so slow that even the most novice of telegraphers could make out what it was saying: dash-dot-dot-dot (B), dash-dot-dash-dash (Y), dot (E), dash-dot-dot-dot (B), dash-dot-dash-dash (Y), dot (E), dash-dot (N), dash-dash-dash (O), dot-dash (A), dot-dot-dot-dot (H). Noah acknowledged this cosmic activity by looking up at the streetlight, then looking down to the ground.

"Mr. Dubain, did you see that?" Noah asked. "Didn't it *not* look random to you?"

Okay, Ralph whispered internally, *if* Noah *can figure that out, then it is definitely not my mind going crazy.* Ralph interrupted Jasper's review of the night's festivities and said, "Why don't I walk home with you all. It doesn't look like you have a flashlight, and I'm so used to living in the dark." The three younger kids were in agreement, but Noah looked like he'd had his tail feathers plucked off and began to show signs of disapproval, like a goose would when they saw something threatening.

"Thank you, Mr. Dubain, but we'll be fine. I've lived here most of *my* life, too, and there was only that streetlight on the corner, then a dark walk home at night. But I appreciate your offer."

How was Ralph going to do this? How was he going to convince Noah not to be alone with the kids, and that there should be another, more mature guardian with them? The message said nothing about the other three kids, though. Nevertheless, who knew what—or **who**—that message was coming from. Noah called for his siblings to return to him so they could finish their walk up Summit Street to their house. Ralph could do no more than stand there directly under the streetlight (where he'd walked the three younger Callahans back to Noah) and watch as the four kids slowly blended into the darkness the further they got from the streetlight. As the kids got even further up Summit Street, the voices and singing began to quiet; Mr. and Mrs. Callahan were very strict about keeping the noise down during the night around the neighborhood.

"But what if something happens to him? What if that silence is stunned shock where the fear steals your voice for a moment of time?" Ralph couldn't figure out what to do. Then there was one more cadence of the flickering streetlamp: dash-dot-dot-dot (B), dash-dot-dash-dash (Y), dot (E), dash-dot-dot-dot (B), dash-dot-dash-dash (Y), dot (E), dash-dot (N), dash-dash-dash (O), dot-dash (A), dot-dot-dot-dot (H), and then it dulled down to the dimness of a night-light. Ralph returned to his rocking chair on his porch and waited to see Doris slow down at that intersection, then turn up Summit Street on her way in from the second-shift rotation and coverage from the hospital. That's all Ralph could do; and think horrible, disturbing thoughts of doom and dread.

CHAPTER 3: WELCOME TO DANVERS

"Good evening. May I speak with Mr. Steven Callahan, please?"

"This is he," Steve replied. "How may I help you?"

"My name is Sir Heath Garrison," replied the caller with a subtle, pretentious English accent and drawn-out vowels, much like you would hear from a television or movie butler. "I represent the National Preservation Council of Historic Landmarks board of trustees here in Danvers, Massachusetts. Is this a reasonable hour to discuss a proposition, or shall we set up a meeting to denim when it is more convenient for you?"

Steve looked at the clock on the kitchen wall from where he sat at the recently cleared dining room table: 6:33 p.m. He turned his focus to the kitchen sink, where Noah and Bekah were washing and drying the pots, pans, plates, glasses, and silverware from dinner. He then turned around to his right, looked across the hall into the living room, and saw Jasper and Holly sitting on the floor watching television. "No. This is a good time to talk. May I ask what this is all about?"

"Oh, it is nothing bad, I can assure you. My apologies if my tone seemed urgent and dire. Mr. Callahan, are you familiar with the Danvers State Hospital here in Massachusetts?"

"I've heard something about it. We have a neighbor down the street who once told me he volunteered at a state hospital in Massachusetts when he was a young man, but nothing other than that," Steve answered.

"Well, for the purpose of this call, the time of day it is, and the main reason I am calling, I will give you a brief overview of the facility and its history. Danvers Psychiatric State Hospital in Danvers, Massachusetts, was built in the year of our Lord 1874. A massive, monolithic, 700,000-square-foot Goliath was constructed of brick and granite, and cast a shadow over all the other facilities in the area. The prominent Thomas Story Kirkbridge was the architect behind this lavish haven for those suffering from a catalog of mental and emotional disorders ranging from depression to paranoid schizophrenia. Thomas had a belief that such a sanctuary would vanquish the stereotypical dreary ambiance often associated with such institutions. It would be a place of stress-free therapy that would make its occupants feel less imprisoned, and more like guests at a hotel.

"The staff consisted of round-the-clock medical professionals from doctors, nurses, orderlies, chefs, maintenance workers, and volunteers. Through many years following the initial construction of the main building, new structures were erected as wings and individual buildings that made up the entire Danvers campus. The hospital, and its adjoining structures, was built upon Hawthorn Hill, which was once owned by Francis Dodge, where the Dodge Farm was located. Its Gothic design and towering rooftops posed such an elaborate structure that it was often referred to as the "Castle on the Hill" by the locals.

"It was a facility that focused on research and cures for mentally disturbed individuals, but all the while treating their patients like people, not case studies. So much so that many of the archaic practices commonly associated with these types of medical facilities were dismissed in order to continue the philosophy of making the patients feel like guests. A 16-year-old patient's mother once called the caregivers the 'Daffodils at Danvers' due to the gentle care and compassionate treatment they showered on the patients, which allowed the patients to be calm, placid, and at ease.

"This hospital remained the leading psychiatric facility until it succumbed to overcrowding between the 1920s and 1930s as the number of patients grew from 400 patients to over 2,000. The original facility was built to support close to 485 patients, and with such an immense increase in numbers, the quality of care began to decrease.

"During that same time of struggle, the financial aid and government funding began to decrease as well. Due to the lack of funds, it made caring for the buildings' structural integrity extremely laborious and time consuming. The board and their financial experts couldn't afford to bring on any contractors or construction crews to repair the crumbling granite and stone. Due to this factor, the once glorious cathedral took on the appearance of the stigmatic psychiatric facility; it became less and less an architectural majesty, and more a decaying, crypt-like fortress.

"In order to control the abundance of patient needs and attempts to maintain treatment and poise, the medical staff decided to adopt the practices of old, which included shock therapy, lobotomies, and straightjackets as a form of maintaining control while being able to tend to other patients with less violent capabilities. Due to the lack of financial assistance from prior investors, as well as state funds, the facility was forced to ship most of their patients to neighboring psychiatric hospitals and, sometimes, out of state completely. From chateau to shambles, Danvers Psychiatric Hospital became more of a blemish on the town than an iconic institution."

"All right," Steve politely responded once Garrison finished his history lesson,
"that is a very interesting story. So are you looking for donations?"

"Not at all, my dear man, I want to offer you a proposal. The National
Preservation Council of Historic Landmarks Foundation is committed to
maintaining the plush, rich history in the region's architectural splendors for
the purpose of preserving the birthplace of America's early cultures. We are
very thorough in our research, and have discovered that you have a great deal
of experience in restoring commercial and industrial structures that have
become decrepit due to neglect or abandonment. We also discovered that you
are a 3rd-generation contractor, preceded by your father and grandfather. It is
that degree of background and experience that caught our eye."

"I appreciate the kind words and approval," Steve interjected, "but I'm more
interested in what Danvers State Hospital has to do with me or my family's line
of work."

"Oh, I do apologize for rambling. The National Preservation Council of Historic
Landmarks Foundation would like to invite you, and anyone you wish to
accompany you, to Danvers, Massachusetts, to assess the condition of the
structures, an estimation for renovation, and potential length of time it would

take you and whatever crews you need to restore the institution's edificial integrity. You see, Mr. Callahan, the Danvers State Hospital used to be the shining beacon for mental health treatment and a mecca for potential patients and their family members. As the region's most illustrious mental institution and its glowing reputation, it became a medical landmark in New England. Since the crisis that the facility experienced in the 1920s and 1930s, it has festered into a blight on our good town and has become more of a sore site than a crowning hope.

"We at the National Preservation Council of Historic Landmarks Foundation are looking to resurrect this once-radiant institution back to its original state. We feel that with the proper restoration and repairs, it will become a place of hope again for many who are struggling with crippling mental disorders, and a place where they can feel safe, proud, and at peace."

"Having done your research, Mr. Garr—"

Steve was cut-off, mid-name, by a huff-toned voice, "**Sir** Garrison, if you don't mind."

"My apologies," Steve corrected. "**Sir** Garrison, having done your research, you must have discovered that my area of work is mostly in the western part of Pennsylvania, with my furthest-west project being in Philadelphia.

Massachusetts is a far way off."

"I **do** realize that this may be outside of your home territory, Mr. Callahan, but I

assure you that you will be generously compensated for your time," replied

Garrison. "We are prepared to offer you first-class airfare to Boston,

Massachusetts, a personal limo service to take you wherever you want to go,

and your own personal quarters for you and any of your guests."

"That's very generous of you, sir, but I do have prior commitments to fulfill

before I can agree to anything."

"Of course, of course. I completely understand. And we at the National

Preservation Council of Historic Landmarks Foundation are very

accommodating and appreciate our clients' valuable time. When do you

believe you would be prepared to make the trip?"

"Well, sir, that's a little difficult to say. The soonest I believe I will be available is

2 or 3 months."

"That would be just fine, my dear man. How does the 8th of August in the year

of our Lord 1983 sound? Is that too soon?"

Steve got up and headed to the kitchen. He retrieved his appointment book from the countertop, flipped through some pages, and then replied, "August 8? Yes, I believe I can make it there at that time."

"SPLENDID," Garrison exclaimed. "We are anxious to meet you and hear of your thoughts regarding the restoration. I thank you for your time this evening. Look for your travel arrangements in the mail this week. Have a wonderful evening."

There was a *click* on the other end of the phone and then Steve hung up the receiver on the kitchen's portable phone charger. "Who was that, Dad?" Noah asked nosily.

"Oh, just a potential client. He's all the way in Massachusetts, though," Steve replied.

"Wow," Noah responded with shock. "That is a long way away. Why would someone in Massachusetts be calling you for a project?"

"Apparently," Steve replied, "the National Preservation Council of Historic Landmarks Foundation did some research and was impressed by my experience with commercial and industrial property restorations."

"Well, I can't say I blame them." Noah winked at his dad after he finished saying this.

On May 6, 1983, a large, thick envelope arrived in the Callahan's mailbox. When Steve returned home that night, he was greeted by four sets of curious eyes, with Holly clutching the envelope in her hands. Steve tilted his head slightly to the right, produced a smile on his face, and said in a very playful tone, "All right, you four, what do you have up your sleeves?"

"**THIS!!!**" Holly exclaimed, and then handed the envelope over to her dad. On the return address was a black-and-white drawing of a palatial structure with the sun shining from behind it and the words "National Preservation Council of Historic Landmarks, c/o Danvers State Hospital Initiative" under it, followed by the address for the hospital: "1101 Kirkbridge Drive, Danvers, MA 01923." All the kids' eyes were wide with anticipation, as if they were at the starting blocks in their living room on Christmas morning, awaiting the go-ahead from their parents. Steve had told the kids about the potential project and how the National Preservation Council of Historic Landmarks Foundation board of trustees had invited him and any guests of his choice to fly over and do an assessment of the buildings and grounds. The Callahans had never been further north than Philadelphia, and the kids thought that they would now have an opportunity to go to the nation's oldest region.

"Now, kids," Steven responded as he gently tore open the top of the envelope, "I don't know how many tickets are in here, so please don't be upset if there's not enough to cover the entire family. This potential client was generous enough to offer all travel expenses, and I didn't want to take advantage of their hospitality; that's the last thing a contractor ever wants to do." As Steven fished through the contents in the envelope, he found seven first-class, open-ended, round-trip tickets to Logan Airport, Boston, Massachusetts, for August 8, 1983, leaving from Pittsburgh, Pennsylvania. He removed the airline tickets, walked over to the dining room table, set down the envelope, and fanned through the airline tickets. His eyes were very wide, and he had unconsciously dropped his mouth open. What kind of people was he dealing with? The kids watched as Steve began counting the tickets and they all nodded in unison with every number that Steve counted off, with widening eyes after each number was counted: "Let's see here, 1 . . . 2 . . . 3 . . . 4 . . . 5 . . . 6 . . . 7!!! **Seven** first-class tickets? Is this for real????" Steve set the tickets on the table and produced a cover letter from the envelope:

Dear Mr. Steven Callahan:

Thank you for taking the time to speak with me the other day.

I am pleased to offer you these airline tickets for you and your

family, as well as one of your professional peers, to join us in

Danvers, Massachusetts, the 8th of August in the year of our Lord 1983. It would be an honor for us to have the lot of you tour our facility, as well as take in some of the breathtaking landmarks and historical attractions Massachusetts has to offer.

We have made arrangements for you and your guests to stay at the Danvers State Hospital for the duration of your trip. We do still have some patients here, but I assure you that your health and safety will never be in jeopardy. We are going to put you up in our staff dormitories located behind the main facility, which are completely segregated from areas that our patients use. The staff dormitory structure is still relatively sound and we feel that the experience there would be both memorable and enlightening. You will have staff chaperones the entire time you're on the grounds, as well as law enforcement for your peace of mind.

You and your guests will have unlimited access to the organization's limousine and all your meals, in and out of the facility, will be covered by the National Preservation Council of Historic Landmarks Foundation. We have also made arrangements for you and your guests to visit some of the top historical sites in our area, as well as reserved box-seat tickets

for the Boston Red Sox vs. the Texas Rangers game on the 9th

of August in the year of our Lord 1983.

We have left the airline tickets open-ended to provide you

flexibility for the stay; where you may, at any time, feel free to

return to Pennsylvania. We are prepared to offer you your

regular weekly profits plus a 10% gratuity for your time and

professional expertise.

Again, thank you in advance for your gracious acceptance to

our invitation. We look forward to meeting you and your

family in person.

Sincerely,

Sir Heath Garrison

"This has to be a mistake," Steve said in a state of stupor. "This is a lot of

money to spend on just an assessment appointment. Perhaps I **am** the guy they

had in mind when they were looking for the best." With that, he smiled at the

four giddily bouncing children who were trying to refrain from screaming

cheers of joy and jubilation. Then his mind switched gears almost instantaneously as he spoke internally, "Oh, wait, can Doris get the time off from work?"

When Doris returned home late that night, Steve was sitting in his plushy recliner and looking through some literature that was also included in the envelope sent by the National Register of Historical Places Foundation. Doris inquired as to what he was reading and why he was up so late. Steve shared all the information that was in that packet and handed her the cover letter included in the contents of the packet.

When Doris finished reading the last line, she looked up at Steve with a stunned expression, her mouth slightly agape, wide-eyed. Steve said, "Do you think you can get the time off from work, honey?" Not able to find any voice in her throat, she nodded rapidly and then leapt towards him and gave him a huge, tight hug.

***

The Callahans arrived at Logan Airport in Boston, Massachusetts, on the afternoon of August 8. They were met at the gate by a guy in a suit with a black cap on, holding a sign that said "Callahan" on it. In the upper right-hand corner was the same insignia that was on the return address section of the envelope Steve had received a few months earlier.

They followed the limo driver from the gate, past the security checkpoints, and into the main area. When Steve turned to head towards the baggage claim area, the limo driver said, "That won't be necessary, sir, we've arranged for airport personnel to retrieve your luggage and bring it out to the car. We will head straight to the car, where you and your family will find beverages and snacks inside." Ronald Boscawen, Steve's financial partner, was also with them as the seventh guest. He was accompanying Steve to take down all of Steve's findings and required tasks/materials needed to perform a complete restoration.

The Callahans and Ronald reached the stretch limo, where the driver opened the door and gestured for everyone to enter. The children were beside themselves, and Doris could barely keep her own composure as well. This was more than just a business trip; it was a lavish vacation. The kids saw the TV in the corner of the cabin, mounted on a polished oak shelf, and gasped with astonishment that a TV was in a car. Three airport personnel retrieved their luggage, brought it out to the limo, and loaded every single piece of baggage into the trunk. Then the driver entered the car and drove off towards Danvers. He lowered the protective, dark-tinted window that separated the cab from the cabin and announced, "If at any time you see something that you'd like to stop and check out, I have been instructed to do just that." Yet it appeared that Ronald and the Callahans had no immediate interest in anything but the elaborate and ornate interior of the limousine.

Ronald and the Callahans arrived at Danvers State Hospital at 5:00 p.m. on August 8. As they broke through the shaded fortress that lined the main road to the institution, a hush fell over them as they got their first look at this gothic-structured facility. The main building didn't seem so dilapidated, but you could see off of the main structure some other adjoining units that were boarded up and sealed. It was almost eerie, but Steve remembered what Garrison had said in the letter, and wasn't worried for their safety.

When the limo drove past the main entrance, Ron and the Callahans noticed a large, 3-story brick building that had a four-white-pillared balcony hanging over the front door. There were two peaked dormers on the far end of the building with circular windows on the one facing the driveway, and the other facing out the back of the building. There were two other entrances that had two smaller green awnings overhanging those entrances.

Garrison was true to his word when he said that the dormitories were not connected to the main building at all, but was rather an autonomous granite and brick habitation for non-resident personnel.

The driver pulled the car up to the main entrance of the dormitories and were greeted by a husky, muscular orderly and a police officer who could've won first place in the Mr. Universe competition. These were two incredibly intimidating gentlemen, but there was something about their expressions and the way they carried themselves that instantly brought relief to Doris, Steve, and Ronald. The kids, however, were in a trance at this foreign place and the men who greeted them at the dormitory entrance.

Putting the car in park, the driver exited the car and walked around to the rear passenger door. The hospital worker and police officer approached the car just to the left of the limo driver. Steve was the first to exit, followed by Doris, and then Ronald; the kids stayed inside until they knew that everything was going to be all right.

The hospital worker, adorned in white slacks and a white button-up dress shirt with the Danvers State Hospital insignia on his left breast pocket, was the first to introduce himself. He was an African-American man in his 30s, standing a

51

towering 6 foot 4 inches, and was built like Arnold Schwarzenegger. If you saw this man on the street at night, you'd be frightened by his sheer size and physique.

"Good evening, Mr. and Mrs. Callahan," he said while extending his right hand out to greet them. "My name is Barry Henderson. I am the head orderly here at Danvers and I've been here for 10 years." Turning to Ronald, he said, "You must be Mr. Boscawen. It's a pleasure to meet you." Barry's voice was so subtle, so gentle, and so calm, that a wave of relief instantly washed over Steve, Doris, and Ron. Barry could easily shake off 10 or 20 people if he were jumped. He was **that** big.

The next person to greet them was the police officer. Another African-American man, in his early 40s, who had the same physique as Barry Henderson. "Greetings, Mr. and Mrs. Callahan, Mr. Boscawen. My name is Reginald Washington, but everyone calls me 'Reg.' I will be your police escort for the duration of your stay here in Massachusetts. Please do not hesitate to ask me any questions or call upon me for assistance at any time."

Doris extended her hand behind her and gestured for the kids to exit the vehicle and meet the two burly gentlemen. When the kids stepped out, they were very much intimidated by these towering, monolithic individuals. When

Barry introduced himself, much like Steve, Doris, and Ron had reacted, you could see a sense of relief wash over the children's expressions. The kids' demeanor had instantly morphed from fear to comfort. Noah looked around and didn't see any patients on the grounds.

"Mr. Henderson—" Noah asked, but was quickly interrupted by Barry.

"Please, young man, you can call me Barry. What can I do for you?" Barry asked.

"Why aren't there any patients or doctors outside? It's only five o'clock. Are they at dinner?"

"No, young sir, this is their 'options' time. They are given a number of different activities to do and they can select the one that they feel most comfortable participating in. We usually have it around 3:00 p.m., but we wanted them to be inside when you arrived, for your own comfort. The patients who are still here are not violent, but we don't take any chances when it comes to our visitors' safety and peace of mind."

Then Barry went to the back of the limo, retrieved the luggage from the trunk, put the bags on a rolling cart, and told Ron and the Callahans to follow him into the dormitory. Upon entering the main foyer, they were surprised to see that it wasn't a dreary, run-down building. The paint was a little faded and there were a few cracks in the granite floor tile, but that was about it. It wasn't at all what they expected.

Barry walked them down one of the main hallways that had glass tear-drop chandeliers with brass finishing hanging down from the tall ceilings and brass sconces just outside each dorm room. The paint was not stained, blemished, or cracked. Each dorm room had a thick, heavy oak door dividing the rooms from the hallways, and the door handles were made of polished brass. At the end of the hallway was a 5-foot gray marble pillar with a flat white marble countertop that held a vase of different wildflowers from the neighborhood and the hospital garden.

The Callahan kids were offered their own individual rooms to choose from, which gave them a great deal of excitement, as they were used to sharing rooms back home. Barry asked each kid which room they wanted, and then he took their individual pieces of luggage into their respective rooms. He then gestured for Doris, Steve, and Ron to follow him down to the end of the hall to the two large bedrooms at the end. Each had their own full bathroom and amenities, while the kids would have to use the community bathrooms: one for the boys, and one for the girls. In each room was a bed that had an 8-inch-thick mattress atop a 6-inch box spring. They were made up with white sheets and a thick comforter, and had a polished oak headboard and footboard. On either side of the bed were oak nightstands and a polished brass lamp with an off-white lampshade. There was a dresser with enough drawers to hold a month's worth of clean clothing. Each room had a 21-inch color TV with cable. It was almost as if they were staying in a 3-star hotel.

Steve looked over at Barry and said, embarrassed, "To be quite honest, I was expecting rooms that you'd see in *One Flew Over the Cuckoo's Nest*."

Barry reacted with a very robust and hearty laugh and responded, "Mr. Callahan, you're not the first one to have said that. Unfortunately, not all of the rooms in the other buildings have been kept up like these. Mainly because the staff takes pride in their living quarters and they, too, don't want to feel like they are in a constrictive sanitarium."

When Ron and the Callahans were all settled into their rooms, Barry led them back up the hallway, turned left, and headed towards the staff dining area. There were a few staff members there having their dinner; a couple doctors, a few nurses, some orderlies, and some of the nurses' aides. They looked up and saw the Callahans and some of them began to gesture to them to come in.

Barry extended his left arm out, with the palm of his hand slightly tilted down as if to say, "Please enter."

Ron and the Callahans sat down at one of the empty round tables that had place settings on them, a soft, white tablecloth over the top of the table, and cloth napkins. There was a small glass vase in the middle of the table that had a scaled arrangement of the one that sat on the pillar in the dorm room hallway. After they went up to get their dinner at the buffet, they returned to their table and were pleasantly surprised at the quality of the food. Ron looked up at Barry and asked, "Do the patients get this same food? This is outstanding."

Barry responded, "Unfortunately, Mr. Boscawen, we don't have the funds to provide this level of food to the patients. But don't let that get you thinking they only eat porridge, bread, and water. I assure you, each patient gets a well-rounded nutritional meal based on his or her dietary needs. Please don't feel guilty; we've tried to have special occasions where we offer the same selection to the patients, but they were so set in their dietary habits that they had no interest in it. You see, for the most part, the patients here have established a daily routine, and most of them become scared or upset if that routine is altered in any way. So you go ahead and eat up, because even if you all weren't here, this is what would have been served anyway."

Following dinner, Ron and the Callahans were invited into the community lounge where there was a coffee maker, a few carafes of hot water, packets of hot cocoa in a soup bowl on the table, along with tea bags and sugar, as well as a glass carafe of cream that was in a stainless steel canister of ice. The room had brass sconces all around, and it was furnished with leather couches, love seats, and recliners. There was a table in the back corner near the windows that had an unfinished puzzle on it, and shelves and shelves of different varieties of books. The floor was carpeted with a red carpet, and the draperies were of a gold-and-red paint splatter design that looked like Jackson Pollack would've painted. There were a series of staff group pictures from different years on the wall. There was a variety of black-and-white photos and color photos, each presenting the outfits and hairstyles common in that era. On the bottom of each of the cedar picture frames were brass plates that read "Daffodils at Danvers" and the year the picture was taken.

The kids went over to work on the puzzle, and also grabbed a few games that were in a lower cabinet. They began to play in the back part of the room while Ron, Doris, and Steve listened to the staff fill them in on a great deal of history about the hospital, as well as answer any questions they had. But there was a dark horror that some of the veteran seniors knew about this institution that they left out of their historical education to Ron, Doris, and Steve; and some of the younger staff members had no idea that such horrors had ever transpired

at the hospital decades before.

CHAPTER 4: LET THERE BE LIGHT

Thomas Story Kirkbridge's plans for the original architecture of Danvers State Hospital consisted of 8 different wings: 3 to the left of the main entrance/administrative building, and 4 to its right. From an aerial view, it looked like a large bat with symmetrically sized blocks acting as steps from the tips of the wings to the bat's head.

The wings were divided into categories to house and segregate patients with particular afflictions. If one was facing forward to the main entrance and could imagine letters on each wing, it would be laid out as such (from left to right): I, H, G, main entrance building, D, C, B, A. The categories and placement of respective patients were:

- Wing A for excitable patients
- Wings B, C, H, and I for less excitable patients
- Wings D and G for convalescing patients

In 1921, the facility added an additional wing for excitable patients (J) that was to the left of Wing I. From Steve's perspective, it seemed the logical thing to do was begin a restoration project from the oldest structure to the newest, and this is exactly how he was to map it out.

On the morning of August 9, Steve and Doris were awakened by small knocks on their door and children's voices coming from the other side. Steve looked over to his right to the clock on the nightstand: 7:00 a.m. In the middle of yawning, Steve said in a higher-than-normal morning decibel, "What do you guys want? It's 7:00 **a.m.** Go find something to do in the lounge for an hour or more."

"But, Dad," Holly squeaked, "there is so much we need to see and we don't have a lot of time."

"Holly, honey, I want to see those sites and historical attractions as much as you do, but I am here to work, as well, and plan on doing that during the day. You, your mom, your brothers, and your sister can go; I want you to enjoy this time while you're here. But please let us sleep a little longer, baby girl."

Steve picked his head up and could see three sets of foot shadows move away and to the right of his door, but there stood one set motionless and unmoved. There weren't any children's voices coming from the other side of the door now, just that shadow of small feet. Plopping his head back down on the pillow with an impatient huff, he said, "Holly, please, give your mom and me another hour. There are games you can play in the lounge." Steve didn't hear anything.

No movement. No motion. No voice. He waited another 10 seconds, picked his

head up, and saw that the two small foot shadows stayed in the same place

they were in.

"Holly, honey, pleeeeeease go with your brothers and sister into the lounge."

He put his head back down. Silence. Another 20 seconds and Steve picked his

head up again, only to see those same two foot shadows not moving. Steve

grunted in a very low whisper, "That's it." He flung the top comforter and top

sheet over his left side, creating a double-cover on Doris. He sat up, swung his

legs over to the right, stood up on weak morning legs, and headed to the door.

He turned the knob, all the while staring at those two small foot shadows, and

while pulling the door open he began saying, "Listen, little g—"

Steve was crippled with a sudden bout of laryngitis as what he saw **wasn't** little

Holly standing there, but just a shadow of two feet and shadows of two legs

that stretched to the wall across the hall, and then disappeared into the wall.

Normally, when you see a person's shadow, they have all appendages; a

bottom, a torso, a neck, and a head. This wasn't the case here. They were

simply two shadows of feet attached to legs that stretched across the hall and

into the wall across the way. Steve wiped his eyes, hoping that by clearing off

the sandman's deposit it would help him get a clearer and more explainable perspective. However, that little maneuver didn't work. He thought the shadows were being cast by something else, perhaps one of the plants atop the marble pedestal. Unfortunately, the sun was not shining into the window at that time of the morning on that side of the building.

Steve had not realized that he had been staring at this shadow for a couple minutes. Doris slightly lifted her head off the pillow, looked over her left shoulder, and saw Steve standing motionless at the open doorway in his purple pajamas, staring down at the floor.

"Steve? What are you looking at?" But Steve didn't respond. He didn't make any gesture or movement that would indicate he even heard her. "Steve?"

Coming out of a trance-like state, Steve turned his head over his left shoulder and said, "It wasn't Holly."

"**What** wasn't Holly?"

"The shadows of feet from under the door. It wasn't Holly's."

"What are you talking about? I heard you tell them to go to the lounge and play so we could sleep a little more."

"Yes, and when I got up to open the door to let, who I believed to be Holly, know she had to go to the lounge, there were those feet shadows and shadows of legs, but no one was there. Come here and look." Steve pointed to the floor and then turned his head back towards the door. Looking down, he saw that there was no shadow. He raised his eyes slowly, like following an imaginary line on the ground, all the way up to the opposing wall. Everything was gone. His mouth was open when he turned back to Doris. With an expression of stunned perplexity, he said, "They're gone."

"**What's** gone?"

"The feet and leg shadows. They just disappeared."

"Honey, you're really freaking me out here; like Jack Nicholson-level scary. Have you also seen and talked to a dressed-up bartender?"

"Oh, I don't know what's happening. I'm probably overtired from everything that's going on, and I haven't had my morning coffee yet. I'm going to head into the kitchen to see if anyone has made some yet." With that, Steve stepped into some slippers that he'd left by the door the night before, grabbed his robe off the end of the bed, and turned right out of the bedroom door. He headed down the hall towards the kitchen and dining room. Doris didn't know what to make of anything that had just happened so she laid her head back down on the pillow and closed her eyes.

The cooking staff had put together a real cornucopia of breakfast foods for the buffet line. The kids loaded up their plates with a towering variety of breakfast foods, and each got a glass of juice to wash it down. They were sitting at one of the dining room tables and Barry, who also had a large plate of food, was with them.

"Good morning, Mr. Callahan," Barry greeted. "Are we all rested and ready for this glorious day?" Steve looked over at Barry with a blank expression on his face. "Oh, come now, are you not a morning person?"

Steve looked at Barry, and with a hushed breath he said, "Shadows." Barry's wide and inviting smile washed off his face.

"Excuse me, Mr. Callahan, what was that?"

Steve repeated what he said in the same tone he had first said it, "Shadows."

Barry got up from the table and the kids watched as this mammoth grew taller with each movement. They were all chewing on bites of breakfast they'd just taken, and followed his ascension with their eyes. Then they watched as he began walking towards Steve. Seeing how there was nothing too interesting about to transpire, the kids turned their attention back to their smorgasbord-piled plates.

Barry reached the place where Steve was standing, leaned in a little and said, "I'm sorry, Mr. Callahan, I don't think I heard you correctly. It sounded like you said 'shadows'; but shadows of *what*?" he asked.

Still unable to change his tone, Steve spit out one word and one word only: "Feet."

"Feet, Mr. Callahan? **Whose** feet?"

"I don't know. There wasn't anybody attached to that shadow. Just feet and shadows of legs that stretched across the hall and disappeared into the wall."

Barry turned to his right, reached for a ceramic coffee cup, depressed the valve on the coffee dispenser nearby, and poured some coffee. He then turned back to Steve and said, "Here. I think you might need this. You're not making any sense."

Steve took the cup of coffee from Barry. Then, as if he were suddenly doused with a bucket of ice water, his tone came back to normal level and he said, "Thank you, kind sir, I think I **DO** need this."

Doris entered the dining room, dazzled by the array of foods that lay before her in the buffet line, and asked, "Is this all for **us**??? Or is this something that you do every day?"

Barry found that charming, welcoming smile again and replied, "No. We do this every day. Then, what we don't eat, we take down to the food kitchen in town, where they can always use extra food."

"That's mighty generous of you. You seem like a good person, Mr. Henderson. This world needs more good souls like yourself," Doris added.

At the end of their breakfast, Doris escorted the kids back to their respective rooms and had them get ready, as she was going to take them out sightseeing so Steve and Ron could begin work. Ron was entering the dining room just as Doris was shepherding the kids out of the room. "Morning, Doris," Ron greeted. "Off for some sightseeing?"

"Yes," she replied. "And this is the hard part: getting the kids ready while there is still daylight." They both had a good chuckle at that and then went their separate ways. Ron grabbed a plateful of food, went over to the table where Steve was sitting, sat down and said, "So, Boss, where do we start?"

As Steve began to lay out his strategy for assessing the structures, Reg came over and announced that he needed to be with them throughout the entire time they were in the Kirkbridge Complex. "For your own safety and peace of mind, I will keep you company."

Steve and Ron went back to their respective rooms, put on their work clothes, and headed out of the staff dormitory, followed closely by Reg. Steve was carrying a floorplan layout that he had printed out from his office printer back in Pennsylvania. He paused, turned to Reg, lifted the paper up to Reg, and pointed to one of the wings. "I want to start here."

"Sure, Mr. Callahan, whatever you feel is best. You're the professional." Reg didn't say that with any degree of sarcasm, but was yielding to years of expertise from a gifted craftsman. "Follow me, then." Reg led them across the road, across the front lawn, and into the main entrance. "Oh, but I must inform you that this is one of the oldest wings, and the first one to have been shut down when this place began going downhill. It was sealed off in 1939. But I have been given explicit instructions to let you into any area you need to be in. We have all the tools you will need to help with your assessment."

"No problem, Reg, lead the way," Steve said with sincere affirmation.

Reg brought them through the maze of wings and finally reached the area where the entrance to the "A" wing was. "Is this an original cement wall? It doesn't match the rest of the facility's cement hue. Why would someone cement off an entrance and not just put up a large piece of wood?" Steve inquired. Steve looked around and found an old lamp stand in the right corner of the room. He picked it up, warned Ron and Reg to stand back, and hammered the stand's lead base into the cement wall. Nothing. Not even a chip of cement was loosened. "Let me try this again." Steve put a little more effort into his second thrust and there was a little chip of cement that broke off and flew towards the wall where the lamp stand was. "This is not working," Steve said. "Do you know if they have anything heavier I could use? Like a sledgehammer?"

"Let me go see. The basement is down this way and we are right over one of the maintenance closets. I'll be right back," Reg replied.

Reg turned and headed down the hallway, just a bit, then turned towards a staircase and disappeared behind the doorway. A few moments later, Reg

appeared from that same doorway carrying a large sledgehammer and asked

with a smile, "Something like **this**?"

"Yes. This should do just fine. Thank you." Steve donned the safety glasses he

always had handy in his pocket, grabbed the sledgehammer, warned Ron and

Reg to step back, and then swung that mighty hammer against the wall with

great force. Again, only a splinter shot off from the wall. "UGH!!!"

"Here, Mr. Callahan, let me give it a shot," Reg offered. He borrowed Steve's

safety glasses, grabbed the sledgehammer from Steve, gestured for Steve to

move back, and then the behemoth of a cop launched that sledgehammer

dead center. A massive crack appeared. Reg turned his head to Steve and

asked, "Shall I continue?" With a look of amazement, Steve just nodded in

agreement. Reg pulled back that hammer again and like a baseball slugger

working towards his 1,000th home run at Fenway Park, swung that hammer

against the wall. No longer was there just a crack, but Reg managed to knock a

small hole in the wall. A few seconds after that, Ron, Reg, and Steve began to

gag as one of the most foul, wretched stenches wafted out from that newly

created sledgehammer-sized hole in the cement barrier. It was one of the

worst smells any of them had ever experienced. It made Ron nearly vomit and

had Reg, the burly giant, almost doubled over. Steve couldn't make out what it was, but he had been around old sewage holds before, and this one definitely

took the gold medal over that smell.

"What the hell is **THAT**?" Steve asked, just after lifting his work shirt up to

cover his nose and mouth.

"I don't know, Mr. Callahan," Reg replied. "Never in my life have I ever smelled

something like this. Do you want me to continue?"

"Hold on a sec," Steve answered. He produced a small pocket flashlight from

his utility belt, approached the wall, and, holding his breath, shined a light into

the small hole. He wanted to find out if he could see anything that was behind

the wall.

"What do you see, Steve?" Ron asked, having followed Steve's lead of pulling

the top of his work shirt over his nose and mouth.

"A very dark hallway, but nothing else," Steve replied. "Reg, give it a few more

whacks and let's see if we can open this up wide enough so I can go through

the wall."

Reg asked Steve to step back again and gave a few more hearty blows to the wall. He was able to produce a narrow opening about 5 feet high and 2 feet wide. "More, Mr. Callahan?"

"No, that should be all right. You two wait here. I'll be right back."

As Steve used his small pocket light to scan the area, he saw that the dorm rooms' doors were missing. The walls were so corroded that chunks of paint were dangling off the walls. He slowly moved forward up the hallway, flashing his light back and forth between both sides of the hallway. When he reached the first room he heard a faint, scraping noise, like something was being dragged across the floor. The hairs on the back of Steve's neck stood up. His heart was beating heavily, and his breathing seemed to become more labored. He flashed his light in the direction of the noise and there was a man, in his late 60s, on the floor, with his arm reaching up and out towards Steve. The man was barely able to get any sound out but managed to say two spine-chilling words, "Kill me." Steve dropped the flashlight, turned around, and sprinted back towards the cement wall. He jumped through to the open hall where Reg and Ron stood and said, "Dear God. Dear **GOD**!!!! Oh my sweet Lord. That can't be possible. That **couldn't** have just happened. Please, God, no!" With that, Steve fell to his knees.

Reg and Ron stood completely dumbfounded and frightfully curious as to what

Steve was saying. "Mr. Callahan? Mr. Callahan! What did you see?" But Steve could not get anything out other than his pleas for a deity to save him from this new mental insanity he had developed. "WHAT'S IN THERE, MR. CALLAHAN????" Reg grabbed his flashlight and took out his police-issued handgun and pointed the light into the narrow passageway that he'd created with the sledgehammer. What he saw next nearly paralyzed him where he stood. He saw an old man dragging himself out of one of the first rooms and turning towards the opening in the cement wall where light was now shining in on the old man's face. The old man stopped, reached his arm up and out to Reg, and repeated what he said to Steve in the same tone: "Kill . . . me." Then the old man's body went completely limp and he just laid motionless on the floor. "How is this possible? This area has been sealed solid for more than 40 years! There was no way for anyone to get in here. This is just not possible." Reg reached for his walkie-talkie, pressed the button to talk, and was only able to get out the words, "Becky, this is Reg over at Danvers. Send help!"

CHAPTER 5: THE PETUNIA BROOCH

The sight could best be described as looking like a presidential motorcade moving down Pennsylvania Avenue preceding the inaugural ceremonies. Red and blues flashed like Christmas lights reflecting off tinsel that swayed in the breeze of a crosswind. There were 4 police cruisers followed by 3 ambulances, followed by 2 firetrucks, and 5 more police cruisers taking up the rear. Reg stood outside on the main entrance of the Kirkbridge Complex. The front four police cruisers turned right into the arching driveway that served as a loading and unloading zone for patients at the main entrance. The four cruisers drove their vehicles to the very end of that looping driveway, allowing the three ambulances to idle right in front of the main entrance. The rear doors of each ambulance opened up and the two paramedics from each ambulance jumped out and grabbed their respective stretchers, raised them up, placed their emergency responder kits on the stretcher, and began making their way up to where Reg was standing.

"So what's going on here, Reg? Did you see a ghost again? Let me guess? Shakespeare this time?" Adam Ransfield, a 24-year-old paramedic, was well known throughout the emergency service community as an arrogant antagonist whose penchant for sarcastic hyperbole often found him on the intolerant side of those usually calm and composed.

The youngest son of the mayor of Danvers, he was protected by his father's politics, power, and influence to the degree that he could say anything he pleased without fear of repercussion or consequences. So long as Adam's dad was in a position of authority, no professional soul wanted to test the boundaries.

Adam was very much aware of this advantage he held over his peers and his superiors, and never hesitated to use the "son of the mayor" card when it best served his purpose. The one and only thing his dad absolutely detested was profanity. He had told all Adam's superiors and peers that if they ever had concrete evidence that Adam so much as whispered a curse word, he would deal with it himself. Adam was keenly aware of his dad's cardinal rule and made sure to pussyfoot around it so he could maintain that Sword of Damocles over the heads of any person that even contemplated crossing him.

"No, Adam, no ghost. But I would much rather have seen a ghost than what I saw," Reg responded. He was doing everything he possibly could to resist the temptation of reaching his arm out, clasping his massive hand around Adam's scrawny neck, picking him up, and reliving his track and field shot put days. However, the intimidation paradigm that Adam held over all his professional cohorts served as an inoculation for obedience and undeserved respect. All Reg could do was cling to the small fiber of restraint he had, and do his best to maintain a civil tone and rational answers, despite the horror he had witnessed. "There really is no way to explain it, Adam; it can only be witnessed."

"Oooooh. You got me shivering in my boots, old man. All right. You win. Let's go see what has Papa Smurf's panties in a bunch," Adam snickered. "Dustin, grab the large neck brace in case we need to revive Father Time here. Wait, a 'large' won't fit. See if the stables have a spare horse collar they can lend us."

Dustin lugged the oversized responder bag over his left shoulder and served as the rudder for the stretcher that Adam was pulling behind him as they entered the main foyer of the administration building. Adam stopped, turned his head to the right and bellowed, "Hey, Papa Smurf, which wing did you see this ghost in?"

"'A' wing, Adam. To your right," Reg replied.

"Is that 'A' like in ancient?" Adam mocked.

No, 'A' as in asshole, Reg thought to himself. He knew if he said something like that aloud, there would be a very interesting conversation that night at the Ransfield's mansion's dinner table. "That's right, Adam, 'A' as in ancient."

Dealing with Adam was a pride-swallowing task for anybody in that service.

With that, Adam turned his head back forward and began pulling the stretcher again as he hollered out, "Hard to starboard, my trusty stretcher lackey!"

After Adam and Dustin turned down the right corridor, heading towards Wing A, Reg hung his head down. He put his right thumb and middle finger on either side of his eyes, closed his eyes, and slowly pulled his fingers together, brushing over his eyelids. He left them pinched up on the bridge of his nose.

Reg felt a warm hand on his shoulder and heard Sheriff Carlton Billings' voice say, "Reg, he's a prick. We all know that. And we all know that not a single one of us would ever want to cross you because you'd crush us like an unstoppable juggernaut on acid." That was followed by a tension-breaking chuckle from the sheriff. Reg dropped his hand from his face, opened his eyes, and turned his head to the right, where he saw the very familiar, reassuring expression from his senior. "So, in your own words, tell me what happened."

"It is like nothing I've ever seen before, Boss. How long have Wings A and J been sealed up?" Reg asked Billings.

"Well, I was in my freshman year of high school and that was in 1927. Soooo,

58 years. But that was only Wing J that was sealed. They kept Wing A open for another five years before they were able to relocate all the high-risk patients to other facilities. So as far as Wing A is concerned, 53 years," Billings replied.

"Is there any possible way you can imagine someone surviving for 53 years in complete darkness with no food or water?" Reg asked.

"Unless they were a zombie, I can't contemplate such a scenario as being possible."

Then Reg looked back up at Billings. Reg's eyes were very wide and his face looked flush. "Sheriff, I was helping Mr. Callahan get an overview of the facility; he was brought in by Heath Garrison. That foundation is looking to put in a considerable financial contribution to the restoration of the buildings here."

"That's right, Reg, the guy from Pennsylvania, right? That's Steven Callahan. He's here with his family and that's why I stationed you here. I needed the best protector on my force."

"Yes, sir. Well, we got up to the concrete wall that sealed Wing A off from Wing B. Mr. Callahan tried to break the wall with the bottom of a lamp stand, but it wasn't strong enough. I went down to the maintenance room in the basement and found a sledgehammer, and gave that to Mr. Callahan. After a couple attempts, he wasn't able to put a dent in that wall. I offered my services and gave it a couple strong whacks and it broke a hole just wide enough for one man to enter sideways. That's when we smelled it."

"Smelled what, Reg?"

"Do you know the landfill on East Coast Road? Do you know how it smells after a heavy thunderstorm in late July? When the humidity begins to lift the methane odor and spread it out over the surrounding area?"

"Well, sure, son, I know that all too well."

"That smells like a bouquet of roses compared to what came out of that hole."

"So it smelled like death?"

"Not just death . . . decay, shit, piss, vomit, mildew, ammonia, sweat, and rot."

"Did Mr. Callahan or his coworker get hurt? Is that why we needed to bring the ambulances?"

"No. They're for the people on the other side of that wall."

"Hold on a second, Reginald, did you say *people* on the other side of the wall?"

"Yes, sir, and one was still alive."

"That can't be possible. In fact, it's inconceivable. Fifty-three years, Reg . . . that place has been sealed off with no way in and no way out for 53 years. How can there be bodies in there, let alone **live** bodies? How many were in there?"

"I don't know, sir. I ran out once I saw the old man pulling himself across the floor from the first room on the right. All he said, in a laboring gasp, was 'Kill me.'"

"I've never known you to lie or make up such outlandish stories, Reg, but I'm just trying to figure out how any of that can be possible."

Louis Peabody and Edward Rivera were walking towards Reg and Billings. They were adorned in full fireman gear, including the helmets, and each carrying industrial-strength axes. Louis and Edward were stepbrothers and of the same age, and both had wanted to be firemen when they were younger. They both joined the academy right after high school graduation, and both boys were very accomplished athletes. They were your stereotypical "gym rats" who started

their mornings, every day, jogging up to the local gym, working out for an hour,

then jogging back to the station house. Both boys were in tip-top shape and

had the textbook definition of healthiness.

Although these two stepbrothers were equally matched in physique, their

personalities were slightly different. They weren't rude, conceited, pretentious,

or cocky, but Edward was a quiet type while Louis fancied being more

loquacious and outgoing. Their hearts were golden and their compassion

immeasurable. However, when it came to their rescuing responsibilities, there

was no margin for error or areas of gray. There was not a soul in the medical

rescue cadre who would dare get in their way on the scene of any trauma.

These boys practiced protocol to the letter, and this is what made them

extremely successful firefighters and rescuers.

When Louis and Ed reached Sheriff Billings and Reg, Louis turned to Reg and

asked, "How's it going, partner? You look very shaken up. Are you all right? Did

you speak with one of the EMTs yet to get checked out?"

"I'm fine, Lou, but there is nothing I can say to prepare you for what you're

about to witness," Ralph replied.

"Do you want to hang back here until we get back? I'm perfectly fine with that. Sheriff?"

"I'm not going to make you do anything you don't want to do, Reg," the sheriff responded. "No one is going to think any less of you. Understand?"

"I'm all right, guys, I just needed some fresh air. Come on, I'll show you what we f—"

Reg was mid-sentence when he was cut off by a panicky Adam, who darted out from the main entrance, his right hand firmly cupping his mouth. He collapsed when he got to the bushes to the left of the main entrance. Not more than a split-second later, there was an eruption of vomit that burst from between his fingers and out from the seal his palm made over his mouth. He had a few more heaving spells and then, while kneeling on the lawn, hung his head down towards the ground. When he was able to gain some semblance of composure, he said in a low tone, but one that Reg, Billings, Louis, and Ed could hear, "It's just not possible. How????"

Louis jogged up to Adam's left side and knelt down on one knee. He placed his right hand on Adam's left shoulder and asked, "Hey, buddy, you okay? What happened?"

"I . . . can't . . . begin . . . to—" Adam quickly cupped his mouth again, with his left hand, but it was as unsuccessful a sealed barrier as the first time and he hurled more vomit out from in between his fingers and the outside edges of his hand. Louis turned his head around to his left, raised his left arm, and gestured for Billings to come over. Billings walking briskly up to the Adam's right, knelt down next to him, and placed his left hand on Adam's right shoulder.

"What is it, son? What did you see?" Billings asked.

"They're alive. They're fucking **alive**!" Adam said, now weeping.

"Who? Who is alive? Mr. Callahan? Mr. Boscawen?"

"The patients. The fucking **patients**, Sheriff!" Adam replied.

Billings looked up over to his left at Louis and said, "Come on, Lou, let's go. Get your brother. Everyone else stays outside for now." Then looking back to Adam he said, "Son, you stay here. Catch your breath."

Billings and Lou shot up light a bottle rocket taking off, jogged towards the main entrance, and Lou called out, "Yo, Ed, let's go!"

The three of them burst through the main entrance doorway as if they were marathon runners breaking through the winning tape. They turned to their right and made their way to Wing A through the zig-zag corridors that made up the preceding wings. They reached the juncture where Wing B ended and Wing A began. They saw the hole in the wall and immediately smelled what Reg had described; but that description paled in comparison to the actual stench. They saw the stretcher in front of the remaining cement wall, but Dustin wasn't there. Steven and Ron were not to be found, either.

Billings put his right forearm up to his face, covering his nose, and approached the hole. With his left hand, he grabbed the flashlight from its holster on his police belt, turned it on, and flashed it inside the hole. He saw an old man lying across the floor. He heard water dripping and a few faint moans coming from further down the hall. He called out, "Mr. Callahan? Mr. Boscawen? Dustin? Are you guys down there?"

There were no other responses besides gasping moans and sounds of cloth scraping across the floors. He flashed his light back and forth, up and down the hall, and saw rat carcasses and bones scattered throughout the hallway. The old man was wearing a hospital Johnny that was up to his knees. He was thinner than the handle of a hammer, with absolutely no muscle tone whatsoever. Billings had to turn his head away from the hole as his eyes began to water from the piercing, wretched foulness that was exuding from the opening of the cement wall. "Mr. Callahan? Mr. Boscawen? Dustin? Anyone?"

He turned back to look into the opening and there were two more emaciated bodies pulling themselves out from two different rooms. It sounded like someone was slowly scraping 80-grit sandpaper over moldy linoleum. He toggled his light between the two beleaguered bodies pulling themselves towards the center of the hallway. They were both wearing hospital Johnnies that were stained brown, yellow, and red. Their hair looked like long, silvery, matted mops shrouding their faces, so Billings couldn't make out if they were women or men. One of the bodies suddenly stopped and collapsed on the floor. The other person continued to pull itself with every last bit of strength. It stopped in the middle of the hallway, then began to turn itself towards the opening in the cement wall. Billings was paralyzed with shock and disbelief. He had never encountered any scenario like this before, and he didn't know how to react. The person slowly inched their way closer and closer to the opening of the cement wall, gasping with each movement. Its matted nest of hair still curtained its face, its gasping growing ever louder as it struggled and struggled to reach the opening.

When Billings was able to break from his horrified trance, he kept the spotlight on this person making its way closer and closer to the opening, but he saw that the body was leaving a trail of blood behind it. He saw what appeared to be a toenail lodged into one of the cracks of the linoleum floor, and continued to hear crunching sounds like tiddlywinks against an oak card table. He looked down and saw that as the body was pulling itself, its fingernails were breaking off, ripping the skin underneath and creating channels of blood that widened the smearing blood trail the body was making with each pull.

"Sheriff??? **SHERIFF**!!!! What's going on?" Lou shouted. "What are you looking at? Move out of the way. Ed and I will break that wall open some more."

"NO!!! Wait. Wait just a minute," Billings responded with a drill-sergeant tone. "Just wait."

Then he looked back in the hole and the body had made its way to the opening in the wall. Its head lifted up from the neck, the hair still dangling over the person's face, and it let out a horrible gurgling sound. There was a pause and then it said in a very low, raspy, scratchy tone,

"A . . . mon . . . tiiiii . . . ahhhhhhh . . ." Then its head crashed to the floor and there was no more movement. No more sounds. No more breathing. No more . . . anything. "Lou, get over here! Ed, go find Dustin, Mr. Callahan, and

Mr. Boscawen," Billings ordered.

Ed wasted no time and turned up the corridor heading towards the main entrance. He got three-quarters of the way up Wing B when he heard retching coming from a door on the right: the lavatory. He peeked his head into the door and called out, "Hello? Mr. Callahan? Mr. Boscawen? Dustin?" He heard a toilet flush, then one of the stall doors opened. It was Dustin. He then saw two sets of outfacing soles under two different closed-door stalls. "Dustin, who's in there with you?"

Dustin cleared his throat and said, "Mr. Callahan and Mr. Boscawen are here with me. Where's Adam?"

"He ran outside. Sheriff and Louis are still at the wall. Is there anyone else in there with you?" Ed asked, now making his way into the lavatory. "No. It's just the three of us. I just couldn't take it."

"It's no problem, dude. You wait there. I'm going out to get a couple of the other paramedics."

Lou turned to the sheriff and asked him, "What was that noise? Was that the person speaking? What did it say?"

"It said something like 'Amontiah.' I'm not sure what that is. Was it trying to say its name?" Billings replied.

The next thing he heard were small footsteps coming from the other side of the wall. This wasn't a scraping noise like the two other patients made, but very distinct and paced steps. They were narrowly spaced footsteps, but something was definitely walking and not crawling. Billings snapped the flashlight back through the opening and saw a small boy walking towards the opening. He was wearing a Blind Cheetah shirt with the word "Pyromania" under a picture of a glass building. He had on jeans that were cut off at the knees and was wearing blue Denim sneakers.

As he got closer, Billings' heart began pounding even faster and his hands began to shake, causing the flashlight to flicker. The boy was halfway up the hall and held up his right arm straight out. He was holding something shiny and round in his hand. His pace continued as he came closer and closer to the opening. When he reached the opening where Billings was standing shining the light through the crevice in the cement wall, Jasper Callahan stopped, holding a brooch with a pink petunia picture in its center. He stared straight into the light and said, "Amontillado."

CHAPTER 6: DAFFODILS AT DANVERS

Mrs. Jeannine Davis-Carpenter was a 45-year-old widow who never recovered from her husband's death while he was serving in the army. He was a captain who was killed by a grenade from a German soldier during the Battle of Passchendaele. Prior to this tragedy, Mrs. Davis-Carpenter's profession was to assist in gathering information for the local paper's gossip column. She spent her days keeping track of different people's lives, habits, and made note of any wrongdoings they were committing. Her main focus was on political figures, as well as municipal workers.

She would often sit on a wooden bench with a newspaper in her lap that was concealing a notepad where she documented persons of interest's activities. At the end of each day, she would fold up her newspaper like a book around her notepad and head over to the print shop where the gossip columnist's office was located. One of the things she would enjoy reporting on the most was the way people performed their jobs. She would watch city workers do road work and see if they put in the required hours the taxpayers were funding. She would pay close attention to how vigorously they worked and if their efforts produced the daily progress expected to complete tasks on schedule.

One spring day, she noticed a construction crew member stop hauling the cement bins back and forth and sit under a tree. It wasn't very hot outside, nor was there any degree of inclement weather, he just sat down. Mrs. Davis-Carpenter jotted down in her notepad: "Martin Dentin lazily stopped working and let his coworkers take on the exhausting task of mixing and hauling cement to and from the truck, thus putting more stress and efforts onto his coworkers who were receiving the same pay as himself. This act of unfair selfishness proves that he is not a good fit for the position he holds." When this got back to the gossip columnist, he reported it to a good friend of his, who was a foreman of that particular construction crew, and without knowing the full story, Mr. Dentin was laid off, cited with performance issues and poor work efforts. A few weeks after that, there was a letter in Jeannine's mailbox from Martin Dentin that read:

Dear Mrs. Davis-Carpenter:

Although I am a fan of your observations that are printed in the local paper, and can certainly appreciate your dedication to protecting taxpayers' contributions to the city, the reports of corrupt political figures, and persons of authority, your unfair and unsubstantiated accounts of my actions a few weeks back caused me to lose my job. I have always been a dedicated, hard worker and have never lazily pawned my responsibilities onto my coworkers. In fact, I would often work harder to help them if they were falling behind on their responsibilities, as true team members are supposed to do.

The day that you observed me resting underneath a tree in the shade while my other coworkers continued working, I had just suffered the loss of a dear friend the day before. He was someone I had known my entire life. You probably know him (Peter Reynolds), as you know practically everyone in this region with the type of work you do. My mind just wasn't in a place where I could focus on the environment I was in, but I had completed my tasks for that day, nonetheless. I was responsible for bringing the cement out to the concrete masons who were filling in part of the sidewalk that had cracked due to frost heaves created over this past winter. They had received all the cement they needed, so I sat down to collect my thoughts.

Because of your absence of investigatory accuracy and haphazard, slipshod degree of involvement in the basis of my actions that day, my family will be in financial strain until I can find work again; which will be difficult in these times, along with possibly a poor reference from my former

employer. I did want to thank you, though, as this incident has

made me keenly aware of how other people can be

destructively judgmental and jump to conclusions they have

very little knowledge of.

I wish you all the best of success with your career path and

pray that no other innocent souls fall victim to your vicious,

superficial depiction of their actions without solid evidence or

full background leading to those actions.

Sincerely,

Martin Walter Dentin

When Mrs. Davis-Carpenter learned of the tragic loss of her husband while he was overseas fighting for the freedom and liberties of his countrymen, she became victim to a flood of regrets and guilt due to the life-altering events she had caused different people with her premature exposure of their actions. Mrs. Davis-Carpenter had taken pride in her skills for snooping, and never considered the conceivable consequences the individuals she reported on would face. It only took a few weeks following that episode that she had fallen into a comatose state of mind and was generally unresponsive to any degree of human connection. Mrs. Davis-Carpenter was found sitting on that same wooden bench, motionless, while it was raining, her head slightly cocked down and to the left, and her eyes were fixated on the tree across the street that Martin Dentin had taken momentary refuge under to collect his thoughts. She realized that his actions never jeopardized his expected results, nor did it cast any additional inconvenience onto the taxpayers. It was this fixed gaze that she maintained from the time Martin Dentin found her on that sidewalk bench in the rain to when she was eventually admitted to Danvers State Hospital.

Besides an estranged daughter who lived out in California, Mrs. Davis-Carpenter had no other family nearby, and her daughter's relocation across the country followed a very heated and hurtful argument when her daughter was 18 years old. The trigger that drove her daughter away was when Mrs. Davis-Carpenter had submitted a report to the local newspaper about her daughter's biology teacher, citing statutory rape, when the facts never even came close to warrant such a horrible label. Her daughter's teacher was let go from his position and was ordered to stay away from school grounds for the remainder of his life.

***

When Ralph first met Mrs. Davis-Carpenter, he was initially intimidated by her lack of movement or response to the caretakers in her unit. Ralph often wondered if she would sporadically, and without provocation, leap out of her wheelchair and lunge at whoever was tending to her, but that never happened. Ralph would usually watch her as he sat at a card table helping another patient with a puzzle, or playing cards, or reading the newspaper while the patient listened intently. Whenever he heard someone tending to Mrs. Davis-Carpenter, he would raise his eyes with curious anticipation to see if she would show any signs of acknowledgement to the caretaker or another patient who was simply passing by to say hello. It seemed like nothing anyone did would elicit any kind of response from her.

Then one day, Ralph was sitting in a recliner across from Mrs. Davis-Carpenter sitting in her wheelchair, still motionless. Ralph had a small flashlight in his right hand, and he was waving his hand in front of the lamp, which created a sequence of fluttering light pulses each time he moved his hand in front of the lamp and then moved it away. On his lap, he had an open book about Morse code, and he was looking down at it while performing these rhythmic hand gestures in front of the light. As he created these illuminated signals, in a hushed tone he would speak different letters in long, drawn-out enunciation, pause after each letter, then move onto the next:

"Ayyyyy, beeeeee, seeeee, deeeee, eeeeee, effffff, geeeee, ayyyyych, eyyyyyye, jayyyyyy, kayyyyy, ellll, emmmmm, ennnnn, ooooo, peeeee, cuuuuue, arrrrr, essss, teeeee, ewwwwwwe, veeeee, dublllll-u, exxxxx, whyyyyy, zeeeee."

He repeated multiple cycles of the alphabet about ten times, then reached down to the book, grabbed the top edge of the right page corner, and turned to the next page. There, he would find small words that put those letters together. He began creating flashing light sequences as he recited each letter in the same long, drawn-out fashion:

"Seeee, ayyyyy, teeeee. Cat."

He went through many different animal words, reached down, and turned to the next page. This page had a little more involved in it, as it was the beginning of practicing full sentences. Again, he brought his hand up to the lamp of the flashlight and began creating a shutter by flipping his palm away and back to the lamp, creating letters in Morse code. The very first sentence on the page was your typical introduction greeting that most people learn with any new language:

"Ayyyyych, eeeeee, ellll, ellll, oooooo. Hello."

Ralph heard a soft and slow tapping. He looked up, but saw nothing. No one was moving around. He noticed an older gentleman in the corner of the room tapping his finger against his chair while reading the newspaper. So he returned to his book and repeated the same word again, practicing with the shuttering effect:

"Ayyyyych, eeeeee, ellll, ellll, oooooo. Hello."

There was a soft, slow tapping again and Ralph looked back at the older

gentleman reading the paper, but his finger was no longer tapping against the

arm of the chair. Ralph looked around to see if anyone was tapping their

fingers against something, but found that no one was. Ralph shrugged his

shoulders, then practiced the word again:

"Ayyyyych, eeeeee, ellll, ellll, oooooo. Hello."

This time, he caught some movement from across the way. Mrs. Davis-

Carpenter was moving her finger up and down on the armrest of her

wheelchair, and then suddenly, it stopped. Her face remained unchanged and

emotionless. Her eyes kept their gaze to the floor. Her head remained slightly

tilted to the left and slightly bent down. Ralph practiced the word, again, but

this time, he did so without looking at the book or reciting the letters as he

created the word with just the light. .... . .-.. .-.. --- (dot-dot-dot-dot, dot, dot-

dash-dot-dot, dot-dash-dot-dot, dash-dash-dash). The indicator for "dot" with

the flashlight is a quick flicker of the light and a "dash" is a little longer exposed

light before closing the makeshift palm shutter. He maintained his focus on

Mrs. Davis-Carpenter while he was doing this. When he was done, she began

tapping her finger against the armrest of her wheelchair, again, in the same

rhythmic cadence that he had performed with the light: tap-tap-tap-tap (pause) tap (pause) tap-taaap-tap-tap (pause) tap-taaap-tap-tap (pause) taaap-taaap-

taaap.

Ralph's eyes began to widen. *Did she just say hello to me in Morse code?* Ralph

thought to himself. *I've never seen her move at all before.* Then he spoke aloud

to Mrs. Davis-Carpenter: "Mrs. Davis-Carpenter, did you just say hello to me?"

Her finger began to move again against the armrest of her wheelchair: taaap-

tap-taaap-taaap (pause) tap (pause) tap-tap-tap. Ralph flipped back to the

original page in the book that had all the letters' Morse code translation. Then

he found each letter that represented the sequence that Mrs. Davis-Carpenter

had created and spoke the letters and the code aloud: "Taaap-tap-taaap-

taaap . . . 'Y'; tap . . . 'E'. Tap-tap-tap . . . 'S.' 'Yes'?" he exclaimed with shocked

excitement. Then his voice calmed back down to a normal conversational tone.

"Do you know who I am?" he asked her.

Her finger began to move against the armrest of her wheelchair again. This

time, the message seemed a little longer. Ralph watched with anticipation and

very closely before her finger stopped moving: taaap-tap-tap (pause) tap-taaap

(pause) tap-tap-taaap-tap (pause) tap-tap-taaap-tap (pause) taaap-taaap-taaap

(pause) taaap-tap-tap (pause) tap-tap (pause) tap-taaap-tap-tap. Then her

finger rested back on the armrest and it didn't move again.

Ralph feverishly began translating the sequence using the Morse code book's alphabet page, again speaking out each letter as he translated: "Taaap-tap-tap . . . 'D', tap-taaap . . . 'A', tap-tap-taaap-tap . . . 'F', tap-tap-taaap-tap . . . 'F', taaap-taaap-taaap . . . 'O', taaap-tap-tap . . . 'D', tap-tap . . . 'I', tap-taaap-tap-tap . . . 'L.' 'Daffodil'?" he asked inquisitively. "No, my name is Ralph Dubain. I've been volunteering here for a few years now. My aunt is Claire Dubain, the head nurse here. Do you know her?"

Mrs. Davis-Carpenter lifted her finger again and began responding with the same series of rhythmic taps: taaap-tap-taaap-taaap (pause) tap (pause) tap-tap-tap.

"Yes?" Ralph responded. Then he continued, "Why haven't I ever seen you move before today?"

There was no movement of Mrs. Davis-Carpenter's finger. There was no response. No reaction whatsoever. Ralph asked again, "Why haven't I ever seen you move before today?" Still, no movement of Mrs. Davis-Carpenter's finger, and no other recognition of Ralph's question. Ralph decided not to press the issue any further, but moved on to simpler questions. "What's your favorite color?"

Her finger began to move again: tap-taaap-taaap-tap (pause) tap-tap (pause) taaap-tap (pause) taaap-tap-taaap, then her finger settled motionless against the armrest.

Again, Ralph looked down onto the alphabet translation page and began breaking the coded message she'd just responded with: "Tap-taaap-taaap-tap . . . 'P', tap-tap . . . 'I', taaap-tap . . . 'N', taaap-tap-taaap . . . 'K.' 'Pink'?"

A few seconds went by and then her fingers began to tap against the armrest, again: taaap-tap-taaap-taaap (pause) tap (pause) tap-tap-tap.

"Do you like flowers?" Ralph asked.

Mrs. Davis-Carpenter responded: taaap-tap-taaap-taaap (pause) tap (pause) tap-tap-tap.

"'Yes'," Ralph affirmed. "What's your favorite flower?"

Her finger began to move again: tap-taaap-taaap-tap (pause) tap (pause) taaap (pause) tap-tap-taaap (pause) taaap-tap (pause) tap-tap (pause) tap-taaap. Her finger rested motionless again.

"Tap-taaap-taaap-tap . . . 'P', tap . . . 'E', taaap . . . 'T', tap-tap-taaap . . . 'U',

taaap-tap . . . 'N', tap-tap . . . 'I', tap-taaap . . . 'A.' 'Petunia'?"

Mrs. Davis-Carpenter responded: taaap-tap-taaap-taaap (pause) tap (pause)

tap-tap-tap.

"So you must like pink petunias, then, right?" he asked.

Mrs. Davis-Carpenter responded: taaap-tap-taaap-taaap (pause) tap (pause)

tap-tap-tap.

Ralph began to smile because he had just discovered there was a way to

communicate with Mrs. Davis-Carpenter. In his excitement, he failed to hear

his mom talking to him. "Ralph, I said it's time to leave now," Doris said in a

little louder decibel. "You need to say good-bye to Mrs. Davis-Carpenter now

because Aunt Claire wants to get back home so there's time to cook dinner,

have your bath, and then get ready for bed."

Ralph then looked up at the clock on the wall: 5:00 p.m. He had completely lost

track of time as he was so enthralled with the communication channel he had

discovered with Mrs. Davis-Carpenter.

Ralph looked back at Mrs. Davis-Carpenter and said, "Good-bye, Mrs. Davis-Carpenter. I'll be back tomorrow."

Mrs. Davis-Carpenter's finger began to move again, but Doris didn't notice: taaap-tap-tap-tap (pause) taaap-tap-taaap-taaap (pause) tap (long pause) taaap-tap-tap (pause) tap-taaap (pause) tap-tap-taaap-tap (pause) tap-tap-taaap-tap (pause) taaap-taaap-taaap (pause) taaap-tap-tap (pause) tap-tap (pause) tap-taaap-tap-tap.

Ralph paused for a moment as he opened the book to the alphabet page, again, and began decoding her message: "Taaap-tap-tap-tap . . . 'B', taaap-tap-taaap-taaap . . . 'Y', tap . . . 'E.' First word is 'Bye.' Taaap-tap-tap . . . 'D', tap-taaap . . . 'A', tap-tap-taaap-tap . . . 'F', tap-tap-taaap-tap . . . 'F', taaap-taaap-taaap . . . 'O', taaap-tap-tap . . . 'D', tap-tap . . . 'I', tap-taaap-tap-tap . . . 'L.' 'Daffodil.' 'Bye Daffodil'." Ralph smiled again. He wanted to give Mrs. Davis-Carpenter a hug, but he didn't know how she'd respond, so he tabled that idea for another time, when he and Mrs. Davis-Carpenter had more time to chat. He joined his mom and they headed towards the main entrance where they met up with Claire, then they all turned and left. All Ralph could think about was getting home and studying harder on his Morse code comprehension. He was too excited to even think about sleeping.

Ralph sprung out of bed the next morning, having devoted his time to

mastering as much of the Morse code skills in the 14-hour period of time

between taking his leave from Mrs. Davis-Carpenter to when he, his mom, and

Claire were scheduled to be back at the hospital. When his mom called him out

to the breakfast table in Claire's kitchen, he sat down with the book of Morse

code in front of him and he was tapping his right foot with speed equal to that

of a rascally grey rabbit. His mom had fixed a plate of pancakes, syrup, and a

slab of butter. She brought it over to Ralph and sat it down to the right of

where his book lay.

"Now, Ralph, close that book and eat your breakfast. Your Aunt Claire has to be

at the hospital in an hour, so we need to hurry along. You can read more of

that book on the way," his mom ordered.

Ralph pushed his book aside, grabbed his breakfast plate and pulled it in front

of him. He picked up the fork that was on the left side of the off-white ceramic

plate and began shoveling the pancakes into his mouth while maintaining his

attention on the translations in the Morse code book. He was so eager to

return to Mrs. David-Carpenter, and hoped he could engage in another

conversation with her through a Morse code medium. Syrup dripped off the

fork and down his chin, onto his shirt, and into his lap. He paid no mind to this,

but continued to shovel those pancakes without even looking down at the plate. When he had scooped up the last bite, swept the plate with his fork to see if there was anything else on it (and finding nothing), he dropped the fork on the plate, pushed it aside, and pulled the book back in front of him with his left hand. He said, "I'm done, Mom."

Ralph's mom came to the table to take his dirty dish away and looked at the sticky dribble of syrup adhered to Ralph's chin. She followed the imaginary line from the syrup on his chin to his shirt and then further down to his lap. "Ralph Dubain!!!! You go wash your face and change your clothes this instant. We are leaving in five minutes." With that, she grabbed hold of the book, closed it, picked it up, and placed it on top of the counter. Ralph did as his mom told him, and soon they were heading out the door and on their way to the hospital.

Arriving at the hospital, Ralph ran around the Kirkbridge Complex into the garden, found pink petunias, picked a handful, and ran back towards the front of the building. He went inside the main entrance and into the recreation hall, where he saw Mrs. Davis-Carpenter sitting in her wheelchair, facing the large windows, her hands motionlessly resting on the armrests of the wheelchair. Her head was still slightly cocked to the left, and she was wearing a pink-and-white floral dress covered with illustrations of yellow daffodils. Ralph stood at the entryway for a moment, a bundle of pink petunias grasped with both hands and held at heart's level, then began walking over to Mrs. Davis-Carpenter. He pulled one of the single chairs from a nearby card table, placed it in front of

Mrs. Davis-Carpenter's wheelchair, and said, "Hello, Mrs. Davis-Carpenter. Do

you remember me from yesterday?"

There was a minute or two pause, and then Mrs. Davis-Carpenter's right finger

lifted off the armrest of her wheelchair and began to tap against it: taaap-tap-

tap (pause) tap-taaap (pause) tap-tap-taaap-tap (pause) tap-tap-taaap-tap

(pause) taaap-taaap-taaap (pause) taaap-tap-tap (pause) tap-tap (pause) tap-

taaap-tap-tap.

Ralph remembered that sequence from the day before and answered, "Well,

actually it's Ralph Dubain, but if you like to call me 'Daffodil,' I'm perfectly fine

with that. Did you sleep well last night?"

Mrs. Davis-Carpenter responded with tapping against the armrest of her

wheelchair: taaap-tap-taaap-taaap (pause) tap (pause) tap-tap-tap.

"That's great," Ralph said cheerfully. "Here, I picked these for you from the

garden outside." He held out the bouquet of petunias he had arranged, but she

didn't move. Ralph was hoping she would reach up, grab them, and smile, but

she didn't do any of that. "Don't you like them?"

Mrs. Davis-Carpenter responded with tapping against the armrest of her wheelchair: taaap-tap-taaap-taaap (pause) tap (pause) tap-tap-tap.

"Oh. OK. Do you want me to put them on your lap?"

Mrs. Davis-Carpenter responded with tapping against the armrest of her wheelchair: taaap-tap-taaap-taaap (pause) tap (pause) tap-tap-tap.

"All right. Here you go." Ralph reached over and gently placed the arrangement on her lap.

Mrs. Davis-Carpenter's finger began to move again: taaap (pause) tap-tap-tap-tap (pause) tap-taaap (pause) taaap-tap (pause) taaap-tap-taaap (long pause) taaap-tap-taaap-taaap (pause) taaap-taaap-taaap (pause) tap-tap-taaap. Then her finger came to a rest on the armrest.

"Oh wait. This is a new one. Hold on." Ralph closed his eyes, and began lip syncing the sequence of taps and reciting them internally. His head bobbed to the pulse of the tapping and then he began to say aloud:
"'T' . . . 'H' . . . 'A' . . . 'N' . . . 'K,' ummmm, 'Y' . . . 'O' . . . 'U.' 'Thank you'? You're quite welcome, ma'am. What kind of music do you like?"

Mrs. Davis-Carpenter's finger began to move again: tap-taaap-taaap-taaap

(pause) tap-taaap (pause) taaap-taaap-tap-tap (pause) taaap-taaap-tap-tap.

Then her finger came to a rest back on the armrest of her wheelchair.

Ralph responded with, "Oh. Hmmm." Again, he bobbed his head while his

mouth moved without producing a sound, reciting the cadence of her tapping

finger and then he said aloud, "'J' . . . 'A' . . . 'Z' . . . 'Z.' 'Jazz'?"

Again, Mrs. Davis-Carpenter responded by tapping her finger on the armrest:

taaap-tap-taaap-taaap (pause) tap (pause) tap-tap-tap.

"I like that kind of music as well. My aunt Claire told me that you were a writer

for the newspaper. I have to write papers for school, and they're usually

reports on history or science. Is there anything exciting happening here that I

don't see during my visits?" Ralph asked with a curious and inquisitive tone.

There was no response from Mrs. Davis-Carpenter so he asked again. "Oh, I'm

sorry. I talk low, sometimes, and often mumble. Mom told me that's something

I need to work on. You probably didn't understand me when I asked that

question. I'm sorry about that. I had asked if there is anything interesting that

happens when I'm not visiting."

Mrs. Davis-Carpenter's finger lifted from the armrest and she held it in the air for close to a minute. Then her finger began to move up and down in response to his question. At the same time, a tear rolled down her cheek: tap-taaap (pause) taaap-taaap (pause) taaap-taaap-taaap (pause) taaap-tap (pause) taaap (pause) tap-tap (pause) tap-taaap-tap-tap (pause) tap-taaap-tap-tap (pause) tap-taaap (pause) taaap-tap-tap (pause) taaap-taaap-taaap. Her finger came to rest back down on the armrest.

"Oh my," Ralph responded, surprised. "This is a long one. Hold on while I figure this one out." With the same actions he had done with the two other sets of code, Ralph mouthed and bobbed his head as he deciphered the message: "'A' . . . 'M' . . . 'O' . . . 'N' . . . 'T' . . . 'I' . . . 'L' . . . 'L' . . . 'A' . . . 'D' . . . 'O.' 'Amontillado'? What does that mean?"

Her hand began to tremble and she responded with: tap-taaap-taaap-tap (pause) taaap-taaap-taaap (pause) tap. Her finger then rested back down on the armrest and her hand's trembling began to intensify.

"'P' . . . 'O' . . . 'E.' 'Poe'? I don't know what you're trying to tell me. What do those words mean?" he asked.

"Ralph, let's go. It's time to leave Mrs. Davis-Carpenter alone. We need to visit with Mr. Murphy now," Aunt Claire beckoned from the other room.

Ralph got up, walked a little past Mrs. Davis-Carpenter's wheelchair, turned to his left and said, "I am going to figure out what you were talking about and then we can talk more tomorrow."

***

In the spring of 1927, after it was determined that the hospital could no longer support the number of patients coming in, the hospital administrators decided to take alternate and barbaric measures to weed through the patients who were "beyond treatment," as some of the head physicians classified. They devised a scheme of nefariously segregating those particular patients whom they knew would never benefit from the therapeutic treatments the hospital provided by entombing those patients in one of the old wings of the complex. It is still unknown as to which criminal director's mind this plan came from, but they administered heavy doses of long-lasting sedatives, placed them in that old, abandoned, decrepit structure with no windows, and seal up the entrances and exits with a 5-inch-thick quick-drying cement mixed with industrial-strength epoxy while the patients were unconscious.

No one in the entire town knew this was happening, especially no courts or medical judicial professionals speaking on behalf of the hospital outside of the facility's walls. The plan included informing the local medical comptrollers that these patients had died, and due to the nature of their deaths and potential health hazards to others from lethal pathogens, the bodies were professionally cremated and the ashes were given to family members; for those patients who had family members, that is. In actuality, the facility directors would have the maintenance crew take lumber that had crumbled from the dilapidating buildings, burn it in the basement furnaces, shovel out the ashes, and put them in cheap urns found at local flea markets. The hospital administrators left the selection of "qualifying" patients up to the medical staff who worked closely with those patients, day in and day out, and would review the patient records filed by the nurses and doctors.

The remaining patients would hear cries and moans coming from inside the adjoining walls, but were not aware of the source or origins behind those noises. The medical directors ordered the caregivers to administer heavy dosages of Alprazolam to those patients who were lucid enough to talk about what they heard to any outsider who may have been visiting (including their **own** family member visitors), which would give those patients' visitors the illusion that the resident was suffering from some form of delusion. Claire Dubain was one of the hospital staff responsible for identifying the patients who were "beyond treatment," and in the spring of 1927, Mrs. Davis-Carpenter was identified as a "beyond treatment" patient by Claire Dubain and became a

member of the walled-in souls.

CHAPTER 7: NOAH'S ARK

Noah Callahan appeared to be a typical jock at Bethlehem-Center High School

in Fredericktown, Pennsylvania; that is to say, he was an active athlete in each

season of the school year and summer vacations as well. Track and field, swim

team, soccer, baseball, and hockey. Although the swimming and hockey sports

were part of the same season, Noah found ways to never miss a meet or game.

In his freshman year of high school, Noah shocked each of his coaches with his

ability for endurance, strength, stamina, and speed. He broke six school records

in his freshman year:

Track and Field

- 1600 Meters: 4:55.48

- 300 Meter Hurdles: 34.17

- 100 Meters: 10.41

Swimming

- 100m Butterfly: 52.38

- 200m Individual Medley: 1:54.67

- 500m Freestyle: 4:45.33

Noah maintained a 4.0 GPA with his top subjects being biology, algebra, and

Spanish. He made honor roll in each semester for two years in a row. By the beginning of his junior year, there were college athletic scouts showing up to get a better look at this seemingly unstoppable force and extremely smart student/athlete. There seemed to be no limit to the success this young man could achieve. Noah impressed many people with all the skills he had, he acquired, and he incorporated into his scholastic career up to that point, but his biggest fans were his parents and his siblings. Noah had the muscular tone of a prized race horse. He stood 5'11" by the time he was 14 years old, sported shoulder-length, golden-blonde hair, and had radiant, sapphire-colored eyes. To put it like Doris used to brag to her friends about him (and would also embarrass Noah, himself, when his friends were around), he was "Prince Charming incarnate"; but then again, what mother **doesn't** say that about their baby boys? Yet, as much of a highly intelligent and youthful athletic Olympian as he was, Noah harbored an alternate personality that was not quite worthy of the same praise and admiration as was his more prominent dynamo.

Steve and Doris had given Noah an old-fashioned cedar storage chest for his ninth birthday in hopes he would learn to keep his room tidy and put his toys in one, sealed area. Before they gave it to him, Steve had scribed the words "Noah's Ark" on the top of the chest with white paint. Noah was the eldest child, and that title usually carries with it a higher degree of responsibility at a young age. With his parents' lines of work and the expectations set upon them by employers and potential clients, Noah started watching over his siblings when he was 12; which, at the time, was the legal age that a sibling could be responsible for watching over his brothers and sisters while the parents were gone.

One of the major differences between the '80s and today is that physical **discipline** (not physical abuse) was not frowned upon or outlawed. In fact, you could usually tell the difference between kids who were spanked or had their mouths stuffed with a bar of soap from those who got "time outs" (or standing in the corner). There was no stigma with physical discipline like there is today. If you go back to the baby boomers and earlier generations, they would've **prayed** for a "time out" or to be sent to their rooms when they disrespected their parents. Because Doris and Steve were members of the baby boomer generation, they knew what acts were considered soap-worthy, what acts were considered spank-worthy, and what acts were considered switch-worthy; all punishments that would land a parent in jail today.

Yet, with the Callahan children having birth-born membership into the Generation X club, jail time was not even a consideration for parents who gave their child a good slap across the mouth (in public) when their child sassed or swore at them. Noah had his fair share of all respective disciplinary measures pertaining to the nature of "the crime." Fewer things brew a child's fear than that immediate realization that you broke a parent's cardinal law and there were inevitable consequences that needed to be reckoned with.

To say that Noah's disciplinary tactics were adopted from his parents would be a farce and a hasty conclusion. In the first few months that Noah was put in charge over ensuring that his siblings were safe, fed, bathed, and tucked in, everyone got along famously and there was no Gregorian dictatorship on Noah's part. All of his siblings listened to him. They thought it whimsical and sprightly, as if they were engaged in a role-playing game where Noah was the dad and they were the obedient offspring. Noah did everything right in their eyes.

"What's for dinner?" the kids would ask.

"Why, donuts and cookies, of course," Noah would respond.

"What's for dessert, then?"

"More donuts and cookies, with a little bit of candy bars splashed into the mix."

"What can we have to drink?"

"Open the fridge, find a container with some liquid substance, open the cap, and drink it."

What child **wouldn't** want that kind of diet in their day-to-day lives? Noah was their hero.

"What time do we have to go to bed?"

"If you're yawning, it's a good sign you should be in bed and falling asleep; don't mind what the clock says."

"Do we have to take our baths?"

"If you're fine with smelling like a rotting groundhog's ass on the boiling asphalt during high noon on a midsummer's day, then you don't need to take a bath."

"Can my friend come over and play?"

"As long as you leave the knives on the counter, knock yourself out."

"Do we have to do our homework?"

"If you're content with being an apprentice janitorial engineer when you get older (no offense to my janitor friends), then no, you *don't* have to do your homework."

"Can I wear this to school?"

"Sure, there is a shortage of entertaining clowns in the state, anyway."

If one could clearly transcribe a child's expressions into words, the young Callahan children's expressions would be saying, "Forget Mom and Dad, we want Noah to be our parents." Then things began to go a little awry.

Bekah had come home from school and had a friend join her in the house. Noah informed Bekah that Mom and Dad wanted him to take her, Jasper, and Holly to the doctors for their annual check-up. Bekah argued that they could **still** go to their doctor appointment, but her friend, Brittany, could stay in the waiting area until Bekah's exam was done and they were waiting for the other two to finish their exams. Noah, having been so lenient and nonchalant with his "parental duties" up to now, was taking his parents' request with great responsibility and accountability. Noah ceased entertaining Bekah's pleas, turned to Brittany and said, "If you want to come over later, that'll be fine. Bekah will call you when we get back." Bekah's face contorted into an expression similar to that of your typical fairytale witch's. Her eyes became

feverishly stern, her mouth snarling, her nostrils flaring, and her demeanor

steadily became more and more in contempt with her brother's inability to

negotiate in her favor. Her back was slightly hunched, as if she were preparing

to charge her brother like a Pachycephalosaurus hopped-up on Red Bull. If one

wasn't physically present when Mount Vesuvius erupted, I imagine they

would've experienced the same cataclysmic precursor that Bekah was now

presenting.

Brittany, not wanting any quarrels with Noah, turned and headed out the door,

closing it cautiously behind her. Not more than a split-second after the door

had clicked shut, Bekah erupted into a frenzy of profanity, degrading remarks,

and flailing arms that closely resembled an octopus falling back to the water

after being cast off the deck of an aircraft carrier. Noah, having a few inches on

her, simply leaned back to protect those flailing tentacles from catching him in

the face and also created a bit of a cushion, enough to grab hold of both

Bekah's arms and use his great strength to restrain her. Somehow, that grip

didn't stop her feet from catching him in the shin and he winced with a shock

of pain, as Bekah had yet to remove her school shoes. Nevertheless, he turned

Bekah around and held both her arms behind her back, then proceeded to push

her up the stairs, push her into her bedroom, slam the bedroom door shut, and

grab hold of the doorknob to prevent her from opening it. There were a few attempted twists of the doorknob, which was soon followed by thunderous strikes against the door from the immeasurably upset girl on the other side.

Jasper and Holly had made their way up to the top of the stairs and stood there watching like rubberneckers on the opposite side of the street where the actual accident had occurred. Noah warned her, "You keep this up, and you're going to be sorry. I am going to give you to the count of ten to calm down and then we can talk about this peacefully. Otherwise, you're not going to like what is going to happen."

Bekah, not swayed by his warning, maintained her jackhammer fist thrusts against her bedroom door, and spouted off inflammatory remarks NO girl should ever be speaking at her age.

"One . . ."

"What's Noah's dick size in inches?" Bekah said with a snarky conviction.

"Two . . ."

"How many times does it take for Noah to find his dick?"

117

"Three . . ."

"Three little bears and their asshole, dickless brother."

"Four . . ."

"What's Noah's IQ?"

Noah's tone was now getting more and more intense. "Five . . ."

"How much would Noah charge for sex?"

The rage and impatience had matured since he'd muttered the number five

because of his sister's defiance and insults. "Six . . ."

"The largest dick Noah ever sucked."

There was no more composure or leniency in Noah's tone. "Seven . . ."

"The second-largest dick Noah ever sucked."

"Eight . . ."

"The number of dicks Noah has sucked at one time."

"**Nine . . .**"

"Oh shit. Noah got to the number nine. Call Guinness."

"**Ten!!!!!**"

Noah twisted the knob with as much strength as he had in his wrist and plowed the door with his shoulder, powering the door open and launching Bekah onto her butt. He then reached down, grabbed her by the ankles, and dragged her down the carpeted hallway on her back. She didn't have the strength to match Noah's muscular abilities so she did the only thing she knew how to do, and tried kicking free of his grasp while continuing to spout off profanities.

When Noah had towed Bekah by her feet into his room, he opened the chest top with the toes of his right foot, pinned Bekah's ankles under his armpit, and grabbed hold of the front of her blouse. Like a WWF wrestler, he picked her up and flung her into the chest, slamming the top down and sitting on the top of the chest. Bekah continued to flail inside for a few minutes until the pounding and screaming began to weaken. He soon heard gasping whimpers rather than shrieks of anger. The pounding had deteriorated to small scratching noises, and then there was nothing. No sound whatsoever. Noah slid off the top of the chest and opened the cover. He saw Bekah lying there passed out, but breathing. He then picked her up, carried her into her room, and laid her on the bed. When he exited her bedroom, he saw Jasper and Holly standing at the top of the stairs with their mouths agape, motionless.

Noah, in a calm and composed tone and mannerism, said, "If you ever act up, you're going into Noah's Ark."

Noah had discovered a newfound disciplinary device to maintain fear and obedience over his siblings and was able to keep order in the house by using the threat of Noah's Ark when Steve and Doris were not home; an effective, albeit barbaric, method of maintaining order.

Jasper was only eight years old when he had his first trip to Noah's Ark. The events leading up to the incarceration didn't seem to warrant such punishment, but Noah's patience was rapidly deteriorating with every defiant response his siblings would give at various times. The kids had just had their wonderfully nutritious supper consisting of Doritos, Chips Ahoy cookies, ice cream, banana-nut bread, chocolate milk, and some brownies. Jasper was cleaning up the table, carting the dirty dishes to the kitchen sink, rinsing them out, then putting them in the dishwasher. As Noah didn't need any cookware to produce the sugary feast, there was nothing more to clean up. Noah peeked his head around the kitchen door frame from the dining room and said to Jasper, "I've filled the bathtub with water for your bath. After you finish up here, I want you to go take your evening bath, get into your pajamas, then go to bed."

Jasper turned his head to the left, with his eyes nearly clearing the line of sight to Noah from just over his left shoulder. He just stared at Noah with a blank expression on his face for what seemed to be more than 15 seconds before Noah blurted out, "**WHAT?**" Jasper turned his head back to focus on the last set of dishes to go into the dishwasher, slid the lower dishwasher rack back into place, then closed the door. He then turned to his left and began walking towards Noah when Noah ordered, "Aren't you going to start the dishwasher, Einstein? Why else would we put dirty dishes into it?"

"I was going to let Mom and Dad have their dinner when they got home, and then there wouldn't be dirty dishes in the sink sitting there overnight while the dishwasher was running and while the clean dishes were drying," Jasper responded.

"Well, that's your chore. You are in charge of cleaning the dishes this week, and

Bekah has that task next week. Then Holly has it the week after. Then I have the week following that. It's a simple rotation of chores. So finish your chore like you're supposed to."

Jasper turned back to the dishwasher. He opened the cabinet doors under the sink and produced the dishwasher detergent. After opening the dishwasher's front door, he poured some of the detergent into the small compartment on the dishwasher door, snapped the cover over the small detergent compartment, closed the dishwasher front door, then turned the knob to wash and pulled the knob toward him. This started the dishwasher whirring and filling up with water. "There," Jasper announced. "Now I've finished my chore."

"Very good, my little amoeba. Now get your foul, pungent ass upstairs and into the tub."

Jasper walked past Noah, turned right into the dining room, then another right into the hallway and ascended the staircase. He turned left down the hall to the bathroom. Noah heard the bathroom door close before he turned and headed to the living room where Bekah was watching *Night Driver*. He sat down at the other end of the couch from Bekah and began watching the television show.

The end credits began to run and Noah realized he hadn't heard any movement

upstairs. He had sat through the entire episode that lasted 30 minutes; it never

took Jasper that long to take his bath. Noah got up from the couch, walked out

to the hallway, ascended the staircase, and turned left down the hall towards

the bathroom. When he reached the bathroom door, he turned the bathroom

doorknob and flung the door open, startling Jasper as he sat with his back up

against the tub with a comic book opened in his hands.

"What the hell?" Noah shouted. "You've been reading this entire time? You

should be in your pajamas and in bed by now!"

Jasper looked up at Noah's scowling face and replied, "I was getting around to

it. I want to finish this story before I take my bath."

"That *isn't* what I asked you to do, you little bastard. Get your clothes off, now,

and get into the tub! You know what will happen if you don't do that, right?

Just ask Bekah."

"But I'm almost d—"

Jasper wasn't able to finish his sentence before Noah burst through the

doorway, lunged towards Jasper, grabbed his t-shirt's collar, and pulled the shirt up over Jasper's head. Jasper began to panic as this towering sibling next grabbed him under his left armpit, pulled him up, then grabbed onto Jasper's shorts and proceeded to de-pants his brother. With Jasper's underwear still on, Noah latched onto Jasper's body, picked him up, and dropped him into the water-filled, porcelain basin. Jasper began to kick and squirm, but he was pinned down by his brother's pillar of an arm pressed against Jasper's chest. Noah then grabbed the bottle of shampoo off the edge of the tub on the other side of Jasper. He flipped open the top of the shampoo bottle with his right thumb, turned it upside down, and squeezed a quarter of the bottle out onto Jasper's head. Noah dropped the shampoo bottle into the water and began to lather up the shampoo in Jasper's hair. He didn't do so with any degree of gentleness or ease, but rather rubbed it in much like you would knead bread dough, all the while maintaining his hold against Jasper's chest. When Noah was done, he took his right palm, rested it against Jasper's head, and with a great deal of force, submerged Jasper's head under the water. Noah then grabbed under Jasper's left armpit, jerked him up out of the water, got him into a full nelson submission hold, and dragged him to Noah's room. With shampoo streaming into Jasper's eyes, as well as being soaking wet and nearly naked, Jasper began screaming in agony. Noah was laughing the whole time he pulled Jasper into his room. He used his right foot to open the top of the cedar chest, heaved Jasper up into the air, and slammed him down into the chest. Jasper felt something snap in both of his shoulders before seeing the top of the cedar chest slamming closed over him. Noah seated himself on top of the chest, just as he had with Bekah, and grabbed a comic from his bed.

"Now THAT's what I call a speedy bath, you little maggot!" Noah hollered down towards the top of the cedar chest. "You want to be a little asshole about things, I can play along. Now stay in there until you dry up."

With sharp pains in his shoulders on every movement he tried to make, Jasper screamed from within the cedar chest, "Noah, let me out! It hurts, Noah, it hurts! I can't move my arms!"

"Good. That will teach you to listen when you're told to do something, won't it!" Noah replied with a smirk on his face.

"Please, Noah, it really hurts! I can't see anything. My eyes are stinging!"

"You're not **supposed** to see anything when you're in a sealed coffin."

Jasper's breathing quickly began to grow more and more laborious and his consciousness began to slip. "Noah, please. Please let me out of here. It hurts."

There was a sudden silence and Noah stopped reading his comic. He waited for a little more than a minute before putting the comic back on his bed, standing

up off the top of the cedar chest, and lifting the top open with his right foot.

Staring down into the hollows of the chest at the small, nearly naked Jasper, he

noticed Jasper's eyes were redder than a ripened tomato and his arms were in

a position that wasn't normal. He reached down, grabbed Jasper by the back of

the neck, and said, "NOW will you listen when I tell you to do something?"

Jasper responded, panting like a dog who had just come back in from a hot

summer's day, "Yes. Yes, I will. Please help me, though. They hurt."

Jasper seemed to be in a daze and when Noah lifted him from the Ark, Jasper's

arms just dangled by his side. Noah had seen this only once before, with a

teammate after he dove a little too deep off the starting blocks. Jasper's arms

were dislocated from the shoulder sockets. Noah's eyes grew wide and he

cradled Jasper under his shoulder blades and knees, turned, and carried Jasper

to his bedroom. He rested Jasper down onto the floor and then recalled what

the swim team's trainer had performed on his teammate. With Jasper sprawled

out on his bedroom floor, Noah sat down perpendicular to Jasper's right arm,

grabbed hold of Jasper's right wrist, braced his right foot against Jasper's right

rib cage, and pulled on Jasper's arm with a sudden jerk, popping the right

shoulder back into the socket. Jasper sat up and howled in blinding pain and

began kicking his feet up and down against the floor.

126

"That's one," Noah said. Noah then got to his feet, went over to Jasper's left side, sat down on the floor, and told Jasper to lay down. Jasper's tears began to stream out of his bloodshot eyes while Noah grabbed hold of Jasper's left wrist, braced his left foot against Jasper's left rib cage, then, without a courteous countdown, jerked his left arm with a mighty force, and popped his left shoulder back into its socket. Once again, Jasper screamed in horrendous agony and began writhing around on his back against the floor. "Stop being such a big baby, the pain will go away in a few seconds," Noah informed his frightened little brother. Noah was so busy playing doctor on his brother's shoulders that he didn't notice that Bekah had made her way up the stairs and into Jasper's room to find out what all the commotion and screaming was about. When she saw her little brother's body laying nearly motionless on the floor, his bloodshot eyes' deadly gaze fixed up to the ceiling, she began to tremble.

"What the hell did you do to him, Noah?" she screamed. "What's wrong with him?"

"The little brat decided to test my boundaries, and I believe he has now learned that this is not a good thing to practice. Isn't that right, squirt?" He looked down at Jasper as he said this and Jasper nodded ever so slowly. Noah got up, grabbed Bekah's right arm, turned her around, and said, "Let's let the little

crybaby dry off and rest." Noah walked into the bathroom, grabbed a towel

from the linen closet, returned to Jasper's bedroom, threw the towel in on top

of him and said, "Now, dry off, get into your pajamas, and get into bed like I

told you originally." Jasper just laid still while Noah grabbed the bedroom

door's knob and slowly closed the door. Jasper laid in that position for well over

an hour, with the towel acting as a makeshift blanket.

CHAPTER 8: JASPER'S SHADOW

On a hot summer morning in August 1984, Ralph was just about to turn in for

his diurnal slumber when he heard Jasper singing along to "Stone of Eras" and

the words "Gumpter gleeken gloughken glophen" are recited to kick off this

song. Jasper was walking down Summit Street towards Chartiers Road. These

words were being sung by John Ellington from Jasper's favorite band, Blind

Cheetah, through thin, foam-covered headphones with a leash that stretched

down to a neutral yellow Stoney portable cassette player, which was attached

to Jasper's waistband.

Jasper began humming and lip syncing along with John Ellington. Next, he

sputtered off a comprehensible line (which Ralph would later learn is one of

the lines of the chorus), "I want rock and roll" followed by a lighter decibel,

almost the same level as a whisper, "Yes I do."

Ralph watched as this miniature amateur rock star sang and moseyed down the

street, with sun shining through small breaks in the leaves and casting a glow

on Jasper's left cheek. Jasper's shoulder-length hair swayed in the morning

wind and he had the demeanor of an individual with absolutely no care in the

world. His posture was not of a hunchback, but rather that of a flagpole. He wasn't walking with any degree of arrogance or pompousness as though he owned the neighborhood, he was simply a child of an emergency room nurse who instilled good posture in her kids. He had a graceful stride, even though the music being blown into his ears was rock and roll.

When Jasper reached the intersection of Summit and Chartiers, Ralph noticed he was wearing a black t-shirt that had a picture of a blue-colored glass building with flames exploding out from one of the upper floors. Black smoke hovered over the flames and in the upper left-hand corner of the image were the words "Blind Cheetah" in a very gothic-like font. Below the image of the blue-colored glass building was a word that had larger spacing between the fire-orange-colored letters: "INCENDIARISM." Jasper had on faded blue jeans that were cut off at the knees, converting the pants into shorts, and had (what seemed to be) a deliberate tear across the left backside cheek. He had his navy-blue, faded denim sneakers on, but wasn't wearing any socks. Jasper had a red-and-orange flamed black bandana tied around his right knee, but Ralph couldn't figure out why. He concluded that it was another generational clothing fad that held absolutely no meaning whatsoever.

Jasper stopped directly under that street's solo streetlight for a moment, and with his head slightly bent down, raised his eyes towards Ralph, smiled, then turned left towards South Fork Tenmile Creek, still singing along with John

Ellington as the song progressed.

This wasn't a smile of embarrassment, though, as if Jasper was caught

surprised by his peering sisters while dancing in his bedroom. No. This smile

had something a little devious in it. Only a few yards down Chartiers Road,

Jasper turned around, his shadow following him with the sun casting ahead of

him, looked down, and said, "Yeah, that's him." He raised his eyes back up at

Ralph, never moving his head, and flashed that sinister smile again. As Ralph

sat in his wooden rocking chair on the porch, absolutely mesmerized by what

he had just experienced, he noticed an anomalous characteristic about Jasper's

shadow. He never picked up on it all the other times he would see Jasper, but

for some reason, on the morning of August 6, 1984, with the morning sun

creating a shadow behind the boy, he realized that the shape of the shadow

was not one proportional to a boy's physique. The curvature of the head was

slightly askew; the bone circumference of the head was more mature than an

8-year-old boy's skull would be, and the shape of the hair was not that of

flowing, shoulder-length hair, but rather the form of an oversized, puffy, cotton

ball. There were also two thin, symmetrical black lines on either side of the

skull, which reminded Ralph of his mom's shadow when she wore her glasses

while out in the sun. There were two half-spheres on either side of the torso,

just about chest level, that would jostle up and down with each step Jasper

131

took. The pelvic area was a little more rounded and bigger than a boy of Jasper's age would ever have. The shadow had a little more girth around the stomach region and protruded slightly on either side of Jasper's shadow. There were very faint lines swaying back and forth on either side of the head, which kind of looked like long earrings one would see ladies wear to festive, special occasions. The thigh area also had a little bit more dimension than Jasper's shape, and the calves seemed to be a lot more muscular than Jasper's frail body's. But the biggest giveaway was that while Jasper was wearing flat-soled sneakers, the shadow showed a gap between the sole of the foot and the ground, which is indicative of a lady wearing high heels.

Ralph had been up all night and this time of the morning, he would have been awake for a full "day" and getting ready for bed. However, this bizarre shadow had really put Ralph's mind in an enigmatic state; there was no way that shadow was being cast by Jasper's body, even though the positioning of the sun to the shadow was spot on. And every step that Jasper took, the shadow kept the same cadence.

Ralph watched as Jasper turned the sharp bend just up a ways from Ralph's house on Chartiers Road towards the creek. Ralph's mind was no longer trying to solve or rationalize this spectacle, but rather trying to dilute the shivering vision that had now been branded in his consciousness. Ralph finally got up from his rocking chair, turned to his left, pulling the handle on the screen door.

He called for Max to go inside, then followed shortly behind. He headed to his

bedroom, took off the denim overalls, then his white t-shirt, pulled on the

faded red-striped pajama bottoms, then finished his wardrobe change by

putting on the faded red-striped pajama top. He meticulously fastened every

nylon button through each of the slits on the adjacent side of the pajama top.

He then pulled the powder-blue blanket and white top sheet back to a perfect

triangle, sat on the edge of the bed, lined up his slippers directly in front of him,

and slid both his feet and legs under the blanket and sheet. Then he pulled

back the linen flap he had earlier created and lay on his back with his head

slightly propped up on his white pillow-cased pillow. He slowly closed his eyes

and was in the right position and place to fall asleep.

***

For many years, it has been postulated that dreams are a random collection of

thoughts, images, and sensations from a person's subconscious while they are

in a state of solid sleep. Many medical professionals will debate the validity of

the dreams, the stories they tell, or if they have any realistic justification to the

individual. Everyone has had nightmares, as well as feel-good dreams. Some

nightmares have been known to startle an individual from a sound REM sleep

so much that they spring up from their bed, face pale-white, body trembling,

perspiring, and in complete horror of the images and sensations they

experienced in their transient dormant state.

There are some psychic practitioners who will argue that dreams are premonitions of things to come, masked with personal historical experiences. For instance, if someone had a dream they were walking their dog on the beach, then looked down only to find a shoe on a leash, that might mean that the individual's dog was going to die, the dog was eating their shoe, or a magical and generous inheritance was in their future; the latter being the foreshadowing we all would like.

There are also those who are prone to sleepwalking during that deep subconscious period, and it has been hypothesized that the sleepwalker is acting out a role they are currently experiencing in the dream. There are no solid scientific facts to corroborate any of these theories, but there are individuals who long to know the translation of the dreams or nightmares they've had.

Dr. Alan Bishop, of Danvers State Hospital, used to classify dreams as a place where your eyes don't go. He further went on to explain that in a deep sleep, your eyes are not experiencing or creating the realm of the dreamscape, but rather your inner mind's eye is performing that function. As a result, when people dream, they are not "seeing" the events that are unfolding, but they are experiencing them. When asked by paranoid or anxious patients what their dreams meant (after they provided the details), Dr. Bishop would often respond with, "What did you feel?" and not "What did you see?"

When a patient would say, "I saw [this]," or "I saw [that]," Dr. Bishop would correct them with his theory that they didn't actually see the vivid images in their deep sleep, but rather experienced a collection of memories woven in an arbitrary pattern with no specific agenda behind that subconscious tapestry. Dr. Bishop would go on to clarify that when you sleep, your eyes don't roll all the way back to the degree where they are literally looking at the brain, and, therefore, can't possibly piece together the different snippets that the subconscious projects into some sane, rational tale. In the chaotic bedlam of dream production, there is no director to provide plot or structured subject behind the images that are laid out before the individual.

Dr. Bishop would placate his patients' concerns by saying, "When you go to see a movie, there is a beginning, a middle, a crescendo, or climax, and then a resolution. Take, for example, the movie E.T. The opening of the movie shows rustling through a wooded area, strange alien vernacular, silhouettes of non-human terrestrials, and a round spaceship adorned with motley-colored glowing lights. When the spaceship takes off because there is a human presence in the area and they forget one of their botanist peers, that begins the rising action to the story line. The rest of the movie follows a structured

sequence of events from when E.T. first meets Elliot, E.T.'s secret houseguest

status, the introduction of feverishly passionate scientists, the increased

physiological bond between E.T. and Elliot, and the escape. The movie climaxes

when the boys rescue E.T. and Elliot from the overzealous, bureaucratic

scientists to bring him to the woods where E.T. would be reunited with his

family. The resolution takes place when the spaceship takes off and Elliot

watches as his new close friend disappears into the night sky.

"Now, these are all events that you experienced with your eyes, your ears, and

perhaps your heart, if you are one who cries during sad parts of movies, as well

as some comic relief in a drama. Your mind adds those images, sounds, and

sensations to the bank in your brain, and performs evening withdrawals when

you're most vulnerable. The only problem is, when your mind goes to release

parts of a memory, the floodgates open and all the stored experiences come

pouring out into a pool of garbled sludge that cannot even begin to follow

standard parts of a story."

***

Due to his sleep cycles, Ralph often had to stay up a little later in the morning

to go and get his groceries, as there were no 24-hour stores in or around

Clarksville. There were small family run shops that had emergency provisions, such as one would find in a gas station convenience store. But as far as regular

household needs and survival supplies, he had to wait for the main grocery

store to be open. Other than that, Ralph would be fast asleep in his red-striped

pajamas during the day.

During the school year, there would be no kids around unless it was a holiday,

vacation, or one of the many other days schoolkids get to stay home from

classes. In the summertime, it was a whole different ball of wax. The Callahans

had moved onto Summit Street when Noah was 4 years old and Bekah was 2

years old, which made Jasper and Holly the only two Callahans to be born and

raised in that house. As a result, Ralph got to watch as Jasper went from a baby

to his current age, whenever Ralph was out running his errands that could only

be done during the day.

Living in a town with a population of just over 200 residents, Ralph often ran

into the Callahans (as well as many other locals) when he went to the store

during the mornings the kids didn't have school. Ralph remembered that, even

as a young toddler, Jasper would often stop and stare at a store shelf, even if

the items there had no relevance to a young boy. Doris was usually trying to

keep her other kids occupied and keep them from running around, but Jasper

never gave her any cause for concern or distraction. He would simply just stop and stare. Now if he had done this towards a human being, there would be some more thought put into this ambiguous fascination of his. But Jasper never **did** stare at somebody; it was always some**thing**.

The first time Ralph noticed the specific unusual act, he instantly looked up at Doris to see if she saw what Jasper was doing and try to get an idea of the expression Doris might have on her face, let alone what she would say to the little boy.

Ralph remembered it as clear as a crystal champagne glass being set down on a lavish table in a fancy restaurant. He was outside the grocery store on a sunny, late-fall morning, picking out the pumpkin he would traditionally carve and set out on his porch for Halloween. The setting was so vivid and familiar, it could've been just the day before that he remembered. There were dried corn stalks arranged in bundles outside the storefront. There were tiers of wooden shelves with different-sized pumpkins on each tier. There were wooden baskets propped at a 45-degree angle that were full of freshly picked apples that would be delivered every morning from Triple B Farms in Monongahela, Pennsylvania.

On the other side of the store's entrance there would be another tier of wooden shelving, with gallons of homemade apple cider and canisters of cinnamon sticks next to each gallon. There were homemade apple pies that Mrs. Daley would make at her place on Cherry Street. And at the corner of the storefront, there was a blue newspaper box with a coin slot and a trusty dispensary.

The air was a crisp 50 degrees, and the festive aroma of seasonal change enveloped the atmosphere. As Ralph was sorting through the wide selection of the ever-popular seasonal orange artifacts, he caught Jasper's presence out of the corner of his left eye. Jasper had made his way to the shelves that had Mrs. Daley's fresh apple pies on them. He was scanning over the many options, and that's when Ralph first noticed this strange action. Jasper looked down to the ground on his left and said, "Not that one. I don't think that's a good one. What about this one?" Jasper was pointing to a larger apple pie whose crust was a little higher than the others, usually indicating that there were more apples used in that pie than the others. With a puzzled look, Ralph continued watching as Jasper was talking to the ground. "Of course I want more apples," Jasper continued. "Why do you think I pointed that one out?" No longer being able to contain his internal perplexity, Ralph said, "Master Callahan, who are you talking to?" Not realizing Ralph was standing right on the other side of the entrance, Jasper flinched as if he were startled by an intruder entering his house.

"No one. I mean nothing," Jasper replied.

Ralph scanned the area before continuing, "Where's your mother? Or is your father with you today?"

Jasper responded, "Mommy's inside. She wanted me to pick out an apple pie for dessert tonight."

"Well, sir, I think that would be a great pie, right there," Ralph said as he pointed to the pie with the bulging pie crust.

"Yeah, that's what I was telling her. I mean it. I mean myself," Jasper stammered. "I'm going to take this pie in to Mom so she can finish her shopping."

With that, Jasper grabbed the apple pie, turned, and hastily walked into the grocery store. Ralph couldn't make heads or tails out of what had just transpired, until it became clearer who Jasper was talking to: his shadow. Jasper was looking down at his shadow and responding to it as if he were talking to a real person.

This wasn't Jasper's typical idiosyncratic behavior of staring at inanimate objects; no, this was something much more eerie. Ralph thought about addressing this with Doris, but then he thought it was just the child having an overly imaginative brain and talking to a make-believe friend. Ralph figured this was something Doris was familiar with already, and there was no need to bring it to light, as it may cause embarrassment or awkwardness. Ralph finally picked out his pumpkin, turned to the entrance doors of the grocery store, and brought it in to purchase.

When Ralph snapped out from his flashback, with a cold sweat covering his face and eyes wider than the moon, he recalled Dr. Bishop's theory that he had read in the doctor's published biography, where he went into theories, and facts to back up those theories. Why was this the first thing that came to mind when Ralph woke up in a panic? Because Ralph realized he knew Jasper's shadow from a memory long since passed: it was the shadow he would see behind Mrs. Davis-Carpenter when he would volunteer at Danvers State Hospital as a young man, and when he and an aide would take Mrs. Davis-Carpenter out to the garden where she could see the flowers the other patients were growing in the motley-colored, massive botanical area.

Ralph was trying to implement Dr. Bishop's theory that his subconscious was toying with the rational side of his brain and the images, memory, and sensations were so real, he felt like he had woken from an astral projection to his youth and one of those days he'd sat with Mrs. Davis-Carpenter out in the sunny afternoon on the Danvers State Hospital's west lawn. Ralph was convinced that he didn't actually see Jasper's alien shadow behind him, but he experienced it in a dream state. He attempted to settle his mind by saying, "It was all just a dream," but unfortunately, he couldn't have been further from the truth.

CHAPTER 9: BOUND BY THE LIGHT

July 5, 1985. Ralph was awakened by the sounds of police and ambulance

sirens. When he rolled over to look at the time, the clock read 8:00 a.m. He

heard a great commotion that sounded like objections from a town hall gallery

of displeased residents. He sprang up out of his bed, ignoring his habitual

stepping into his bedside slippers and throwing on his bathrobe, and ran from

his bedroom to the living room where he found Max standing on his hind legs,

looking out the window. Max had made his way behind the opaque draperies

so that only his paws could be seen by the window. Max began barking at the

approaching thunderous sirens and racing engines as the emergency vehicles

sped their way up the country road.

Ralph paused for a brief moment, reflecting on the prior evening's encounter

with the Callahan children and the encrypted message from the streetlight

before and after the children were present. His face instantly grew pale, his

heart began racing with the speed of FASTCAR vehicles zipping around a

racetrack, and his legs seemed to lose all strength.

When he was able to compose himself enough to bring his attention back to

the commotion taking place outside his living room window, he expeditiously made his way to the window and ripped open the draperies to find a large

group of residents, some in their evening sleepwear, standing in front of the

streetlight. Max continued to bark out the window at the concert of gasps and

tears taking place 15 yards from the house.

Ralph had difficulty making out what they were looking at. Without any

consideration for the attire he was adorned with, he made it to the front door

with great haste, turned the doorknob, and pulled the door open with the

strength of two military police officers. He took three quick steps out onto the

front porch when he was instantly gripped in a paralyzing stance as he finally

saw what the townspeople were looking at. There was a boy in his boxer shorts

and tank top and bare feet, suspended halfway up the lamppost, his head

hanging down and over to the left, and his face as pale as a billowy cloud. It

looked as if he had been magnetically adhered to the steel lamppost and left

there to perish. His legs had been broken and wrapped behind him around the

back of the lamppost, and his arms had been dislocated and wrapped behind

him against the lamppost. There was no blood. There were no cuts or bruises.

There were no signs of any other bodily damage other than the broken legs and

dislocated arms. It was as if someone strung him up like garland around a

Christmas tree.

The next thing Ralph noticed was agonizing screams coming from up Summit

Street, and they quickly grew louder as they neared the intersection. It was a man's voice crying out and a woman's shrieking that Ralph couldn't quite make out. There were also sounds of children crying a little bit behind the man's and woman's voices.

Steve was the first one to come into Ralph's view, with Doris closely behind him. One of the town's residents ran up and met the children and barricaded them from progressing any further down the road. Their screams quickly turned to forceful objections, and another neighbor had to run up to join the first man who went to prevent the children from moving any further down towards the corner of Chartiers Road and Summit Street.

Steve reached the lamppost and quickly began trying to pry his son's lifeless body off the steel post his son had been hung on. His screams grew louder and louder as all his attempts were failing. Doris reached the light post and began pulling at her son's body but had the same results as Steve; nothing. Doris was working off of an adrenaline rush that is most often found in a mother when her child is in perilous danger, and where some cases have reported that the mother was able to move a parked car off her child. This degree of adrenaline seemed to rage through her body like a toxin, taking over all other normal physical functions.

Bekah had broken free from the restraining clutches of the two men holding

them up in the middle of Summit Street and she emerged into the center of the

intersection, where she quickly collapsed in horrific screams as she saw her

brother's lifeless body wrapped around the single lamppost in that area of the

neighborhood. Bekah had great difficulty breathing between her screams of

horror and uncontrollable cries.

Midway up Summit Street, you could hear two small voices crying out, **"What's**

going on???? What's happening????" As they were not hearing any responses

to their frightened inquiries, the volume of their voices grew increasingly

louder with each round of those same questions pouring from their mouths.

When Ralph finally made out who the male voice was coming up from the

middle of Summit Street, he realized it wasn't Jasper up on that lamppost, it

was Noah.

The first emergency vehicle to arrive on the scene was the town sheriff's

cruiser, instantly followed by two other police cruisers. The ambulance was last

to arrive. The cruiser doors were flung open and the officers and sheriff bolted

from their vehicles without paying any mind to the car doors as they sprinted

towards the small crowd. They plowed their way through the townspeople and when they saw Noah's body up on the lamppost, each one of the officers froze

with stunned disbelief. Never in their entire professional careers as law

enforcers had they ever witnessed something as profound and brutal as what

they were now seeing.

When the sheriff was finally able to recover from his own crippling shock, he

waved his hand at the EMTs who had made their way out from the back of the

ambulance and had begun rolling a stretcher towards the scene. As the EMTs

emerged from behind the crowd of witnesses, they, too, stopped dead in their

tracks with immeasurable disbelief and shock. Much like the police officers and

the sheriff, they had never experienced a sight like this one. They had tended

to severe motor vehicle accidents and the gory aftermath of farm vehicle

accidents, but this spectacle went beyond any rational explanation. There,

straight in front of them, was a boy's body suspended halfway up a light post

with no binding rope or restraining shackles of any kind. They had no training,

whatsoever, to handle a situation like this. How could they? There is nothing in

emergency manuals about tending to a lifeless body mysteriously adhered to a

metal light post.

A large fire engine quickly appeared down the Chartiers Road a bit, with a

deafening sound of sirens consuming the air. The truck hadn't even come to a

full stop when two of the firefighters leapt off the truck and ran up to the light post. With the same reaction as the police department, sheriff, and EMTs, they paused momentarily to try and compose themselves after witnessing something that could never be included in any degree of emergency services training.

One of the firefighters turned to the fire engine and simply yelled out, ""**TWELVE!!!!**" Two other firefights produced a 12-foot ladder and sprinted over to where the first firefighter was standing, directly in front of the light post and directly under the boy. Two of the police officers had made their way over to Steve and Doris and, with every ounce of strength they had, wrestled the hysterical parents away from the pole so that the emergency responders could tend to the boy.

Douglas Mansfield, the senior firefighter on the company, ascended the secured ladder until he was parallel to Noah's body. He first drew his attention to the boy's arms that had been dislocated and wrapped behind him around the lamppost. He was looking for whatever might be adhering his hands and arms against the pole, but couldn't find anything. No handcuffs. No rope. No industrial adhesives gluing his limbs to the pole. It was simply . . . just . . . stuck, without any humanly devices. Trying to be as respectful and gentle as he could, he began trying to pry the boy's legs from around the pole, with as much success as Steve had when he tried: zero. Still in human restraint, Steve and

Doris continued their attempts to wrestle free from the clutches of the two

officers, but found it more and more difficult to overpower these two

musclebound men keeping them from advancing at all.

Then, an unusual and cosmic event occurred that instantly stunned the entire

crowd, including the rescue professionals, and Steve and Doris. The streetlight

came on. The streetlights in the town had all been programmed to turn on

depending on the amount of natural light that was in the sky. At 8:00 a.m. in

the month of July, it was already too bright to trigger those sensors in the

streetlight and cause the light to come on. Then the light began to flicker, just

as it had when Ralph and the Callahan kids witnessed it just nine hours earlier.

It did one round of flickering, then it stopped and dimmed down until it shut off

completely. No one knew what it meant, but Ralph stood there and repeated

the cycle of flickers in his head until he came up with the message the

streetlight had sent: dash-dot, dot, dash-dot-dot-dash, dash. Sheriff Robinson

turned to see Ralph standing on his porch in his striped pajamas, looking

hypnotically stunned at the streetlight. Knowing Ralph's military station, his

brow turned into a quizzical expression, then turned back towards the

streetlight.

Without any warning, without any force of nature, Noah's body was dislodged

from the post and slammed into the pavement just beneath the lamppost. The

two officers restraining Steve and Doris lost all strength in their horrific

amazement, which allowed Steve and Doris to escape the grips of the officers,

race over to their son's body, and collapse on the ground next to him. All the

other rescuers had no idea how to react to what had just happened. By all

accounts, there were ominous forces beyond explanation that were involved

here.

Jasper and Holly had found a way to escape the restraints of the two

townspeople holding them back and made their way to the intersection. Holly

exploded into tears of terror as she collapsed to the ground next to her

parents. Jasper stood there, looked down at his brother's body, then looked up

at the light post. Jasper didn't shed a tear. Didn't react like everyone else did.

Didn't lose all muscle strength in his legs.

Ralph then saw something that was both chilling and haunting; Jasper looked

back up at the light post, nodded his head two times as if he was responding to

someone asking a question, then moved his focus back down to his brother's

body.

Ralph was haunted by Jasper's behavior while he stood beside his older brother's body. He's always known Jasper for his fascination with manmade structures and how sometimes, when he was alone, Jasper would simply stop walking and stare at something for a few minutes before continuing on. Normally, boys his age would be skylarking about the streets, woods, and fields, looking for something to keep them entertained, but Jasper was unique.

The explosive epidemic of doctors hastily labeling kids with Attention Deficit Disorder (ADD) hadn't entered the mainstream medical field yet, and Jasper was just classified as a boy with a curious imagination. Yet when Jasper stood under that lamppost, looked up, nodded his head twice at the dimmed light, then looked back down at his brother, it was a very peculiar action from a boy who just watched as his mangled brother lay motionless by his feet.

What or **who** was Jasper acknowledging? Ralph began to believe he was the only one to notice this, as the other witnesses were focused on his parents' traumatic grieving and a lifeless young boy lying now on the warm pavement. *Did any of the emergency rescuers see it?* he thought. Ralph **couldn't** have been the only one to see that remarkably abnormal gesture at a time such as this. Then, like a lightning bolt hitting a large oak, his mind sharply snapped into a vision he hadn't even thought about until then: "Jasper's shadow," Ralph whispered to himself.

Even though the rest of the onlookers left the horrific scene out of respect for the deceased, Doris and Steve still knelt by Noah's body. One of the Callahan neighbors had taken Bekah, Jasper, and Holly to their house to remove them from area and not have them continue to stare at their oldest brother's body. As Ralph sat on that rocking chair in his red-striped pajamas, he experienced that ghostly feeling one gets when they feel someone is staring at them. He looked up and saw Jasper standing halfway up Summit Street, motionless and still, like a marble statue. The morning sunlight shone through the trees and cast a faint glow on Jasper's face and he was staring directly at Ralph with a villainous, chilling smile. Ralph felt surges of electrical pulsations throughout his body and his heart began to race. He turned to look behind him to see if Jasper might possibly be looking at someone else, but as he turned back to Jasper, he noticed the boy's expression had not changed. His stance had not changed. His eyes maintained their fixation on Ralph's eyes. And that smile was still unwavering on his face. The only thing Ralph could do was look back at the young boy. He was crippled in a stupefying trance and his mind's only focus was on this boy's maniacal gaze. Without warning or any sign of provocation, Jasper slowly raised his right arm out in front of his body with his index finger pointing directly at Ralph, with Jasper's expression never shifting.

"Morning there, Ralph. What's on your mind, Master Chief?" It was Sheriff Langdon. Ralph hadn't even noticed the sheriff heading up his walkway, as he was still spooked by the little boy up the way on Summit Street, ominously glaring at him and holding out a steady arm with his index finger pointing at him. When he heard the sheriff's voice, he was whipped back into a conscious awareness of his immediate surroundings. "You probably already know this, Chief, but I do have to ask you a few questions, seeing as how your property faces directly out onto that intersection."

"I understand, sir," Ralph replied.

"Thanks for being cooperative. I knew I could count on you for that. Were you up during your usual time last night and through this morning?"

"Yes, sir. I went to bed around 5:00 a.m. like I usually do."

"And were you out on the porch during that time? As you normally are?"

"Yes, sir. Max was right next to me, as he is now, and I had my cup of coffee and cigar."

"Did you notice any suspicious or abnormal behavior around the neighborhood during that time?"

"No, sir. It was very quiet and peaceful as usual."

"Have you seen any strangers in town in the last few days?"

"Not really, sir. The Browns had family visiting from Connecticut for the weekend, but they left before the holiday. Other than that, I haven't seen any unusual activity happening around here."

"Were you aware of any enemies Noah Callahan had, or perhaps anyone who was angry at the family for any reason?"

"No, sir. The Callahans are good folks. This is just so horribly tragic what happened. How is it possible for a young boy to be suspended up on a lamppost without any adhesive or securing mechanisms?"

"Well, Chief, we're still working on that, ourselves. Trust me. Do you know of any domestic issues the Callahans were having?"

"Not at all, sir. Those parents love their children immeasurably. You'd be hard-pressed to find **anyone** who knows them to say anything to the contrary."

"Perhaps you might have experienced the brother and sisters arguing with

Noah?"

"No more than siblings usually argue, sir. You remember how you and Flo used

to fight all the time? Sure, there were fistfights that led to some light bruising,

but nothing ever escalated beyond that."

"This is very true, Chief. But if such sibling altercation ends in one of them

being brutally mangled and mysteriously suspended from a lamppost, then that

is something I would need to know. You might remember the incident where

little Jasper was in the emergency room up at Brownsville Memorial. Both his

shoulders were dislocated, and Noah helped him set it back in. We investigated

this to see if there was any mistreatment from Mr. or Mrs. Callahan, but found

out that little Jasper and Noah were play wrestling and Noah forgot the extent

of his strength. In the end, we determined that there was no foul play, but

rather just two brothers having a fun wrestling match. Damn television and

that WWF wrestling. Kids will emulate any celebrity figure and their actions."

"Yes, sir, I do remember that incident. It seemed to be the talk of the town for

a short period of time. Poor Steve and Doris, they were getting stares for the

next few months after that and giving gossip hounds and knitting circles plenty

of ammunition for inappropriate judgment; when in fact, they have to be a

couple of the most compassionate, nurturing, loving parents this town has. But even if there was a sibling altercation that was exacerbated to something much more violent, like a mangled murder, none of those other children have the slightest ability, physical or emotional, to hang their oldest and strongest brother on a lamppost. They would've needed a ladder and hoist. I definitely would've heard that."

"This is true, Chief, but we can't write off even the most remote possibility that there was someone else involved, one who had the physical capacity to commit this kind of murder, to be doing that dirty work for one of the siblings looking for severe payback."

"Sheriff, I will not subscribe to any such degree of retaliation from any of those kids. Noah was a kind and nurturing brother who would do anything for his siblings and had a parental role when Steve and Doris couldn't be home."

"I understand, Chief, but as the good Sherlock Holmes said, 'Once you eliminate the impossible, whatever remains, no matter how improbable, must be the truth.' Do you know of any enemies young Noah may have made in school?"

"I have never heard of such a thing. Even when I have to go grocery shopping during the mornings, key shopping times for the gossip crows, I have never heard anything of the sort from that clique."

"Your living room window faces that streetlight and your bedroom is separated by a wall with the door to the living room. It is very quiet out here, void of any city traffic-level commotion or business. I would think you'd be able to hear the screams of a boy even through that setup. After all, breaking a leg accidentally is painful enough. Breaking both legs and dislocating both shoulders with force should produce a great deal of anguishing screams of pain. You heard nothing like this?"

"No, sir, it was as quiet as it usually is."

"Did you take any medication, prescription or over-the-counter, that would cause drowsiness before you went to bed?"

"No, sir, I have no afflictions that would require such medications."

"One last question, then I'm going back to the scene: the streetlight came on and flickered shortly before young Noah fell from the lamppost. I looked up over to where you were sitting and you had a stunned and fearfully shocked expression on your face. Why was that?"

"I was still in shock of what I, and everyone else, was experiencing. Something completely unexplainable and bizarre."

"All right, Chief. I may be following up on some additional questions once the department gets a chance to sit down and work through the evidence collected. Thanks for your time."

"Any time, Sheriff. Don't hesitate to call on me if you have any other questions. I hope you can find who did this heinous crime."

With that, Sheriff Langdon turned and headed back down Ralph's walkway and crossed the road, ending back at the streetlight. The EMTs had placed Noah's body on the stretcher and loaded him in the back of the ambulance. Ralph was able to see Doris and Steve enter the back of the ambulance just before it slowly took off from the scene. Ralph quickly returned his gaze back up Summit Street where little Jasper had been staring and pointing at Ralph, only to see that the boy was gone. Ralph simply could not tell the sheriff that the flickering lights spelled out the word "next" in Morse code. Ralph believed that kind of information would only be necessary if asked directly. He wasn't prepared to offer up such details that the sheriff might find completely random and outlandish.

Ralph began to engage in an internal conversation with himself. *And what is with that one word the streetlight gave, "next"? What is that supposed to mean? Is there someone else destined to suffer the same morbid fate that befell young Noah? And why Noah, anyway? What did he do that was so intense it would warrant such an atrocious act of violence?*

Shortly after the ambulance left with Noah's body, Doris, and Steve on board, the fire department and most of the other law officers left. There was a small sedan that pulled up to the streetlight. Two men stepped out, with one going around to the back of the vehicle, opening the trunk, and producing a box that looked like a medium-sized toolbox that you would see a carpenter carrying around. Ralph recognized these individuals as Trevor Martindale and Scott Percival, the two most intellectual forensic investigators in that county. Trevor was carrying the toolbox and met up with Scott at the area where Noah's body had landed on the pavement. Trevor knelt down, set the toolbox next to the preliminary chalk outline of Noah's body, and began producing instruments and vials of chemicals used for gathering forensic evidence. He handed some items to Scott, who took them over to the lamppost and began conducting his due diligence in obtaining any evidence that was not naked to the human eye. For the next hour, the two young men performed their research, and Ralph couldn't bring himself to abandon his station on the front porch. He was so mystified by everything that happened and that was currently taking place, he felt compelled to maintain his position in the rocking chair, even though he was

having trouble keeping his eyes open.

CHAPTER 10: LECHEROUS PROCLIVITY

Tenmile Creek. Not only the scene of Mother Nature's local aquatic recreation, but the hunting grounds for William (Billy) Donnelly. Billy was a 10th-grader who used the area for his voyeuristic fantasies and the creek bank's wooded terrain as his nest for covert observations. His prey of fancy were young girls between the ages of eleven and fourteen years old. He had a post that spanned two hundred yards of the riverbank's tree line where he would take up daily residence to spy on the young girls who would engage in leisure water activities during the torrid summer seasons and early fall after-school congregation.

As a child of physical and mental abuse, Billy would often flee to Tenmile Creek for refuge following the malicious, violent beatings and abhorrent exploits by his alcoholic stepdad. Before Michael Nichols began serving his lifetime sentence, with no parole, for domestic violence and severe child abuse in the winter of 1981, he committed a great deal of lifetime damaging acts on Billy, Billy's mom, and his younger sister, Jenna. Under the influence of frequent alcohol-induced rage, Michael would physically beat Billy's mother with brute force and any object that was in reach, and while she was in a stunned, beaten state, he would bind her to the steel radiator with her mouth gagged. Michael would then bind Jenna's hands and feet to the four bedposts and stuff a dirty sock in her mouth. With a gun pressed against Billy's mom's head, he ordered

Billy to perform unspeakable, sickening, and abominable acts with his younger sister while Billy's mother was forced to powerlessly witness these vile acts of abuse. While tears flowed from each of Michael's victims' eyes and moans of excruciating pain and objections were heard, he would stand there with his gun in one hand and a bottle of Jack Daniel's in the other and laugh, all the while blurting out derogatory insults at both Billy and Jenna. When Michael was finally satisfied with the atrocities he'd forced upon Billy's mom, sister, and Billy, he would order Billy to unbind his sister and mother from their roped restraints, proceed to force them into the closet, and lock the closet door with them inside the dark, tight quarters. The three of them would be encased in this unlit prison for hours before Michael would release them.

When one of the neighbors, a new resident to the town and a retired counselor for victims of abuse, picked up on the signs of physical abuse, she phoned the authorities and Michael was hauled away to the Fayette State Correctional Institution in La Belle, Pennsylvania. During the trial, when Billy's mother was asked why she'd let these acts take place, not report Michael to the authorities, or escape to a safe place, she said what most victims of spousal abuse would say: "He was going to counseling and I hoped he would change."

Billy's lascivious intentions were believed to have originated from the horrors he was forced to engage in when he was younger. He would perch himself atop trees that put him close to where girls would frolic in the water and stare for hours, feeding his fantasies for preadolescent paraphilia.

He was a savvy charmer with boyish good looks and was considered to be one of the cooler, popular kids in his school. It was not uncommon for a group of young girls to adoringly giggle as he passed them by in the hallways or on the street. Billy was keenly aware of his effect on the schoolgirls and would use this to his advantage when his pubescent urges throttled up.

The school had an incentive program for the students to interact with each other with the hopes of increasing their interpersonal skills while improving their scholastic comprehension. It was called "Power in Numbers," and those who participated in the program would be rewarded with increased grading on their efforts, which contributed to the overall grades for the quarter. As an average student, Billy would partake in this program with the soul intention of seducing his female classmates, but never for the academic focus of the program.

One of Billy's successful measures of gratifying his libidinous desires was to coerce young girls to Tenmile Creek using promises of potential stardom through modeling opportunities. He had crafted believable credentials and created professional-looking business cards and would give the illusion that he was acting as a freelance photographic scout for girls interested in a modeling career. He persuaded his prospective naïve models that the amateur shots would be submitted to a variety of girl-targeted magazines and apparel retailers. Billy would tell his starry-eyed prospects that they shouldn't tell any adults because otherwise, the companies he was "working for" would not accept their candidacy for potential stardom, as parents are well known for being overzealous when it comes to their children's success and achievements. Amber Robertson, a 13-year-old modeling enthusiast with severe insecurity, fell victim to this scheme.

On an unseasonably warm September afternoon, Billy (knowing Amber's desire to be a model for a national apparel retailer) approached Amber in the schoolyard.

"Hey there, Amber. KD Quarter has asked me to submit photographs of local rural girls for a clothing line with a farming theme. I understand that you want to be a model when you get older, but this might be an opportunity to achieve that before you're an adult. Do you have any interest in posing for some pictures that I can submit to them?" Billy asked.

A wide-eyed, giddy Amber replied, "OF COURSE!!!! It would be a dream come true!"

"Excellent," Billy replied. "I can meet you at Anglers Point at 4:00 p.m. You can't tell your parents because KD Quarter won't consider you for photos for publishing until a decision is made. You're a size 5, right?"

"Yes. How did you know?"

"I've been doing this for more than a year now. When you work with potential models for that long, you get a pretty good idea of clothing sizes."

"I never thought of that. But you're right."

"All right. I'll see you at Angler's Point at four. You can bring a friend if you want, but don't go telling everyone because it will get really busy and I won't be able to focus, all right?"

"It's a deal. See you there."

Anglers Point was the section of South Fork Tenmile Creek where intersecting bodies of water produced a great amount of fish and found a lot of fishing enthusiasts casting their lines out from a small beach under a train trestle about 200 yards south of Center Street in Clarksville. This was also a popular

swimming and wading area for kids and teens around the neighborhood. It

wasn't unusual to find a group of kids splashing in the water and hanging out

on the small beach in this area.

About 50 yards east of Angler's Point was a smaller clearing on the creek's bank

that was sheltered by a group of trees, and an area risqué teens would utilize

for evening skinny-dipping events. This smaller area was known to the younger

generation as "Skin Beach," named for the indicative nude aquatic activities.

Even though the spot was known to the adults in the area, the popular

clothing-free youthful pastimes were kept in secret by the teens and kids.

Billy arrived at Angler's Point and walked through the short tree line divider

and began setting up his camera equipment; a gift given to him on his 12th

birthday by his grandparents. He also had a suitcase full of different pieces of

girl's apparel. With the temperature in the 80s, he would have no trouble

getting Amber to wear a bathing suit and be in the water for some of the shots.

After he was all set up, he walked back through the small tree line and hung

out under the train trestle, awaiting Amber's arrival. He was hanging out no

longer than 10 minutes before he heard a couple of girl's voices coming

through the trees along the east side riverbank. Billy recognized Amber's unmistakable sweet voice, but the other girl's voice was unfamiliar. Billy began

to panic a little. He thought, *What if this other girl doesn't know me or is aware*

of my photographer facade? I won't be able to get some of the shots that I

prepared for. Or maybe this other girl might be interested in posing as well.

Don't worry about it, Billy, you're smart and can finagle some arrangement.

Amber appeared out from the tree line by Angler's Point, walking her bike

alongside her. To her right was the other girl, whom Billy recognized right

away: Bekah Callahan. Bekah was also walking her bike out from the wooded

area.

"Hey, Billy," Amber greeted, "I brought Bekah with me because she is

interested in becoming a model as well, and I told her that you wouldn't mind if

you had photos of both of us to submit to KD Quarter. She didn't tell her

parents about this, mainly because they are both still working. And she won't

tell her parents, either, because I told her what you said to me about KD

Quarter not accepting the pictures if we told any adults." Amber turned to

Bekah and said, "You won't tell them, right?" Bekah shook her head and had a

bashful expression on her face. She had a major crush on Billy and was just

thrilled to be in his presence.

"Sounds good to me," Billy responded. "I set up the equipment over at Skin

Beach so we won't be interrupted if anyone else decides to hang out at Angler's Point due to the hot weather. So let's head over." Billy turned and headed to the small tree line with Amber and Bekah closely on his heels. When they reached Skin Beach's clearing, Amber and Bekah saw the camera mounted on the stand and an opened suitcase filled with different kinds of girls' attire.

"Let's get started. The first thing I need to do is get pictures of you in your regular clothes, what you are wearing now, so that the people at KD Quarter can see what you look like without the clothing you'll be modeling in. So, Amber, come over here and Bekah, you stand behind the camera for now."

Amber walked up to where Billy was standing and Bekah moved to a spot behind the camera stand. Billy then went over to the camera and began shouting out directions to Amber while he was bent slightly over and looking through the view port of the camera: "Very nice. Now fold your hands and place them in front of your belly. Excellent. Doing good. Now put your right hand on the back of your head and your left hand down by your side. Perfect." With each direction that Billy called out, Amber happily, and with a wide smile, complied. "That was great. Bekah, your turn."

Amber walked towards the spot where Bekah was standing while Bekah

simultaneously began moving towards the area that Amber had been posing at.

"All right, show me what you got." Billy called out the same directions as he

had with Amber, and then told them that that part of the photo shoot was

done.

Bekah made her way back towards Amber and stood next to her while Billy

knelt down next to the suitcase and pulled out a sheer white bathing suit that

had small roses randomly scattered around the whole thing. With the bathing

suit in his hand, he stood up and extended his right arm out to Amber and said,

"Now we need to take photos with swimwear. Go ahead and put this on."

Amber took the bathing suit from Billy's hand and said, "All right. I'll be right

back."

As Amber began turning and walking towards the wooded area, Billy stopped

her by saying, "No. We don't have time for that. We only have an hour or so

and it's getting darker, sooner, now. Change right here while I set up for the

next set of shots." With a great deal of insecurity and nervous embarrassment,

she did what Billy instructed her to do because, after all, he had worked with

many different models and probably saw this all the time. Amber turned her

back to Billy and began to undress. Billy was now in front of the camera, at the space where both Amber and Bekah had posed for the first set of preliminary photos, and began setting up some props that were going to be used in the next series of photos. He would glance up, from time to time, as Amber removed all her clothes and began putting on the bathing suit. When she was done, she turned towards Billy and said, "I'm ready."

Billy instructed her to join him at the area where the next photos were to be taken. When Amber was standing next to him, he began to move her into specific poses with his hands, then said, "That's perfect. Hold that pose." He returned behind the camera, bent over slightly, and took three pictures of Amber in that pose. "That's excellent. Now, these next shots require a wet look. So why don't you go into the water and dunk under the water so you are completely soaked." Amber slowly entered the water, turned around, and fell gently backwards into the water. When she emerged, Billy said, "Now stand up, stay right there, and put both of your hands on the back of your head." Amber did as instructed. With the type of fabric she was wearing and being completely soaked, there was little left to the imagination. Billy's heart rate began to increase with arousal. With multiple clicks of the camera's shutter capturing this innocent young girl wearing a very wet, very revealing bathing suit, Billy began to provide more directions: "You're doing great. They're going to love these shots. Now turn around. Bend over just a little bit. A little bit more. Turn your head to the left to face me. Perfect. Now put both your hands on your hips. Outstanding." The clicking of the shutter was almost constant as Billy took multiple pictures during the poses, as well as the transition between poses.

Bekah stood behind Billy witnessing all of this. A wave of insecurity washed over her. Even though she had a crush on Billy, she didn't want to expose herself to the degree that she saw Amber exposing her body to Billy. She definitely didn't want any pictures like that being sent to a major clothing company. Bekah also began to worry about whether or not Billy would find her attractive after he saw her in such skimpy attire. She grew more and more anxious with every click of the camera's shutter. Then she spoke up: "Billy, I actually have to get going. Mom wanted me home for dinner by four forty-five and I have to be home for that."

The camera's clicking came to a sudden stop. Billy stood upright, turned to Bekah and said, "Well, I can't submit any of your pictures without a swimsuit series; that includes the original shots in the clothes you're currently wearing. You wouldn't be considered for modeling their spring clothing line without these. Are you sure you want to leave?"

Bekah stood there for a moment, her eyes rolled up and to the left as she contemplated his words, then looked back at him and said, "Oh well. Maybe another time. Amber, are you ready to go?"

Amber turned around, now facing Billy and Bekah, and responded, "Well, that depends on how many more clothing variations we need to get through so I can make sure the judges at KD Quarter will consider me for their spring lineup model." She then focused her gaze onto Billy. "How many other outfits do you need before the people at KD Quarter will consider me to be their model?"

Billy looked at the top of the camera at the number of exposures he already had and said, "Well, we still have some shorts and t-shirt clothes to get on film, but I have 36 pictures already. They require a minimum of 40 pictures, so let's just take 4 more and then we'll wrap this up."

Amber agreed and then looked at Bekah and said, "Can you wait a few more minutes so I can walk home with you?" Bekah nodded and then Amber turned her attention back to Billy. "Okay, what do you want me to do next?"

Billy replied, "Come out of the water and sit down on the beach." Amber did as he instructed. Then Billy continued: "Now bend your knees up, hold them both with your hands, and stare over your knees like you were spying over a wall." When Amber got into the pose he said, "Wait. Lay your right leg flat on the ground, put your right hand behind your back, keep your left hand on your left knee, and lean back a little."

Amber got into the pose that Billy just instructed her to do and said, "Like this?"

Billy replied, "Yes. That's great." There were four clicking sounds and then Billy said, "That's a wrap. You can go ahead and get changed."

Amber got up off the ground, headed to the spot where her clothes were, picked them up, and began walking towards the woods. Again, Billy stopped her by saying, "Where are you going? Change right here on the beach while I put my camera equipment away. I don't want you running off with my stuff. Don't worry, I won't look." Amber complied with Billy's request while Billy began packing up his equipment, all the while sneaking glances at Amber while she dressed back into her original outfit.

When she was done, she held out the soaking wet bathing suit and asked, "Where do you want me to put this?"

"Go ahead and put it in the suitcase, even though it's wet. Don't worry about it. You did excellent, by the way. KD Quarter shouldn't even hesitate to offer you the position. Wait till I hear back from them before telling anyone." Then Billy turned his gaze over to Bekah and said, "That goes for you as well. You wouldn't want to risk Amber not being offered an opportunity because you went and blabbed to your or her parents, right?" Bekah nodded with a degree of shame, and then Billy continued by saying, "Wonderful. I'll see you both later. Thanks again."

With that, the girls grabbed hold of their bikes' handlebars, kicked up the kickstands, and began pushing them towards Angler's Point. They were shortly out of Billy's sight when he sat down on the beach, laid back on the sandy ground, put both of his hands under his head, and laid there, smiling. He was victorious with his intentions and pleased with satisfaction. His smile had a sinister smirk to it because the girls didn't know that there wasn't any film in the camera. Their naivety and quest for fame made them completely unaware that this charade was a complete farce, and only performed to satiate his lecherous proclivity.

CHAPTER 11: THE SILO'S SECRET

Long before the national Amber Alert law was enacted in the new millennium, there was the town of Clarksville, Pennsylvania, Amber Alert. When Doug and Marie Robertson first made the call to the sheriff's department, it had been five hours from when Amber left Bekah Callahan at her house and went to continue down Summit Street towards her home.

"Good evening, this is Rose, the sheriff's administrative assistant. Is this an emergency call?" Rose VanTrose was known by the entire town—heck, the entire region—as the sheriff's assistant, because she made it very clear each time she answered the phone; and not just the one in the office. Rose had this feeling that such a position held a level that warranted praiseworthiness, adoration, and unsolicited respect. Even the sheriff didn't use his title for bloated pride and pompousness.

Doug, knowing full well who was answering the phone in the sheriff's office, answered, "Rose, this is Doug Robertson. Our daughter, Amber, has not come home, and she was last seen with Bekah Callahan at 4:45 p.m. this evening."

"Did you contact Mr. or Mrs. Callahan to see if Little Miss Bekah knew whether Amber had an alternative destination?" Rose asked with a hint of narcissism.

"Bekah Callahan is the one who told me what time she last saw Amber, as Doris

Callahan is at work and Steven Callahan is still en route from Philadelphia,"

Doug huffed back on the phone. "When I asked Bekah what the two of them

were doing before Amber separated from Bekah, all Bekah said was that they

were hanging out by Angler's Point. After that, they walked their bikes home,

gave each other a little hug at the end of the Callahan's walkway, and went

their separate ways."

"Were they with anyone else at Angler's Point?" Rose asked.

"No. According to Bekah, they were just skipping rocks over the creek."

"When was the last time **you** saw Amber?"

"Just before she left for school at seven thirty this morning. Marie said that was

the last time she saw Amber as well."

"Who?"

"Ummm, my wife, Marie Robertson."

"Ahhh yes. Sorry about that. Thanks for clarifying. Well, I can send an officer over to your place to get more information."

"Any chance you can send the sheriff himself, Rose?"

"Well, Mr. Robertson, this isn't exactly a pick-and-choose service. But if the sheriff is available, I will request he go over. Is that fair?"

While rubbing his palm on his forehead from irritability and frustration, he responded, "Yes, that's fair, Rose. Thank you for your help this evening."

There was a knocking on the door a few minutes later, and when Marie answered it, it was Sheriff Langdon himself. "Good evening, Mrs. Robertson. Your husband called a little while ago. I heard the report go through the radio from Rose and, well, here I am."

Despite what some people have to say about small-town law enforcement being a little more timid than the big-city cops, that's not at all what the Marianna County law enforcement subscribed to. The sheriff was actually off normal work hours and was driving home from the grocery store across town. Even though he had perishable food and drinks in the car, he didn't hesitate to swing up the road a few miles to check out this child's disappearance.

177

It was just Doug, Marie, and Amber left in that house; Amber's older brother, Julius, was a freshman at Penn State University and lived on campus. "Oh my, Sheriff, thank you for coming personally. This means so much to us," Marie responded. "I don't know what to do. This has never happened to us nor anyone else that I can think of; and I've even tried calling different people to ask."

"Now, Mrs. Robertson, there is nothing to worry about until there is something to worry about, correct? By the way, how is young Julius doing up at Penn? I remember my son's freshman year there was so challenging."

"He's doing quite well, Sheriff, thank you for asking. Can we talk about Amber now?"

Sheriff Langdon always tried to calm the tension and emotion in the air if there was ever any that came to be. "Of course, Mrs. Robertson, of course. Rose filled me in on the high-level information that your husband provided to her, so I have the gist of what is happening. Aside from the Callahans, did you call anyone else or go anywhere to look for her? Perhaps some of her known favorite hangouts?"

"Well, we did call the Hurlberts, Fords, Carrs, and the Woodlawn girls from Amber's class, but they didn't know anything, nor had they seen her since school was dismissed. After we talked to Bekah Callahan, Doug went to Angler's Point to look around there while I came back to the house to wait and see if she came home."

"Sheriff, thank you for coming so quickly," Doug said, surprised. He wasn't even paying attention and had no idea who was talking to his wife at the front door. "We really appreciate it. Has my wife filled you in on any of the additional information Rose didn't provide? Marie must've mentioned that I went down to Angler's Point and saw the tire treads from their bikes, but nothing other than that. There were also spots where some small rocks had been pulled up out of the earth, but that goes along with Bekah's story of how they walked their bikes down there after school and were just skipping rocks on the creek."

"You didn't see anything else that may seem a little out of place or curious?" Langdon asked.

"Just saw burnt pieces of wood, but we all know the teenagers hang out down there and have little beach parties."

"Yes, Mr. Robertson, that's true. Don't remind me. And I had to bust **you two** when you were in high school. Of course, I was just a rookie, and looking for as many brownie points as I could get." They all had a moment of comic relief, accompanied with chuckles. "Do you know of any enemies or bullies Amber might have at the school or neighborhood?"

"Oh, not Amber," Marie responded with supportive accolades, "Amber is a sweet little girl and I don't know why anyone would have any issues with her. She is so courteous, compassionate, polite, and—"

"And 13 years old," Langdon interrupted.

"Yes, sir," Marie said awkwardly. "And 13 years old."

"You said that you called her female classmates. Did you think to call any of her male classmates? Or do you know of a boy she may have a crush on?" Langdon inquired.

"A **crush**? Amber? Ha-ha-ha-ha-ha. I guess you don't know Amber that well, Sheriff," Marie responded. "She is 100 percent focused on her studies and athletics."

"You don't say," Langdon said, while sneaking a wink over Doug's way. "Well, I would start calling all of her classmates and see if they have any information.

I'm going to head down to Angler's Point and see if I can find anything down

there." Langdon reached for his police radio he had on his left hip. "Langdon to

Jackson."

A static-y voice came over the speaker, "Go for Jackson."

Langdon continued, "I'm here at the Robertson house responding to a missing

persons call. Their daughter, Amber, hasn't been home since she left for school

this morning. She was down at Angler's Point with Bekah Callahan. Mrs.

Robertson reached out to Bekah, and Bekah said she last saw Amber at 4:45

p.m. this evening, and believed Amber was heading back to her house. I'm

going to head down to Angler's Point, now and look around some more. I need

you to come over to the Robertsons' and stay here in the event that Amber

shows up or they receive any word of her whereabouts."

"You got it, boss. I'll be there in five."

Langdon then turned back to where Marie and Doug were standing. "Officer

Jackson will be here soon and will stay with you in the event that Amber comes

home, calls, or you learn something new when you contact her other

classmates. I'm going to head down to Angler's Point and look around the area some more."

"Thank you, Sheriff," Marie responded. "We really do appreciate this, as well as everything you do for this town."

"You're very welcome, ma'am. And I enjoy what I do." With that, Langdon turned towards the front door, twisted the door handle, opened the door and stepped outside. He turned back and looked through the doorway and said, "Everything will be all right, folks, we'll find Amber."

Jackson drove up to the side of the road in front of the Robertsons' house not five minutes after Langdon drove off. The driving distance between the Robertsons' and Angler's Point was less than five minutes. Jackson was talking to the Robertsons when their phone rang. In anticipatory hysterics, Marie darted for the phone, ripped the receiver off the hook and answered in a frantic tone, "Hello???"

"Mrs. Robertson, this is Sheriff Langdon. May I speak with Officer Jackson?"

"Is everything all right? Did you find something? Why couldn't you call him on his radio?" Marie responded.

"Yes, Mrs. Robertson, everything is all right. I need to speak with Jackson about some police matters and it is protocol that these conversations not be conducted over the radio. But everything is all right."

"OK," Marie responded, still in hysterics. "Here he is." She handed the receiver over to Jackson.

"Jackson here. What's up, boss?"

"I found something here at Skin Beach that could be nothing. We all know that the teenagers use this secluded spot as a means to entertain themselves in skinny-dipping escapades, but I found something that is a little curious. I need you to keep the Robertsons calm and not mention this to them. Tell them something like I found nothing here and that I'm heading over to the Callahans' to talk to Bekah, all right? We don't need to cause any additional stress on the Robertsons. Plus, like I said, this could be nothing."

"Will do, boss."

Langdon went back to Angler's Point from his car where he'd called Jackson. He walked through the small tree line between Angler's Point and Skin Beach, knelt down, and picked up a pair of jean shorts, a pink t-shirt that had a My

Little Pony picture on the front, a pair of soiled socks, a pair of white sneakers,

and a pair of white underwear. As he flashed his flashlight back and forth, he

noticed a small patch of dried blood on the sandy ground underneath the

underwear he had picked up. There was a beach chair and an inflatable beach

ball near the water's edge, and several footsteps too big to be made by the

white sneakers he found.

When he shined his flashlight back to where the blood was, there was an

indentation in the sand of a square shape with a cylindrical protrusion pushed

out in front of the box and an outline of what appeared to be a strap of some

kind connected to the box. It didn't take Langdon too much time to be able to

identify that shape as a camera.

As he moved the light back and forth some more, he saw lines in the sand that

looked like a broken-up "X." One led to a tree, another to an adjacent tree, one

led to a large boulder by the water, and the other one led to a tree to the left

of the boulder. These were obviously rope lines used to restrain something.

Moving the light back up to where he picked up the clothes, he saw a large box

indentation, but had no idea what could've made that shape; it could have

been a number of things. There were more large footsteps leading to the

woods behind Skin Beach, and he noticed a smearing in the sand that looked like something was being dragged up the bank and into the woods. He followed

the path of pressed plants and foliage that went all the way up to the

pavement of Center Street, where the trail ended. There were no tire tracks to

determine what happened next, nor any kind of evidence to identify anything

further.

He knew what he needed to do next, which was to show the clothing to the

Robertsons to see if they could identify it as one of Amber's outfits; a task he

always dreaded.

Arriving at the Robertsons', Langdon sat in his car for about five minutes, trying

to compose himself as he was experiencing fear, nervousness, and sadness. The

evidence he'd captured at Skin Beach had shaken him up, and there was truly

only one explanation for the whole thing. At this point in an investigation, it

was protocol to disclose any and all findings to the parents.

With a trembling left hand, Langdon reached for the door handle of the

cruiser's driver-side door, opened it, and got out of the car. With weak legs he

began up the walkway to the Robertsons' front door. He had a bag in his right

hand.

He knocked, and Doug answered the door. He saw Langdon standing there with the bag in his right hand and an expression of concern on his face. Doug's eyes widened and the sheriff said, "Doug, I need to share some information that is going to be difficult to hear."

Doug collapsed to the floor, as he could only imagine what was in the bag that the sheriff was holding. Jackson was standing next to Doug. Marie had come out of the kitchen to see her husband kneeling on the floor with his hands over his face, and she could hear muffled sobbing coming from him. She noticed the bag that Langdon was holding, screamed a shriek of horror, ran over to Doug, and knelt next to him.

Langdon looked up at Jackson and shook his head back and forth. After a minute or two, Jackson reached under Doug's left armpit and Langdon wrapped his arm around Marie's shoulders. Both Jackson and Langdon guided Doug and Marie to their feet, escorted them to the living room, and sat them down on the couch. The sheriff then began to remove the articles of clothing from the bag and describe the scene he saw at Skin Beach.

A massive search effort began that evening and continued for the next two months, which included extensive interviews with the residents of the town, all school persons and faculty, businesses, and neighboring townspeople. Out of shame and guilt, Bekah kept the secret of the events that had transpired the

last time she saw Amber. She believed she would be arrested and incarcerated

for withholding pertinent information that could lead to finding Amber. Though

Bekah's heart was filled with grief and sadness for Amber's disappearance, she

couldn't bring herself to reveal the secret she possessed. Bekah was conflicted

between her fear of being arrested and having everything taken away from her,

and her guilt of what happened that day at Skin Beach. She believed her secret

might lead to finding Amber, but her fear held greater control of her conscious

faculties.

Doris Callahan was gathering laundry in Bekah's room one Saturday afternoon

and unearthed a small red book that had the word "Journal" on the cover. She

had no idea that Bekah kept a journal. As a typical curious parent, she opened

the book to the first page, sat down on Bekah's bed, and began reading

through the many pages. The contents were familiar as to what you would find

in a teenager's diary: boys, clothes, shopping, events with girlfriends, boys,

activities at school, and boys. Doris chuckled over some of the entries because

she thought they were cute and silly. She was a little uncomfortable with the

entries that referenced boys, but the way it was written seemed innocent and

harmless. There was nothing in there to indicate sexual activity; and this was

something a lot of teenage girls would document. Then Doris came upon a

page that sent a shiver of horror up her spine:

Friday, September 6, 1985: Had a photo session with Billy Donnelly at Skin

Beach. He is so cute. He was collecting pictures to submit to KD Quarter for their

1986 spring clothing lineup. Amber Robertson was with me. He took pictures of

us in our regular clothes, then had Amber change into a see-through white

bathing suit (with little roses on it) right in front of us. He had her get into the

water, took pictures of her when she was soaking wet—and you could see

everything through that bathing suit. I was nervous and embarrassed and didn't

want to have those kinds of pictures taken of me. Billy would think I wasn't

attractive enough to date me. I told him I wasn't going to pose with that outfit

and I had to get home for dinner. He told me that he needed to have those

pictures to send to KD Quarter or I wouldn't be considered for the modeling

position. Amber did everything Billy asked and I believe she will be offered the

modeling job, as she wants it most. Now we just have to wait and hear from KD

Quarter and then we can tell Amber's parents.

Doris darted up from Bekah's bed, went over to the staircase, and hollered out,

"Bekah, can you come up here please? Right now."

Bekah, startled by her mother's tone and decibel level, got up from the couch

and headed over to the stairway. She stopped, looked up at her mother and

asked, "Why? What's up?" Bekah then noticed her red journal in her mother's

hand and Bekah's face went pale.

"I need to see you up in your room **now**!"

Bekah began ascending the staircase, maintaining eye contact with Doris the whole time. When Bekah was three-quarters of the way up the stairs, Doris turned and headed to Bekah's bedroom, stood next to the open door, and waited for Bekah to enter the room.

Upon Bekah coming into the room, Doris closed the bedroom door, looked at Bekah and said, "Have a seat on your bed. I found this under a pile of clothes while I was gathering your laundry to wash."

"You didn't read any of it, did you?" Bekah asked with a nervous tremble in her tone. "That's private information."

"Yes, I did. Everything was harmless until I reached your entry for September 6, where you were with Billy Donnelly and Amber Robertson at Skin Beach; yes, I know all about Skin Beach and what happens there," Doris responded.

Bekah had a keen recollection of what happened that day and the entry she'd put in her journal for the events that transpired. "So?"

"Why didn't you tell your father or me, or the **authorities** of this? That was the evening that Amber disappeared, and this could've helped the police find Amber. You withheld very important information. Why? What would cause you to keep this information from those who could help Amber???"

"It was a secret, and if the adults knew, Amber wouldn't be able to fulfill her dream of becoming a model."

"But why, even days into the investigation, did you not say anything? This is absolutely inconceivable, young lady."

With great frustration and disbelief, Doris turned to the bedroom door, opened it, then stormed towards the stairway and made her way down the stairs. She turned left into the dining room, then continued through to the kitchen. Bekah raced down behind her, screaming, "Mom, what are you going to do? You're not going to tell anyone, are you? You can't do that! That's private information!"

"No!" Doris snapped back as she lifted the receiver off the charging base. "Kissing a boy or revealing silly activities during a slumber party is private. Information that could aid in the discovery of a missing child is **not** private information."

Doris dialed the number to the sheriff's office and Rose answered in her typical

snide and pompous tone, "Sheriff's department. This is Rose, the sheriff's

administrative assistant."

"Hi, Rose, this is Doris Callahan. I need to speak with the sheriff **now**!!!"

"Calm down, Mrs. Callahan," Rose replied. "What is the nature of this call?"

"I have information that could help in the search for Amber Robertson and I

need to speak with the sheriff **immediately**."

"Well, Mrs. Callahan, Sheriff Langdon is out at lunch right now, so I'll give him

your message when he returns."

"WHAT??? Are you kidding me, Rose? This is a life-or-death situation. You **need**

to put me in touch with the sheriff right now! This can't wait until he gets back

from lunch. Do you understand?"

"Settle down, Mrs. Callahan. Let me see if I can get a hold of him." Rose placed

Doris on hold, picked up the police radio, pressed the talk button and said,

"Rose to Sheriff." A few seconds passed by before a voice came over her radio.

"Go for Sheriff."

"I have Doris Callahan on the line who says she may have information about Amber Robertson. I told her you were at lunch and would get back to her when you return."

There was a momentary silence on the radio, and then Langdon responded with great irritation in his voice, "You must be joking, Rose. Someone calls with information that could lead to the discovery of a missing child's whereabouts and you tell them I'm at **LUNCH**?? This is completely unacceptable. I'll deal with you later. Tell Mrs. Callahan I'm heading over there now. I can't believe you, Rose. Not wise. Not wise at all." Langdon dropped his fork, grabbed his hat, and raced to the door and out to his car. He sped over to the Callahans' like a FASTCAR driver on his last lap of a race.

Doris was standing out on the front steps of their house when Langdon arrived. She held the red journal in her hand. Bekah was standing next to her, looking down at the ground. The sheriff slammed the brakes so hard it created burnt tire marks on the pavement.

He leapt out of his car, the cruiser's red-and-blue lights flashing, and ran up the walkway to where Doris and Bekah were standing. Doris handed the journal to

192

Langdon that she had opened to the entry about the photo shoot. After reading through the page, he slammed the journal shut, turned around, and raced back to the car. He pulled the police radio from his belt loop, pressed the talk button on the left side of the radio and said, "Langdon to Jackson."

"Go for Jackson."

"I need you to get over to the Donnelly house right away. Have McCormick, Rogers, and Middleton meet me there as well. Don't let **anyone** leave that house. Do you understand?"

"I understand, boss. What's going on?"

"Just get over there. And have an ambulance meet us there as well."

Langdon reached his cruiser, got in, slammed the door, then peeled out, heading towards the Donnellys'. His heart was racing and his body was trembling with fear and anticipation. He had no idea what to expect.

When he reached the Donnelly home he saw Jackson's, McCormick's, Rogers,' and Middleton's cruisers there. He could see Middleton standing at the rear corner of the house, McCormick and Rogers flanking the sides of the house, and Jackson standing at the front door. Slamming the brakes again, Langdon

threw the cruiser in park, thrust open the door, got out, and ran up to where

Jackson was standing. He then went past Jackson and pounded on the front

door of the Donnelly house.

"This is Sheriff Langdon. Open up!"

Billy opened the door with a frantic expression on his face. "What is this all

about, Sheriff?"

Langdon had the journal open to the page with the September 6 entry, put it in

front of Billy's face and said, "Would you mind explaining this?"

Billy cracked a smile on his face; the kind you would see on a magician's face

after he shocked an audience with an illusion that left them stupefied. "Oh,

that," Billy replied whimsically and with a calm tone. "We were just having

fun."

"You never mentioned this to us when we interviewed you about Amber

Robertson's disappearance. Do you mind telling me why?" Langdon responded

with an irate and impatient tone.

"It wasn't important information. We were having a fun photo session and then Bekah Callahan and Amber went home. That's all. Nothing worthy of sharing with anyone else."

Langdon slammed the book shut and dropped it on the ground. He grabbed Billy's arm, spun him around, produced the handcuffs from his police belt and said, "William Donnelly, you are under arrest in connection with Amber Robertson's disappearance and withholding information from the law." During this entire process, Billy's expression never shifted. It was like he was proud to have been discovered.

When they arrived at the police station, Langdon got out of the cruiser, walked around to the back passenger door, opened it, and ripped Billy out from inside. He forcefully shoved Billy into the police station and over to the interrogation room. Langdon then pushed Billy down onto one of the chairs next to the table in the room and said, "Now listen, young man, you'd better start singing like a canary. And I mean **now**."

Billy maintained that proud expression on his face and said only two words before refusing to say anything further: "Grain silo."

Langdon dispatched all his officers to each of the grain silos in the area and told

195

them to report on anything they found. Jackson went to the Bates Farm and

had Arnold Bates escort him to his grain silos and assist in searching inside each

of them. Amber's body was found halfway down one of the grain silos. While

Jackson and Arnold were still in the silo, Jackson removed the radio from his

police belt, depressed the talk button, and with a sobbing tone, recited two

words: "Found her."

Amber Robertson's body was discovered in one of the grain silos at the Bates

Farm off Leonard Road in Clarksville, Pennsylvania, three miles north of

Angler's Point. She was wearing a translucent, white bathing suit with small

roses on it. Her neck had been snapped and both of her legs broken and

dislocated from the hip sockets. There was bruising on both her upper arms, as

well as rope marks around both wrists and both ankles. There was dried blood

on the crotch area of the bathing suit, and blood-matted hair dried against her

face. Her body had not decomposed due to the pressurization within the grain

silo, even though she had been missing for two months.

CHAPTER 12: THE SWIMSUIT RECKONING

Ralph Dubain opened the front screen door of his house, let Max exit the house first, then followed closely behind him. Ralph had a cup of coffee in one hand, an unlit cigar in the other, and a newspaper wedged between his side and arm. He walked over to his chair, set the cup of coffee down on the table, placed the unlit cigar in the ashtray on the table, then grabbed the newspaper from under his arm. He turned around and sat down.

It was a chilly November evening, but not so much that Ralph required a hat, thick winter jacket, or gloves. Ralph had been stationed on a naval ship through all seasons of the year so one thing he had no trouble enduring was cold temperatures. One might say that he had become immune to them and could tolerate sitting outside in zero-degree temperatures. At this point in his life, he would much rather be sitting outside in his trusty wooden rocking chair than cooped up inside his empty house.

He set the newspaper down on his lap, reached over to his left, grabbed the cigar and book of matches he kept on the table, and proceeded to light his cigar. He took a few deep drags to get the embers burning brightly, closed his eyes, lifted his head up, and exhaled the smoke he had collected in his mouth from the cigar. He opened his eyes and began to lower his head when he was gripped with a ghostly fear at a vision in front of him.

Jasper Callahan was leaning up against the lamppost across the street, looking in Ralph's direction with that same sinister expression he wore on the morning of Noah's dead body discovery. The streetlight above cast a 10-foot semi-circle of soft amber light underneath it, making it appear as if Jasper were on center stage under a spotlight. It looked as though Jasper was a mannequin propped against the streetlight, as he was hauntingly motionless with the expression of insidious plot on his face. His gaze was firmly fixed on Ralph's face as if Jasper was peering into the darkness through a telescope and studying the dimly lit glow of Ralph's face. Jasper's left leg was bent at the knee and his left foot was resting on its toes on the pavement beneath him, forming a figure "4." His arms were folded across his chest with his hands tucked beneath each elbow. He was wearing blue-and-red flannel pajama bottoms and a pajama top that had a large shape-shifting robot cartoon image on the front. He was wearing navy blue slippers that covered everything up to his ankles. Jasper's hair was scruffy, with no one hair going in the same direction. He had a gold brooch pinned above his left breast, and Ralph could barely make out the image of a pink petunia in its center. It was as if he was sleepwalking and took post at the streetlight. This was not the place where a 10-year-old boy should be at 10:00 p.m. on a chilly November evening wearing only pajamas.

Max began barking, breaking Ralph's paralyzing stare at Jasper. Ralph turned to

Max, put his hand on Max's head and said, "Shush, boy." Ralph never broke his

focus on young Jasper's ominous pose. "Yeah, buddy, it's kind of freaking me

out, too." He then spoke up out into the night air, creating an echo through the

stillness: "Master Callahan, what are you doing out so late? You're going to

catch a cold with just your pajamas on in this temperature."

There was no movement from Jasper, no recognition of Ralph's words, and no

shift in his expression. Instead, the streetlight began to flicker: dot-dot-dot, dot,

dash-dot, dash, dot, dash-dot, dash-dot-dash, dot-dot, dash-dot, dash-dash-

dot.

Ralph spoke aloud again in a confused tone, "'Sentencing'? What or **who** are

you sentencing?"

Jasper spoke not a word. Instead, he slowly rolled his eyes up and delicately

moved his head facing up the lamppost. Ralph followed Jasper's line of sight

and dropped his cigar in horrified disbelief. There, about halfway up the

lamppost, was a boy, no more than 16 years old, suspended against the

lamppost. He had been squished into a translucent white girl's bathing suit with

little roses all over it that was one-third the size of what would fit the boy. The outfit was so tight around him that the fabric had begun to tear along the sides. It was compressing his torso and abdomen to the point where his body took on the shape of a pear. His man parts were pushed out from the crotch area of the bathing suit due to the pressure the swimsuit was putting against his groin. The boy's legs were broken and bent reversely at the knees, making it so his kneecaps were behind his legs. His shoulders were dislocated at the socket and dangling only by muscle, tendons, and skin. His neck had been broken and spun around so that his chin was directly over his spine facing the lamppost. He had bruises on his upper arms, and red rope burns on both his wrists and his ankles. The blonde hair on the back of his head was stained with dried blood and matted against his skull. There was a red strap around his neck that led to a black 35mm Minolta camera that was resting against his compressed chest. He was spattered with thin, fibrous strands of hay, as if someone had tarred and feathered him with honey and straw.

Ralph tried to wrap his mind around this violent display of vicious brutality. His mind instantly went to the sight he'd experienced when he saw Noah suspended up on that very same lamppost only a few months before. Except this time, it was different. Noah's arms and legs had been wrapped around the lamppost as if he were tied to it by his limbs, which might indicate how he stayed suspended up on the post. With this boy, there were no limbs wrapped around the post, so the mystery of how he remained suspended was even greater. Ralph then saw something that made him wish he was dreaming, and

provided an inconceivable explanation as to how the boy was held up against

the post.

There was a shadowy ring around the boy's midsection that looked like arms,

and in the center of his gut was the shape of fingers interlaced, with the palms

resting on the boy's stomach. Ralph slowly looked up to the boy's contorted

neck and he saw a shadowy head hanging off to the side of the lamppost. Not

against the lamppost, but in the air next to the lamppost, as if someone was

peeking their head out from behind the post. He could make out a set of eyes,

but they were more like dim white holes and not eyeballs. He could see the

outline of hair, but it was the same kind of shape you would see if someone

was on the beach and the ocean wind was blowing through their hair, creating

a wave pattern of hair at the top of their shadow's skull. The eerie factor, in this

case, was that there was absolutely no breeze, but the shadowy outline of hair

seemed to blow around in the air. A ghostly white smile began to appear where

the shadow's mouth would be, starting on its right side and growing

counterclockwise to the left, revealing a grim smirk. The light that created the

shadow's right eye began to narrow until there was no more light from that

side of its face. It was winking at Ralph. This ominous presence was actually

winking at Ralph. There was no more mystery involved here; what he was

seeing was a dark, ghostly apparition of Mrs. Davis-Carpenter clutching the young boy firmly against the metallic light post.

Ralph remembered the puzzled expressions on the rescuers' faces when they were trying to figure out how Noah was being affixed to the light post. They thought it might have been an industrial adhesive or some other means that could explain how Noah's body was suspended halfway up the streetlight's pole. When Noah's body finally separated from the lamppost and flopped against the pavement, the mystery was heightened. Perhaps the industrial adhesive had weakened from the boy's weight. Or if he were suspended there by nails, perhaps the body's skin and muscles ripped through the steel spikes, dislodging Noah's body from the lamppost. But none of that happened. There was no evidence of an adhesive or piercing spikes that would explain Noah's captivity to the lamppost. He simply, just, fell off.

Ralph was hit with a gruesome epiphany that the shadowy apparition, now restraining this new victim against the lamppost, was the same mechanism used to suspend young Noah, but because it was morning and the sun wasn't hitting that area of the streetlight enough to cast shadows, the spectral shadow wasn't visible. However, there was no light now to lead back to a physical form. It was just a gloomy shadow. Yet, how can a shadow, a lack of light, possess any degree of strength to have impact on a physical object? None of this made any sense.

When Ralph finally found enough muscle to stand up, he walked hastily towards Jasper and the streetlight, panicky and in terror. Jasper never shifted his stance but kept his glare on Ralph as Ralph grew nearer and nearer. "Jasper, my dear boy, what have you done?"

Jasper just continued to look up at Ralph with that unaltered expression on his face.

"Young man, what have you done? Answer me. Who is this up on the lamppost?" Ralph inquired, while pointing his finger up at the lifeless body suspended against the pole.

Again, Jasper did not speak a word, move a muscle, or show any signs of recognition of Ralph's questions.

"You stay there, Jasper. I'll be right back." Ralph turned and began walking cautiously away from Jasper and the lamppost, turning his head to the left every now and then to see if he was being followed, or if the ghostly apparition released the young boy from the pole, or something more evil was following him. Yet, everything remained as it was. No one was following him or posing a threat to his presence.

Ralph reached the front steps of his house, opened the screen door, and made

his way into the living room. He picked up the phone's receiver and dialed the

sheriff's number. On the third ring, the phone went dead. Ralph thought that

someone picked up the phone on the other end of the line and began to shout,

"Hello? Hello? Sheriff? Rose? Someone? Please respond if you're there!" Yet no

one responded. The line just went dead. Ralph replaced the receiver back onto

its base, picked it back up off the base and put it to his ear, hoping to hear a

dial tone. There was silence. A terrifying silence. Ralph began hearing breathing

through the earpiece of the receiver. It was very light breathing. Ralph began

speaking again. "Sheriff? Rose? Is that you? Who is this?"

Ralph was petrified when the breathing stopped and a child's voice responded,

"Uh-uh-uh. You don't want to do that." The child's voice began to giggle in a

high pitch with such frolic amusement like you'd hear if a child was being

tickled. Ralph dropped the phone and darted over to the living room window

that faced the streetlight, ripped open the curtains, and saw Jasper still leaning

on the lamppost in the same position he was when Ralph left him. The

shadowy arms were still gripped around the young boy's body against the

streetlight's pole.

Ralph ran back to where he'd dropped the phone's receiver, picked it up off the floor, and stretched it as far across the room as he could so he could look out the window and still hold the earpiece to his ear. That childish giggle continued on the other end of the phone. "Who is up on that post?" Ralph ordered in a tone that you would hear coming from a drill sergeant during boot camp.

The childish giggle continued but grew stronger with gleeful exuberance. "Uh-uh-uh, secrets, secrets."

Ralph saw that Jasper's mouth was not moving. It was if someone had poured liquid nitrogen on the boy and he was put into a cryogenic state. But it was HIS voice on the other end of that receiver. It was so recognizable. He'd talked to Jasper a few times and it was incontestably Jasper's voice pouring through the phone's earpiece. "What secrets, Jasper?" Ralph asked, now growing more and more impatient.

"Let's play a game, Master Chief," the Jasper voice said.

Now this was getting creepy. Jasper knew Ralph was in the military, but Ralph had never told him what his rank was while he was in the navy. How could Jasper have possibly known his rank? Did his dad tell him? Or somebody else in town who knew what Ralph did in the navy? "What kind of game, Jasper?" Ralph asked.

"A *quid pro quo* game," the voice snickered.

Ralph began to think internally, *This is enough. How does a 10-year-old boy know what quid pro quo means, and even more, how to engage in it?* Then Ralph spoke aloud, "All right. I'll go first."

"Uh-uh-uh, Chief, that's not how this game goes," the voice responded in a disapproving tone.

"All right. What's your question?" Ralph asked.

"What was the name of that state hospital in Massachusetts where you volunteered as a child?"

"Danvers State Hospital."

"Very good. Now your turn." The voice said this like a kid who just said "go fish" while playing cards with his grandparents. While Ralph maintained his focus on Jasper, he continued to see that Jasper's mouth wasn't moving, nor were any of his facial muscles twitching while Ralph was hearing the voice through the receiver.

"What's the name of the young boy up on that lamppost?"

"Uh-uh-uh. You don't just go groping for an answer like that. You have to warm your way up to it."

"But that is my question. Now tell me who that is up on the lamppost."

The voice's tone changed from a childish giggle to a deepened, demonic, authoritative gurgle and hollered back through the line with great anger and fury, "No, asshole, this is my game and you will play by **my** rules, or you die!" The voice then returned to the cute, childlike tone and continued, "Now, ask a different question."

Ralph noticed that Jasper's expression went from the sinister state to an infuriated scowl when the voice changed pitch, then returned back to the original expression when the voice told Ralph to ask a different question. "All right, Jasper, I didn't mean to upset you. Ummm, how old are you?"

The voice responded, "Ninety-eight years old. My turn. What was your aunt's name who worked at the state hospital?"

"Claire Dubain." Ralph began wondering where Jasper's questions were heading. Still shaken by the change in the tone of Jasper's voice when he was trying to force the name of the boy out of him, Ralph asked, "What is your name?"

"Uh-uh-uh. Secrets, secrets. Ask me another question."

"OK, ummm, where do you go to school?"

"I don't go to school, silly, I'm 98 years old. My turn. What was your favorite meal at Danvers when you volunteered?"

Ralph had no idea. And what's more, Ralph had no idea how Jasper would know the answer to that question. But now he began thinking to himself that it wasn't Jasper he was talking to, it was Mrs. Davis-Carpenter speaking through Jasper's voice box. "The meatloaf and mashed potatoes," Ralph replied with a lack of confidence in his answer.

"NO. THAT'S WRONG!!!! Think, you miserable old fart. Try again, or there'll be a penalty." This order was said in the same demonic tone that had responded when Ralph tried to force the name of the dead boy earlier.

"Oh wait, that was my second favorite. My favorite was the chicken parmigiana with spaghetti," Ralph answered.

One of the shadow's hands holding Billy up against the light pole released its grasp around Billy's waist, then shot towards Ralph's living room window, hitting it, causing the glass to implode and spray against Ralph's face. Small shards of glass lacerations appeared on Ralph's face and the gashes began to bleed almost instantaneously. Ralph had no time to shield his face, nor had he expected any such action to occur. He then noticed the shadowy arm slowly recede back towards the light post, return its position around Billy's midsection, and interlace with the left hand's fingers as Ralph had originally seen. "You want to try again, or should you suffer another penalty?"

Ralph, now straining and attempting to unlock that memory vault in his brain, was feverishly hunting around for what his favorite food was while he volunteered at Danvers, decades ago. He kept coming up with the same two meals he answered, but knew if he said one of them again, there would be repercussions. The childish voice on the other end of the line began saying, "Tick . . . tock . . . tick . . . tock . . . tick . . . tock." In a panic of fear and terror, Ralph blurted out, "Macaroni and cheese!!!"

"Very good," said the sweet child's voice. "That wasn't so hard, now, was it?

Your turn."

"What's your favorite flower?"

"Pink petunias. My turn. At Danvers, one of the patients mentioned two words

to you: 'Amontillado' and 'Poe.' Did you ever figure out what that patient was

trying to say?"

Ralph vaguely remembered these words from one of the conversations he'd

had with Mrs. Davis-Carpenter, but also remembered he never followed up

with her on whether or not he figured out the message she was trying to

convey. He responded, "It's Edgar Allen Poe's poem *The Cask of Amontillado*. I

read it in my freshman year of high school. My turn. What happened on the

night that Noah died?"

"Bad boys need to be punished. Noah was a bad boy and imprisoned his

siblings in a cedar chest to hurt them. That act should never go unpunished. My

turn. Why didn't you do your homework after the patient gave you those two

names and find out what the patient was talking about?" The voice never

referred to the patient as Mrs. Davis-Carpenter, but rather addressed her in the

third-person.

"I was only nine. I couldn't figure out what those words meant. How was I to know? I was still reading Archie comics back then."

The voice's pitch returned to the demonic tone. "Yes, but you were old enough to read books on Morse code, now, weren't you? You could've asked your mom or aunt, now, right? Instead, you were being a lazy little shit without concern or interest in the patients you were with!"

"I didn't think they would know what I was talking about."

"You never tried, you poor excuse for a scholar. Because of you, and you alone, many of us died in horrible, inhumane ways. Your laziness killed us!"

"Killed who? I was told you passed away and your body was cremated. They even showed me the urn. It had a pink petunia on it."

"Such a naive little boy." The voice returned back to the childlike tone. "Next question, you selfish little prick."

With blood continuing to flow from the cuts on his face, Ralph asked, "Why are you doing this?"

"No one else will."

The shadow's hands quickly drew away from the boy's body, causing him to fall

to the ground. The shadow began to recede into the blackness behind the

lamppost, where the tree line began. Jasper reset his right leg to a proper

standing position, stood upright, winked at Ralph, then turned and began

walking back up Summit Street towards his house. Ralph stood in his living

room, wide-eyed, the phone's receiver pressed up against his ear, blood

painting his face. He began yelling into the phone, "Wait. Come back! Hello?

Jasper? Hello?" There was no response, and Jasper was out of sight. Ralph

dropped the phone onto the floor, raced to the front door, threw open the

screen door, nearly knocking it off its hinges, and began jogging up Summit

Street as best as an old man can jog. When he reached the Callahans', he ran

up the walkway and began pounding on the front door. "Mr. Callahan? Mrs.

Callahan? Are you awake? It's Ralph Dubain. I need to talk to you."

Steve Callahan opened the door in an excitable state. "What's going on, sir? It's

late. Why are you yelling and pounding at our door this time of the night? What

happened to your face? You're bleeding profusely!"

Ralph responded with impatience, "Where's Jasper? I just saw Jasper out at the

streetlight. Is he here? Did you hear or see him come in?"

"Mr. Dubain, sir, Jasper is asleep, and so are the other children. Please lower your voice."

"That's impossible. I just saw him down at the streetlight. He was wearing pajamas with a cartoon on it. I saw him leaning against the lamppost. Can you go see if he is in his room?"

"Mr. Dubain, you're beginning to worry me. Jasper has been asleep in his room for the last three hours. How do you know what kind of pajamas he is wearing? Are you spying on him? You're making me very uneasy talking about seeing my 10-year-old boy standing in his pajamas this late at night out in this temperature. Please go home or I'll be forced to call the sheriff."

"But, Mr. Callahan, sir, would you just go see if Jasper is still in his room?"

"Good night, Mr. Dubain. Please leave my home. And get those cuts looked at." With that, Steve slammed the front door shut in Ralph's face. Ralph looked up to the windows on the second floor and saw Jasper looking out from one of them with that sinister expression. Jasper raised his right index finger to his lips in a shushing gesture, then slowly disappeared into the darkness of the room behind him.

CHAPTER 13: CONTAGIOUS PERPLEXITY

"Sheriff's department, Officer Jackson speaking."

A frantic voice came over the line, "Officer, this is Ralph Dubain on Chartiers Road. I'd like to report a dead body."

"I'm sorry, Mr. Dubain, can you repeat that last part?" Jackson responded.

"A dead body. There's a dead body under the streetlight at the intersection of Summit Street and Chartiers Road."

"Do you know who it is, Mr. Dubain?"

"No. I haven't gone up close to see it. But I know it's dead."

"Mr. Dubain," Jackson continued, "I just got off the phone with Steven Callahan, who told me you were frantically pounding on his door asking about his son, Jasper. He told me you said you saw Jasper underneath that same streetlight you're telling me about now, and how you described the young boy's pajamas, which made Mr. Callahan uncomfortable. I was actually going to give you a call next."

Ralph's heart began to race. There was only one reported pedophile case in all the years that Ralph had lived in that town, and the townspeople persecuted and professionally crucified him before any real evidence came to light. Ralph couldn't even begin to fathom harming a child in any manner, let alone an act as inexcusable and evil as sexually assaulting a child. Yet here he was, thinking that he was being painted as a pedophile for identifying someone's child and the pajamas the child was wearing.

Ralph was in hysterics over what he'd witnessed, and he wanted to make sure that the young boy was in no danger to himself or anyone else, which is what prompted him to race over to the Callahans' to begin with. When it comes to reports of that nature, it's "ready, fire, aim" instead of the other order of "ready, aim, fire." If someone is arrested or suspected of being a murderer, the law will arrest and detain the suspect and then perform investigations that will either convict or acquit that individual. However, when it comes to child abuse of any kind, the suspect is oftentimes convicted guilty by the general populous before any investigations commence. Ralph was already fearing for his life from a shadowy apparition, but now he began fearing for his life from an angry mob of local residents by accusation alone.

"Officer, I had no intentions of harming that boy or any child, ever. I **did** see

Jasper leaning against that lamppost wearing only his pajamas on a chilly November evening. Surely that is not a criminal act to make sure that the boy was safe in his own home!"

"Of course not. I imagine the way you did that, with the intense amount of emotion and persistence, led Mr. Callahan to worry. I know he doesn't think you're a child predator, but he said that you had lacerations on your face and were bleeding, as well as acting hysterical at ten o'clock at night. Put yourself in his shoes. How would you have reacted if he appeared on your front porch in the same manner demanding you go check on your child, who you believe to be sound asleep in his bedroom?"

"I see your point, Officer. Now that I reflect on it, I must've appeared like a raving lunatic. I wasn't composed enough to be stampeding to someone's house so late at night, causing a disturbance, and scaring a parent. Is he going to file charges?"

There was a slight chuckle on the other end of the line and Jackson replied, "Of course not, Mr. Dubain. You are a well-respected individual in this town and everyone, **including** Mr. Callahan, knows that you would never harm a child in any way. He told me to put your mind at ease by letting you know he wasn't going to say anything to anyone, either, and that he wants to stop by your place in the morning and calmly discuss things with you."

There was a very noticeable sigh of relief and then Ralph said, "Thank goodness. But Officer, there **IS** a dead body under that streetlight. Can you come out or send another officer out, please?"

"I'll send Middleton over. He went over to the gas station to pick up some stale donuts and burnt coffee for us." There was more chuckling from Jackson before he continued, "Give him a few minutes and he'll be there."

"Thank you, Officer, I really do appreciate that, and your reassurances."

There was a click on the other end of the phone line, then Ralph returned the receiver to the phone's base, stood there for a moment, looked out the broken living room window, and set his focus onto the lifeless body that was laying underneath the solo streetlight on that road. For a split moment, he could swear he saw the body twitch slightly, even from the distance he was standing. But he quickly washed that thought away, convincing himself that he was still very shaken up about the events that had transpired within the last hour.

When Ralph was running back to his house from the Callahans' to call the police, he didn't think to stop and try to identify the boy's body before continuing on to his house. Ralph thought that Officer Middleton might ask this question, so Ralph turned towards the front screen door, opened it, walked out on the porch, and stood motionless for a few seconds. He descended the three steps off the porch and slowly made his way over to the boy's body. The body was lying flat on its stomach, but its head had been broken and twisted 180 degrees around his body, so he could identify the face without having to move the body at all. When he looked down at the boy's face, he was able to identify him as Billy Donnelly, the boy who had abducted, raped, and murdered Amber Robertson. Ralph began to whisper aloud, "How is this possible? William Donnelly is in jail, and there were no warning calls to the residents about an escaped convict to look out for. Who would do this to the boy, anyway? And how can I tell the police what I saw without them thinking I am absolutely loony? How believable would a story be about a shadow brutally murdering a person, dragging them up a streetlight pole, and suspending them there? Oh, Mr. Dubain, you've found yourself in quite a quandary here."

Ralph looked up and noticed some bright headlights approaching in the distance. The only people who would be driving down the road at this time of the night were police and 2nd-shifters. Ralph didn't want to take the risk of having Officer Middleton discover him standing next to the dead body when he arrived at the scene so he double-timed it back to his house, leaped onto the porch, and sat down on the rocking chair. As this was his usual place to be found, he didn't think it would arouse any suspicion from the police. There was one thing Ralph completely failed to remember, as his body was completely numb to any sensation other than panic and worry: he still had a bunch of cuts on his face and would have to explain this to Officer Middleton when he arrived.

A police car pulled up in front of Ralph Dubain's home without the lights flashing or siren blaring. Officer Middleton did not want to incite any kind of commotion from curious residents; and flashing reds and blues and deafening sirens would be like a hypnotic draw to any curious minds. People would actually get into their cars while still in their nightclothes and follow emergency vehicles to the scene; such is the draw of excitement in a small town.

The door to the police cruiser opened and out stepped a 6'2," musclebound, bi-racial man whose heart was bigger than the sun, but whose massive body could easily intimidate. Officer Middleton would visit the schools as "Officer Friendly" and teach the kids about safety, accountability, and respect. He would teach the kids things like don't take candy from strangers, never get into a vehicle when you and your parents don't know the driver, never be afraid to call the police if you believe someone is doing something bad to another person, never play with a weapon if one is found in the open, be extra careful when it comes to fireworks and always have an adult around when using them (if they're even legal where you are), always wear your helmet when riding a motorized bike or four-wheeler, cow-tipping is not allowed, and if you see someone in danger, don't try to help them if it will put your life in danger as well.

Officer Middleton was also an accomplished guitarist who formed a local band with other officers in his area. They would play out at fundraisers, special events, and holiday concerts. This group not only provided great music and entertainment, but also showed the audience and townsfolk that police are people, too, and that they shouldn't only be seen as authoritative officials. Granted, neither Officer Middleton nor any of his police brothers would ever fall short of performing their duties to the full extent of their abilities, and could take on the toughest assailants, but they also had a personal side that they wanted the residents to know.

One of Officer Middleton's biggest fans was young Jasper Callahan, as Middleton's band played modern rock music and songs that Jasper saw on MTV. It wasn't unusual to find a star struck Jasper pressed up against the stage where Middleton's band was playing. Middleton was even asked for his autograph by his adoring young fan, which Jasper pinned up on his bedroom wall under his poster of Prince, also one of Middleton's favorite musicians.

Officer Middleton noticed Billy's body as he was approaching the scene. When he stepped out of the car, he glanced over at Ralph, then redirected his attention to the body lying under the streetlight. He walked over and knelt down next to the body. He put his right index and middle finger against the carotid artery on Billy's neck, held it motionlessly there for about 15 seconds, then took his hand and moved it to where Billy's mouth was. Middleton was almost certain he wouldn't find a pulse or signs of life when someone's neck was snapped and twisted halfway around his body. However, that is something that all emergency responders do to ensure that someone is unconscious or dead. Middleton noticed that the arms were dislocated at the shoulders and both legs were broken at the kneecaps, making his legs shaped like a chicken's legs. Middleton was also a bit thrown off by the attire the 16-year-old boy was scrunched into: a girl's bathing suit three times smaller than the boy was. Middleton was very composed for someone who had just seen a mangled body lifelessly laying on the pavement, but it wasn't because he was masochistic, it was because when it came to his job, Middleton maintained professionalism whether or not anyone was around to see him performing his duties.

Middleton stood up, reached for the police radio on his left hip, brought it up to his face and pressed the talk button. He said, "Middleton to Jackson."

Jackson replied, "Go for Jackson."

"Wake the sheriff up and send him over to the corner of Summit Street and Chartiers Road. We have a dead body here. Looks like Billy Donnelly, but he's supposed to be up at Fayette State awaiting sentencing. Would you call up there and have them check to see if Donnelly is still in his cell?"

"I was just up there this afternoon for a prisoner transport from Fayette State to the hospital. I'm sure they would've noticed if Donnelly wasn't there. He's in a solitary cell for his protection against the other inmates. But I'll call up, nonetheless. Do you want me to send McCormick over to your location as well?"

"Yes. That's probably a good idea," Middleton agreed.

Jackson set down his police radio on the desk, picked up the telephone receiver, and dialed Langdon's home number. Langdon picked up the phone. He didn't say hello, but rather said, "I'm on my way, Jackson. Let Middleton know I'll be there in less than 10 minutes. And send Rogers over to sit out front of the Robertson house just as a cautionary measure. If word of this incident hits them before we have everything under control, we're likely to have a highly emotional crowd parading around and contaminating the scene."

"Sounds good, boss," Jackson agreed. "I'll get right on that."

Middleton looked up and over at Ralph's porch and saw him sitting in his wooden rocking chair. Ralph got up and raised his right hand to greet Officer Middleton. As he was raising his right hand in acknowledgement, they were both startled by a distant car radio blaring and slowly growing louder as the vehicle worked its way up over the hills and wound through the country roads, heading directly to the intersection of Summit Street and Chartiers Road. They could see the headlights cast a glow on the trees and pastures as it drew nearer. They could hear the driver singing out loud, and could only deduce that he had the window open, as both Ralph and Middleton could hear the song as clear as a bell. "Ohhhh I know that it's getting late, but I don't wanna go home. I'm in no hurry, baby, time can wait, 'cause I don't wanna go home. Listen to the man sing his song, but I don't wanna go home. I don't mind, baby, stay all night long, 'cause I don't wanna go home." The car sped along with no regard to the posted speed limit signs, its engine revving with the rumble of an 8-cylinder sports car.

Middleton raced back to his cruiser, opened the door, dove in, put the car in gear (as it was still idling while he was examining the body), and floored the accelerator pedal in the direction of the oncoming car. He got no more than 200 yards down the road when Ralph saw the police car's brake lights flood the area with a red glow. Ralph noticed Middleton exiting the car, go around to the

trunk, lift up the trunk's top, and produce a couple sticks in his hands. With the

help of the brake lights, Ralph saw Middleton handling the sticks, and then

there was a burst of sparks and red-pinkish glimmer from the top of the sticks.

Middleton had retrieved a couple road flares and activated them.

Middleton took the flares and walked about 20 feet in front of the cruiser, laid

both flares down on the road, then went back to his car and turned on the

police lights. When the oncoming car rounded the corner and saw the flares

and flashing lights of the cruiser, it began to slow down and stopped only a few

yards from the flares. The radio was still blaring the music, "I know it's time to

go, but I don't wanna go—"

The music went dead as the driver-side door opened on the fire-engine-red

1983 Chevrolet Camaro and the driver slowly exited the vehicle. He noticed

Middleton standing in front of the police cruiser. "Is that you, Middleton?

What's going on here?"

"Julius? Julius Robertson? Is that you?" Middleton replied, raising his right hand

over his forehead, trying to shield the bright headlights on the vehicle that was

now parked in front of him. "What are you doing home?"

Julius responded, "It's Thanksgiving break, Jay. I'm just getting into town from Penn. Was I playing the music a little too loud this time of the night? I think road flares and the reds and blues flashing are a little bit of overkill for disturbing the peace. Did Old Man Jones hit another cow crossing the road?" Julius chuckled as he spoke.

Julius Robertson and Jay Middleton had been teammates on the high school swim team, with Jay being four years Julius's senior. Middleton went right into the police academy when he graduated from high school. Julius continued on with his swimming success and was awarded a scholarship to Penn State in his senior year. Julius always respected Jay for his sportsmanlike conduct, support, and leadership as team captain. He and Jay would have their own practices off-season, and Jay would work with Julius on improving his strokes and stamina to get better times during swim meets. To say they were good friends would be an understatement.

"Still being the same old smartass, huh, Julius? And why the hell are you still listening to Southside Johnny and The Asbury Jukes? Did your dad lend you his 8-track?"

"Ha, ha, ha. Very funny. But I still remember your time for the 50-meter butterfly improved by two seconds while you were swimming with this song piping through the speakers around the pool. So, mock all you want." Julius had

made his way up to where Middleton was standing and extended out his right

hand to greet him. Middleton responded in kind and grabbed hold of Julius's

hand, then pulled Julius in for a bro-hug. "It's great to see you."

"Hey, man," Middleton responded, "I am still so sorry for what happened with

your family. I wondered why you went back to Penn so soon after the funeral. I

would've thought you'd take the rest of the semester off. I'm sure the school

board would've approved a hardship leave with no risk to your grades."

"Dude, I would've gone crazy sitting in that house with memories constantly

around me. It was actually my *parents'* idea for me to go back to school. They

said Amber would want me to continue with my life and I should honor her by

returning to school. So **that's** why I left. I know there were some people who

thought poorly of me, but my parents were right. I'm dedicating all my efforts

and achievements in memory of Amber."

"Don't sweat it, bro. You did the right thing. And screw those few who thought

poorly of you. They have nothing better to do in life but cast judgment on

others."

"So what **is** going on here, Jay?"

"There was a water main break at the intersection of Chartiers Road and Summit Street. I know you have to get through here to get to your house on Mahle Road. I hate to do this to you, man, especially after you've just finished driving from Penn, but I need you to go back up to 7 Creeks Road, down Bacon Run Road, and loop back around to the other end of Chartiers Road. Nobody is being allowed to pass through here due to the amount of water pooling up in the road. I know that is a very roundabout way to get home, but there's nothing more I can do."

"No worries, Jay. To paraphrase Southside Johnny and The Asbury Jukes, I just wanna go home." Julius laughed, then shook Middleton's hand again and headed back to his car. He got in and made a K-turn, heading back to 7 Creeks Road. As Middleton watched the Camaro's red running lights turn up onto 7 Creeks Road, he grabbed the police radio off of his left hip, brought it up to his mouth, pressed the talk button, and said, "Middleton to Sheriff."

"Go for Sheriff," Langdon replied.

"We have a problem. I just intersected Julius Robertson on his way home from Penn. I laid out some flares and blocked the way to the corner of Summit and Chartiers before the bend in the road. I told him there was a water main break at that intersection and I was rerouting all traffic up 7 Creeks and Bacon Run to get to the other end of Chartiers." Middleton paused then began talking on the police radio again: "Middleton to Rogers."

"Go for Rogers," said a voice through the police radio.

"Did you catch that?"

"Roger." Rogers said this with a hearty laugh.

"All right, boys," Langdon chimed in, "let's be professional, and everyone maintain their posts. Middleton, stay where you are for now in the event Julius circles back or any other vehicles head that way. Rogers, let us know when Julius pulls into his driveway. If he comes over to you to ask why you're parked in front of their house, tell him it's a new neighborhood watch program we've put together in Amber's honor."

"Roger that, boss," Rogers replied, again with a snicker.

Langdon showed up at the scene, noticed the body, then turned his head to the left and saw Ralph standing on his front porch looking over at the squad car. Like he had done with Middleton, Ralph greeted the sheriff by raising his hand in the air and waving it back and forth. Langdon opened his car door, got out, and headed over to Ralph without examining Billy's body first. When Langdon got three-quarters of the way up Ralph's walkway, he greeted Ralph: "Good evening, Chief. Looks like we have another mangled body here. Do you want to tell me what you know about it? Did you see who did it? Any information can help."

Ralph hesitated, then said with a nervous tone, "I didn't see the actual murder take place, but if I told you what I **did** see, you wouldn't believe me. In fact, you might think I was on some medication with a side effect of hallucinations."

"In a scenario like this one," Langdon replied, "any information is valuable."

Ralph returned to the rocking chair, sat down, took a deep breath, and proceeded to disclose everything he had witnessed, down to the very last detail. While he was sharing the information with Langdon, the sheriff's face began to contort into an expression of enigmatic disbelief. His brow stretched down as he pressed his eyebrows together. His eyes completely fixated on Ralph with his pupils slightly dilated. His lips seemed to form a straight line across his face, rather than the normal curvature. When Ralph had finished his recounts of what he witnessed, there was a seemingly lengthy silence, then Langdon spoke up.

"Well, Chief, that is certainly some tale. I can't, for the life of me, figure out why you would concoct such an unbelievable story, but I must say that I'm having difficulty believing that a shadowy spectacle gruesomely tortured young William, then hoisted him up on the lamppost and secured his body against the streetlight pole, using nothing more than phantom arms. I'm even trying to wrap my head around why a 10-year-old boy would be standing there in the November air at ten o'clock in the evening. Do you have any tangent evidence to corroborate your story?"

Ralph paused for a moment, trying to think of something he could provide to the sheriff as concrete proof, but was coming up empty. "Well, there is the broken living room window there," Ralph responded while pointing to his right at the blown-in window, "and there is young Jasper. Perhaps you can go over to the Callahans' and talk to them yourself, and see if what Jasper is wearing fits my description. Also, check out his slippers to see if there is any evidence that he would have walked down here. Maybe some kind of dirt? I'm grasping for any other possible proof that I could provide."

Langdon reached down to his left hip and grabbed the police radio. He brought it up in front of his mouth, pressed the talk button, and spoke: "Sheriff to McCormick."

A few seconds later, a voice came through the speaker of the radio: "Go for McCormick."

Langdon continued, "What is your location?"

"I'm en route to your location."

"All right. What's your ETA?"

"Be there in three."

"Roger, that." Langdon returned the police radio back to the belt strap over his left hip. "Chief, I will go up to the Callahans' when McCormick gets here. You stay here with McCormick. I'll let you know what I find out."

"Thank you, sir. I appreciate your patience through this whole ordeal."

A few minutes later, McCormick's cruiser pulled up behind Langdon's car. The driver-side door opened and McCormick stepped out. He began making his way towards Ralph and Langdon. Langdon turned and began walking down Ralph's walkway, and met McCormick near the end of the walkway. "I'm heading up to the Callahans' to check something out. I want you to wait here with Mr. Dubain until you hear from me. Understand?"

"Certainly do, boss," McCormick replied.

Langdon continued walking to his car, got in, and turned right up Summit Street. When he arrived at the Callahans' he got out of the car, headed up the walkway, and began feeling that eerie sensation one gets when they believe they're being watched. Langdon stopped halfway up the walkway, looked to his left, looked to his right, then looked up at the windows on the second floor of the house. He scanned the windows and froze when he got to Jasper's fully opened bedroom window. There, standing in the window wearing a shape-shifting robot cartoon pajama top, was young Jasper. Jasper had a haunting, unsettling expression on his face, complete with an ominous smirk and dark eyes that seemed to look right through Langdon's body and deep into his soul. He was wearing a gold brooch that had a pink petunia in its center. The glow from a nightlight radiating from an outlet under Jasper's bedroom window was the only illumination provided.

Langdon raised his hand in the air and waved it back and forth, smiling up at Jasper. Jasper's expression never shifted, nor did he make any movement to return Langdon's greeting. Already, Ralph's description held true.

Langdon continued up the walkway, reached the front door, and knocked gently so as not to create a thunderous echo that would stretch to the neighboring homes. A few seconds later, Steve Callahan opened the front door and was stunned to see Langdon standing there.

"Good evening, Mr. Callahan. I apologize for the late hour, but I was talking to Mr. Dubain and I need to go see your son, now." Langdon had a calm but authoritative tone. Steve opened the door all the way up and gestured Langdon to enter.

"Can you tell me what this is all about, Sheriff? It is very late and I don't want to wake my son if it is at all possible."

"I'll try to be as quiet as I can be. Is your wife home?"

"No, sir, she is at work up at the hospital. I must say, Sheriff, this whole thing is making me extremely uneasy."

"I understand, Mr. Callahan, but this is very important and cannot wait any longer."

"All right, Sheriff, follow me."

Steve turned to the stairway that was behind him, across a small foyer where the front door was, and began walking up the stairs, with Langdon following. He turned to the left down the hallway, stopped at the first door on his left, then carefully turned the bedroom doorknob. Steve proceeded to stealthily push the door open and looked inside the darkened room, with only the small nightlight providing a soft glow. He gestured for Langdon to enter. Langdon quietly began walking over to Jasper's bed and saw Jasper sleeping on his side, his left hand wedged underneath his pillow covered with a He-Man pillowcase, and a thick comforter pulled up all the way over his neck. There were soft breaths coming from Jasper's slightly agape lips, and Jasper looked peacefully at rest. Langdon turned around to Steve, who was still standing just inside Jasper's bedroom door, and whispered, "I have to see what Jasper is wearing. Do you mind? I will be as delicate as humanly possible so as not to awaken the boy." With an awkward and uncomfortable expression, Steve nodded.

Langdon reached his left hand down to the top of the comforter, being as gentle as possible, and grasped the top of the comforter. He slowly began to drawn it back and down towards the end of Jasper's bed. As Jasper's body was slowly being revealed, Langdon's eyes began to widen with disbelief. Jasper was wearing a faded yellow pajama top that had a picture of Machiavellian yellow canary cartoon on the front. As he continued to pull the comforter

down, he saw that Jasper was wearing the same color faded yellow pajama

bottoms. Langdon finally had completely uncovered Jasper's sleeping body to

see that the pajama bottoms were the type that had white slippers sewn into

the end of the pajama legs fabric. With the comforter still in his grasp, Langdon

began to slowly pull it back up over the boy all the way to Jasper's neck,

replacing it just as he'd found it.

Steve stood by the door with his right eyebrow raised and the left eyebrow

slightly lowered down. Langdon, completely dumbfounded, began looking

around the bedroom floor for dirty clothes to see if he could spot the shape-

shifting robot cartoon pajamas. He thought it was completely impossible for

the boy to change between the time Langdon saw him standing in the window

to the time when he and Steve got to his room. The bedroom window was

closed and the room had no evidence of the cold that would have seeped into

the bedroom from the opened window. Langdon turned back to Steve and

whispered, "May I check the hamper?"

Steve nodded again with an uncomfortable, curious expression on his face.

Langdon turned to his right and walked over to a white hamper, carefully lifted

the lid, and looked inside. If Jasper **had** been able to change that fast, then

Langdon was sure he would find the shape-shifting robot cartoon pajamas either on the floor or on the very top of the pile of clothes inside the hamper.

Yet, Langdon didn't see any of this. Langdon slowly placed the hamper's lid

back down, being very gentle so as not to create any sound that would wake

Jasper. Turning back to Steve, he asked, "May I check the dresser drawers?"

Steve nodded, and Langdon made his way over to where the dresser was,

which was behind where Steve stood. Langdon reached for the wooden knobs

on the top dresser drawer, delicately pulling the dresser drawer open, then

looked inside. There inside, he saw neatly folded socks, underwear, and t-

shirts. He pushed the drawer back into place, maintaining the same soundless

manner he'd used to open the drawer, then released his hold on the wooden

knobs. He grabbed hold of the next set of wooden knobs on the drawer just

below the top drawer and quietly pulled it open. Within that drawer were

neatly folded shorts and pajamas. He reached into the drawer and began sifting

through the various outfits until he reached the bottom of the pajama pile.

There, undisturbed, were symmetrically folded shape-shifting robot cartoon

pajamas, so meticulously folded in a manner that no 10-year-old boy would do;

this was more the work of a skilled housekeeper. Langdon paused, looked up at

Steve with a perplexed expression, then proceeded to remove the shape-

shifting robot cartoon pajama top from within. He raised the pajama top in

front of his face and inhaled deeply from his nose. There was no mistaking the

aroma of fabric softener that emanated from the outfit. Langdon held the pajamas up in front of Steve and asked, "Does Jasper have a second set of these pajamas?"

Steve replied, "No. That is the only pair of Transformer pajamas that Jasper owns."

He returned the carefully folded pajama top to its original spot, slowly closed the dresser drawer, and turned to Steve. "Where does Jasper keep his slippers?"

With widened eyes and a baffled expression, Steve responded, "Jasper hasn't worn slippers for years. His pajamas have slipper bottoms attached to the pant legs."

Langdon remembered what he saw Jasper wearing when he'd uncovered the boy. Ralph had definitely identified the shape-shifting robot cartoon pajamas, and Langdon had just seen the boy standing in the window with them on, but Langdon was confused as to how the shape-shifting robot cartoon pajamas were clean, meticulously folded, and placed at the bottom of the pile of pajamas in the dresser drawer when he had just witnessed Jasper wearing them not but a minute or two earlier before entering his bedroom with Steve.

There was also no conceivable way that Jasper could be as peacefully and soundly asleep in that same length of time. Langdon was very disconcerted by this whole thing.

Langdon gestured to Steve that he was ready to exit the bedroom and began making his way back to the bedroom entryway. When Langdon had completely exited the bedroom, Steve followed and carefully closed the door behind them. They both headed back to the stairway and began to descend when Steve spoke up.

"All right, Sheriff, can you tell me what this is all about?"

Langdon proceeded to share everything that Ralph had told him and include what he had seen while walking up the Callahans' walkway.

"That doesn't make any sense, Sheriff," Steve responded after Langdon finished filling him in on Ralph's account. "There is no way my boy was down by the streetlight, in his pajamas, wearing slippers, and being a witness to a horrific murder. Mr. Dubain must have mistaken Jasper for a different boy. Still, I can't believe that any boys around here are capable of such an act."

"I understand, Mr. Callahan, but we cannot dismiss any possible leads. You understand, right?"

"I guess I do, Sheriff. I'm just still baffled by Mr. Dubain's testimony."

"I've disturbed you enough this evening, Mr. Callahan. I'll be on my way. I'll let you know if I need any further information while conducting my investigations. Thank you for your time and again, I do apologize for the late-hour visit. Good night, sir."

"Good night, Sheriff."

Langdon turned to the front door, and Steve opened it for Langdon to exit. Langdon began walking back down the walkway towards his squad car. When he reached the bottom, he turned his head back around to the right, looked up at Jasper's bedroom window, and saw the boy standing there in his shape-shifting robot cartoon pajamas, wearing a gold brooch with a pink petunia in the middle, and glaring at Langdon with a cold gaze. In a state of paralyzed perplexity, Langdon raised his right hand, waved it back and forth, and waited for Jasper to respond; which he never did. Langdon turned to his car, got inside, grabbed the police radio from the dash of his car, pressed the talk button and said, "Boys, this is going to be a long one."

CHAPTER 14: JASPER'S CHALLENGE

"Jasper to Sheriff."

The tender, youthful, chilling voice called through the police radio, startling

Langdon while he stood next to Billy Donnelly's lifeless body with Vernon

Harbinger (the region's medical coroner) kneeling on Billy's right. Langdon was

flooded with shivering chills causing the hairs on the back of his neck to stand

up. Vernon whipped his head up to Langdon, then they both looked at the

police radio on Langdon's hip. A minute passed by that seemed like an eon to

both Vernon and Langdon.

"Jasper to Sheriff." The voice introduced a hint of impatience to the childlike

tone.

Langdon produced the police radio from his left hip, brought it up to his mouth,

and responded, "Go for Sheriff?" Langdon's response was in the form of a

question, as he could not believe that young Jasper could get a hold of a police

radio, or any mechanism, for that matter, and call through the same

confidential frequency that only the police radios were on. Langdon was both

inquisitive and horrified.

"I would like to play a game," the voice continued.

"What kind of game? Who is this? Is this Jasper Callahan?"

"Uh-uh-uh. Secrets, secrets."

Langdon sharply recalled Ralph's description of the voice that was coming through the receiver of his phone while he stared out the window, staring at the shadowy apparition and a motionless Jasper leaning against the lamppost. Langdon began to wonder if all of Ralph's story was not actually a ploy to conceal the murderer's true identity, but a factual account of what he'd witnessed. This was both frightening and bloodcurdling. Langdon pressed the talk button and spoke in a petrified, yet authoritative, tone: "Son, this is a restricted frequency. You are not allowed to be on it. You're interrupting an investigation and distracting my officers in the process."

"Are you sure?" the voice responded with a malevolent snicker.

"Yes, I am sure." Langdon paused for a moment, pressed the talk button, and said, "Sheriff to Jackson."

"Go for Jackson."

"Are you getting all this?"

"All what, boss?"

"Jasper Callahan is calling me on the police radio. Surely you all heard it."

"That's a negative, boss."

"This is not the time for games, Jackson."

"I'm not playing any games. I didn't hear any 10-year-old boy's voice coming through my police radio. Are you all right, boss?"

"No. No, I'm not. I need you to pay close attention to any calls that come through your police radio and let me know when you hear Jasper's voice."

"Roger that, boss."

The voice began to chortle with great amusement through Langdon's police radio. "I guess it's just you and me."

"Sheriff to Jackson."

"Go for Jackson."

"You must've heard that. He just spoke through the radio again."

"Boss, you're starting to give me the willies. I'm not hearing any child's voice on my radio. I just hear you talking to someone but nothing more."

"Sheriff to Middleton."

"Go for Middleton."

"Do you hear Jasper's conversation through your radio?"

"I'm sorry, boss, all I hear is silence out here, except for the person you're talking to. Are you sure you're not accidentally pressing the talk button while speaking to someone next to you?"

"I'm not pressing the talk button. Young Jasper is talking to me through the radio. Keep listening. Maybe our equipment is malfunctioning."

"**Everyone's** equipment, boss?"

"Just keep listening."

"Roger that, boss."

The haunting voice came back through Langdon's radio, maintaining an uneasy, snickering laugh. "Shall we continue, or do you wish to test my patience any further?"

Without hesitation, Langdon replied, "Let's continue. What is this challenge of yours?"

"Noah and Billy were very naughty boys. But they are not the only ones. There are two other revolting souls out there who have done inexcusable acts to children. That is a big no-no."

"I agree, Jasper, harming any child is not only criminal, but detestable. Who are these two boys you're talking about?"

"Who said anything about them both being boys?"

"So they're both girls?"

"Uh-uh-uh. Secrets, secrets."

Langdon was beginning to grow more and more anxious. "Are these individuals adults?"

"No."

"Do any of them live in Clarksville?"

"Yes."

"Where can I find these culprits?"

"*Quid pro quo*, Sheriff."

In the same manner that Ralph had pondered, Langdon was flabbergasted by the notion that a Lilliputian, 10-year-old boy knew what quid pro quo meant and, furthermore, how the process would be performed. "All right, young Callahan, who goes first?"

"That would be me, as this is my challenge."

"Makes sense to me. Ask your question."

"Joe was 13 years old yesterday. He will be 16 years old next year. How is that possible?"

Langdon dropped the police radio to his side. He had heard this riddle when he was younger, but didn't remember the answer. He looked down at Vernon, who was listening intently to the conversation between Langdon and Jasper. Vernon rolled his eyes up and to the left, attempting to recall the answer to the riddle himself.

"How is this possible, Sheriff?" Jasper repeated. "Come on. You're a smart man. You can figure this out. Tick . . . tock . . . tick . . . tock."

Finally, Vernon's eyes returned to Langdon's face and he whispered, "'He' is Joe's friend's name."

Langdon returned the police radio back up to his mouth, pressed the talk button, and answered, "'He' is Joe's friend's name."

"Very good, Sheriff. Next time, try to get the answer on your own, without Dr. Necrophilia's help."

Langdon glanced down at Vernon, who wore a stunned expression. Langdon wasn't pressing the talk button on the radio, so how could Jasper have known he had given him the answer to the riddle? Langdon began to wonder if he really needed to talk through the microphone on the radio if Jasper could hear what he was saying with the talk button depressed. Langdon then pressed the talk button and said, "Quid pro quo, Jasper. Are the two culprits' ages 13 and 16?" Langdon was utilizing the contents of the riddle as possible descriptions of the offenders Jasper was speaking about.

"Yes. Very good, Sheriff. I see you are using your brain now. Except one of the culprits is 15, not 16. Quid pro quo, Sheriff. I sit on a bridge. Some people will look through me while others wonder what I hide. What am I?"

Yet another riddle Langdon remembered from his youth. However, he had recently heard it from one of his grandchildren. He responded right away, without drawn-out hesitation or any help from Vernon. "Sunglasses. Quid pro quo, Jasper. Do the culprits often hang out at Angler's Point or Skin Beach under the train trestle?"

"Definitely. You're doing very well, Sheriff. I expected a lot worse from you and your early stages of Alzheimer's."

This last statement bewildered Langdon the most. No one, not even his own wife, knew of the diagnosis he'd received only a month earlier. This information was strictly between his primary care physician and himself. Langdon was keeping this a secret so as not to cause alarm or be forced into early retirement due to the risk that memory loss can pose in his line of work. Again he looked down at Vernon, who was staring up at him. But when Vernon's and his eyes met, Vernon slowly lowered his head and began examining Billy's body again. Langdon was worried that perhaps Jasper made it so that the other officers could hear that last bit of information, but muted the rest of the discussion.

"Quid pro quo, Sheriff. Four fingers and a thumb, yet flesh and bone I have none. What am I?"

"The Great Lakes," Langdon answered nervously, for he truly had never heard that riddle before.

"Wrong. Uh-oh. Now you must receive a penalty." Langdon dropped the radio to his left side again and began to frantically look around for any dangerous items that could inflict harm on him or Vernon. But he couldn't see any

projectiles heading his way. He couldn't hear any kind of approaching noises

that would indicate a charge against him. He couldn't feel any kind of physical

assault to his body. But he felt a cold sensation rush through his body from the

back to the front, and there was no breeze.

Without warning or provocation, Billy's body lifted off the ground, knocking

Vernon on his backside. He was able to brace himself with his arms slightly

behind him with the instinctive aid of involuntary reflexes. The lifeless body

launched towards Langdon, who had no time to react. The intense force,

coupled with the full weight of Billy's body, caught Langdon's torso and

abdomen, causing him to be knocked back about five feet from where he

stood. Billy's body then fell on top of Langdon as he laid flat out against the

pavement.

Billy's head hit the ground, creating a cracking sound as his skull splintered

under the skin. Billy's dislocated right arm flopped heavily against Langdon's

mouth, splitting his bottom lip open and causing blood to immediately begin

flowing down the left side of his cheek and chin. Gravity elongated the stream

of blood down Langdon's left side of his neck and it began dripping, creating a

small, crimson pool of blood on the asphalt.

When Langdon came to his senses, he pushed Billy's flaccid body off to his right, causing Billy to flop against the pavement and produce a squishing sound. Langdon brought his left hand to his lips, made one swipe over his lower lip, then raised his hand to see his fingertips coated with a red liquid. The stinging sensation that ripped through Langdon's lower lip as he brushed his fingers across was enough to make him flinch with discomfort.

Langdon put both hands on the road, pushed himself upright, then repeated the same action of brushing his left hand's fingers across his lower lip. Again, he held out his hand in front of his face, and saw that the color and coating of blood on his fingertips had increased in area.

A few feet from Langdon's right leg he heard a devilish cackle coming from the speaker of the police radio he had dropped when Billy's body collided with him. "Try again."

Langdon found the strength to get on his feet. He walked over to the police radio, bent down, swiped the radio from where it was laying, and said, "Listen, Jasper, that was completely uncalled for and my patience has run out. I don't want to play your games anymore. Now just tell me who these two transgressors are."

The voice morphed into a deep, demonic, low gurgle and shouted back through the radio's speaker with violent outrage, "You will play my game or you will suffer further, more dire consequences! Do not test me. You've already witnessed what I am capable of. Now try again."

This new voice caused Langdon to emotionally cower like a dog who has just been reprimanded by his owner. Langdon brushed his left hand across his lower lip again, raised his hand in front of his face, pushed the talk button on the radio, and said, "You're a glove." It was as if the knock down from Billy's body broke open an unconscious, scholarly part of his brain and he instantly knew the answer; though he had never heard that riddle before. In a defeated tone, he said, "Quid pro quo, Jasper. Is there a glove at the scene of the assault?"

"Ahhh, I see I shook some of your calculating intellect loose. I thought that might help. Yes, there is a glove at the scene of the assault." The voice had returned to the seemingly innocent, unripened, child's tone. "Quid pro quo, Sheriff. There is a black dog sitting on a black road. There is no moon, or any other means of illumination. A car speeds down the road with no headlights or running lights on, but steers around the dog. How did he know the dog was there?"

This one Langdon knew right away; it was a brainteaser he had presented to his

oldest grandson. "It was daytime. Quid pro quo, Jasper. Would I only be able to

find this glove during the day with a police dog?"

"I'm impressed, old man. You're getting good at this. Only a few more to go."

"Jasper, it's getting later and later. Can we please hurry this along? If the victim

is still alive, we need to find him or her before it's too late."

"Uh-uh-uh. Patience, my geriatric pet."

Langdon sighed impatiently and then said, "Quid pro quo, Jasper. Is the victim a

boy or a girl?"

"Actually, it's both. Quid pro quo, Sheriff. A young boy leaves home. He goes 59

feet and turns a corner. He goes another 59 feet and turns another corner.

Soon, he rounds one more corner. As he's returning home, he sees two masked

men. Who are they?"

"An umpire and a catcher. He's a baseball batter. Quid pro quo, Jasper. Does one of the assailants play baseball, or does one of the victims?"

"Okay. I wasn't going to help you out here, but you've been a sport with all this; no pun intended . . . hehehehe. One of the assailants is a baseball player. Quid pro quo, Sheriff. A woman sees a murder in the field near her home yet doesn't report it. Why?"

"She saw a group of cows, and groups of cows are known as 'murders.' Quid pro quo, Jasper. Does the other assailant live on a cow farm?"

"No, but he helps work at one. Quid pro quo, Sheriff. Look at the numbers on my face, you won't find 13 any place. What am I?"

"A clock. Quid pro quo, Jasper. What happens at one o'clock tomorrow?"

"Outstanding, Admiral Asshole. I am truly in awe of your problem-solving abilities. You have until 1:00 p.m. tomorrow to apprehend the two criminals. If by then you haven't done so, I will leave a little gift for you. Now hurry along, my fossil friend, hurry along. Tick . . . tock . . . tick . . . tock." There was a static snap from within the police radio's speaker, then the patronizing child's voice was no more.

"Jackson to Sheriff."

"Go for Sheriff."

"What was all that about? Were you answering riddles? What happened there? Are you all right?"

"This is the weirdest night of my life, Jackson."

"So what happens at one o'clock tomorrow afternoon, boss?"

"We're going to be back here scraping a couple more dead bodies off the pavement if we don't find two teenagers who assaulted a couple kids, and if we don't find the victims. I need you to call everyone in, including the fire department. Everyone meet me here immediately. Middleton, Rogers, McCormick; that goes for you as well. We're not even going to consider any of the Robertsons suspects. I'll explain when you get here."

"I heard you say Joe's friend, 13- and 15-year-old boys or girls, sunglasses, Angler's Point, glove, daytime, police dog, baseball, cow farm, and one o'clock. Are these supposed to be clues?"

"That's right, Jackson. Now stop talking to me and get on the horn to the rest of the department, as well as the fire department."

"Roger that, boss."

CHAPTER 15: A DIAMOND IN THE ROUGH

Samantha Richards, a splendidly gorgeous blonde-haired, blue-eyed woman, held a black ballpoint pen in her right hand. She was tapping it on the dark oak kitchen table, gnawing the pen's cap between her back right teeth, and staring down onto a slip of paper (that her daughter Wendy had handed her five minutes prior) through her oversized, gold-rimmed glasses. The lenses were a bit thick for a normal 35-year-old mother, but Samantha's eyesight had been damaged in a fireworks accident ten years before.

Clarksville Parks and Recreation Athletics Programs Permission Slip

*I, Samantha Richards, give my (enter age of child) 15-year-old son/daughter/dependent **(circle one)**, Wendy Richards, permission to participate in the following athletic teams and competitions:*

☑ Baseball ❑ Basketball ❑ Canoeing ❑ Cheerleading

❑ Cross Country ❑ Field Hockey ❑ Football ❑ Golf

❑ Gymnastics ❑ Lacrosse ❑ Soccer ❑ Softball

❑ Swimming ❑ Tennis

I, understand, as the parent/guardian, I am responsible for ensuring that my child/dependent attends all required practices and competitions. I furthermore accept responsibility over my child's/dependent's actions and sportsmanlike

behavior, and will do my part in ensuring that his/her participation is done so

with respect for their opponent(s), teammate(s), and coach(es). Additionally, I

acknowledge that any athletic equipment that is not provided by the parks and

recreation department will be supplied by myself. If my child/dependent

behaves in an unruly and disrespectful manner to his/her coach(es),

teammate(s), or opponent(s), I agree to accept my child's/dependent's

dismissal from the program.

The Clarksville Parks and Recreation Department's mission is to see that all

youth have opportunities to engage in athletic events, as well as nurture their

interpersonal skills. The Clarksville Parks and Recreation Department does **NOT**

condone, nor tolerate, any degree of unsportsmanlike conduct, bullying,

derogatory remarks, racial discrimination, prejudice, or obscene

language/gestures.

The Clarksville Parks and Recreation Department would also like to make it

vividly clear that we expect sportsmanlike conduct from our parents/guardians

when attending practices and/or competitions. In the event that a

parent/guardian becomes unruly and violates the same code of conduct we

mandate for our young athletes, you acknowledge that this will result in the

immediate dismissal of your child/dependent from the program.

The Clarksville Parks and Recreation Department appreciates your cooperation with our program's policies and procedures and we look forward to welcoming your child/dependent into our program(s), to nourish athletic capabilities and engender a sense of acceptance and inclusion.

Signature: _____

Date: _____

Samantha was staring at the paper as Wendy had checked off the "Baseball" program instead of the "Softball" program. Additionally, Wendy had filled in her mom's name, Wendy's name, and age. Wendy seemed under the impression that she'd just give her mom the form to sign, Samantha would sign it without reading it, and that would be that. However, as her mom was a proofreader for a law firm, this was very poor judgment on Wendy's part. Behaving like a typical teenager, Wendy believed that her mom, tired after a long day of work, would be too exhausted to read any kind of document, no matter the length.

The fact that Wendy wanted to participate in the town's parks and recreation athletics program didn't bother Samantha; it was that Wendy selected baseball instead of softball. Samantha was aware of her daughter's enthusiasm for the game and was an avid Pirates fan. Wendy had posters of her schoolgirl crush, Don Robinson, hanging on the wall next to her bed and scattered around the room. Wendy never missed a single game that was aired on the television. Her prized possession was an autographed baseball from Don Robinson that he'd signed for her when Samantha took her to the Pirates vs. Padres game on her 10th birthday. Wendy kept this in a glass case on top of her vanity. Additionally, Samantha knew of her daughter's freakishly powerful pitching abilities that would rival a minor league baseball player's. Where softball pitchers throw underhand, Wendy had a massive overhand pitch that would register 91 miles per hour on radar guns; even the boys on the Clarksville Parks and Recreation baseball team (the Hornets) could ever only get up to a 50-mile-per-hour fastball. Wendy had tried out for the team the last couple years, but they told her she could only play softball because the two programs, softball and baseball, were "gender specific." Although both Samantha and Wendy objected to this policy, the decision to not accept her onto the boy's baseball team never wavered. After both decisions, Wendy would go to her room, grab her Don Robinson autographed baseball, lie down on her bed, hold the glass case against her chest, and cry uncontrollably.

Samantha wasn't ready to watch her daughter go through that again, so she went to scratch out the "Baseball" checked box, and then check in the "Softball" box, when she heard a voice coming from the kitchen doorway.

"Mom, I know what you're thinking, but I want to try again this year."

"Honey, I respect your perseverance, but I can't see you suffer like you did the last two years. It is incontestably unfair that the town has that policy between softball and baseball players' genders, but we can't really do anything about it."

"But this year it's going to be different. The Parks and Recreation Department has a new director, and she is a *female*. So maybe she'll sympathize with me. Bekah Callahan said that she and the new director's niece are pen pals and that the new director agrees with co-ed baseball teams. Please let me try out again this year . . . **please**!!!!"

Samantha stopped tapping the pen on the solid oak table, stared at her daughter's pleading expression, and gave in to Wendy's blue, sweet china doll eyes. "All right, honey, but if for some reason they don't accept you on the baseball team this year, will you consider trying out for softball?"

"I can't throw underhand, Mom, you know that. I'm liable to hit the batter in the head with the ball if I do pitch underhand. I'd rather not play at all than

play softball."

Samantha let a few seconds pass by, looked back down at the paper, put the

black pen to it, and signed and dated the bottom. "All right, Wendy, one more

time. That's it. If for any reason you're not accepted on the team, I don't want

to have this discussion again next year."

Wendy folded her hands together, held them to her heart, and began jumping

up and down while wearing the brightest smile a girl could have. Her should-

length, blonde hair bounced up and down in cadence with Wendy's hopping.

She looked like a fan at a rock concert fawning over the lead singer. It was

actually a cute, innocent sight, and one that was always welcomed by

Samantha. When she was done, Samantha set the pen on the table, grabbed

the left side of the permission slip, picked it up, and held it out to her daughter.

Wendy snatched the permission slip as sharply and quickly as a crocodile would

grab a gazelle. She then turned and went squealing with blissful glee up to her

room. Samantha looked down at the pen and said, "Please, George, please let

her get in this year. We can't handle another year with a long spell of hysterical

sadness."

It was George Richards who had taught his daughter the art of pitching. He'd spent hours with her in the yard, showing her the different techniques with overhand pitches. George worked at the Hibbet Sports store, in Waynesburg, Pennsylvania, as a manager. As such, he received employee program discounts and incentives. With Wendy being his only child, he wanted to be able to pass down all his sports skills to whatever offspring he had.

Even though the Clarksville Parks and Recreation Department had policies against co-ed baseball teams, George didn't subscribe to that same philosophy. If his child wanted to learn a specific sport, he was going to teach them. In the fall of 1983, George was diagnosed with terminal brain cancer and passed away only a few months later. Samantha would often wonder if Wendy's emotional breakdowns after trying out for the town's baseball league might be the result of some misguided feeling of disappointing her father. If so, those thoughts would be squashed immediately if George was around to tell her she could never disappoint him. Samantha was a firm believer that when your soul leaves your body, it doesn't leave the Earth, but rather stays and protects its loved ones who are left behind. Because of this, she would often have vocal conversations with her late husband and feel that her thoughts and decisions were influenced by his soul's presence.

***

Early the next morning, having received her mom's blessing and permission to try out for the Hornets baseball team again, Wendy awoke, produced a Pittsburgh Pirates uniform from the closet (that Samantha had given her that past Christmas), pulled out a dented and faded blue shoe box, opened it up, and pulled out the pair of cleats she'd got from her dad's store. Wendy then stood up, reached her arm up high, stood on her toes, and pulled down a plastic bag from the top shelf of her closet. In the bag was the baseball glove George had given her the spring before he passed away. It was a special edition Wilson pitcher's glove, and Wendy took extra-special care when handling the glove. Wendy set all these items on her bed, walked over to the vanity, picked up a brush and a hair elastic, and proceeded to brush her hair into a ponytail. She went over to her bed, sat on the head of the bed (near her pillows), grabbed the framed photo of her dad that was on her nightstand, and while looking intently at it, said, "This year, Dad . . . this year, it will be different. You wait and see."

She returned the framed photo back to its original position on the nightstand and proceeded to get changed out of her nightgown and into the baseball uniform. Tryouts began at eight that morning, but Wendy's anxious excitement found her awake and fully prepared by 5:30 a.m. She sat back down on her bed, took a deep breath, looked over at the picture of her dad, and said, "I'm doing this for you, Dad."

The turnout for the Hornets' tryouts was unexpected. Thirty-five kids sat in the bleachers waiting for their turn to give a demonstration of their skills to the coaches and managers of the Parks and Rec department. Wendy's nervousness was very apparent in her leg as she lifted the heel of her right foot up and down at a rascally grey rabbit's speed. It was causing the weathered aluminum bleachers to creak and wobble. Wendy paid no mind to these sensations, but rather focused her full attention on each candidate showing their batting and fielding skills.

When Marcus O'Neil set down the bat next to home plate, took off his batting helmet and began walking back to the dugout, one of the coaches looked at his clipboard, then looked up to the bleachers at a little over a couple dozen impatient expressions and said, "Wendy Richards . . . you're up!"

Wendy stood up, hiked down from the top seat of the bleachers, walked down the dusty dirt path next to the fence that separated the spectators section from the ball field, and slowly made her way to the opening in the chain-link fence where Coach Morrison stood. Wendy had been wearing the pitcher's glove the whole time she was waiting and now it was damp inside, caused by her sweaty palm.

Coach Morrison was looking back down at his clipboard when Wendy reached the spot where he was standing. "Ahhh, so I see this is your third tryout with the Hornets. It says you're a pitcher, here. Is that true?"

"Yes, sir, that's true. My dad taught me how to pitch when I was a little girl."

"Well, Miss Richards, we pitch overhand in this league. Is that something you can do with enough control to get it out over the plate into a batter's strike zone?"

"Sure is, sir. I can't pitch underhand; my dad never taught me that."

"Is your dad here with you today?"

"No, sir, he passed away a couple years ago."

"Oh, I'm sorry to hear that, Miss Richards. I'm new to this county so I'm not familiar with the people or their history yet."

Wendy developed a slight twinkle in her eye as she felt that Coach Morrison's unfamiliarity with her prior year tryouts would be to her advantage. After all, who has ever seen a 15-year-old girl throw a 91-mile-per-hour fastball before?

Coach Morrison took a baseball out of his side ball pouch, held it up in front of Wendy's face with his thumb, index, and middle fingers, and said, "Well, Miss Richards, let's see what you can do." He then released the ball into Wendy's glove. Wendy produced that same exuberant smile she had when Samantha had signed the permission slip. Wendy then jogged over to the pitcher's mound, stood on the plate, and swung her right arm around in a circle, loosening up her right shoulder. Coach Morrison set his clipboard down on the bat box and walked over to home plate. He picked up the bat young Marcus had laid down moments before, stood to the left of home plate, swung the bat a few times, then said, "Let me have it."

Wendy stood bent over on the mount with her left arm down by her hip, her right hand grasping the ball, and staring directly at Coach Morrison. A few seconds went by before she brought both hands together at her stomach, bent her arms up, stood up straight, stretched her right arm back, and pitched the ball towards home plate. As she released the ball, she made a slight girly grunting sound while her left foot flew up, nearly touching her back. The ball rocketed towards home plate where Coach Morrison was standing. When it got to the sweet spot of the batter's box, Coach Morrison swung his hardest at the ball, missing it by only a split-second. The pitch was at waist level and he was slightly bent forward in a typical batter's stance. The ball was also directly in

266

the middle of the plate, which, combined with the height of the ball, is the

perfect strike. Coach Morrison snapped his head to the right and down at the

catcher, who still had the ball in his glove; the glove was at his chin level and his

eyes were wide open in disbelief. Then the coach looked sharply at Wendy,

gestured for the catcher to throw the ball back at her, and said, "Let's see that

again."

Wendy was given the ball back. She repeated the same stance as she initially

did, wound up, and launched the baseball directly over the plate at Coach

Morrison's waist level. He swung with all his might and missed the ball zooming

by. Strike two. He and the catcher were sharing the same expression of

amazement. Coach Morrison gestured to the catcher to throw the ball back to

Wendy before saying, "All right. One more time, Miss Richards."

When Wendy wound up again and released the ball, she put so much strength

into it that she tripped up a bit, but didn't fall. She got the ball over the same

area of the plate. Coach Morrison swung with every ounce of strength he had,

but again, missed the ball. He turned his head to the assistant coach holding a

radar gun and asked, "How fast?"

The assistant coach looked at the LCD display on the radar device and

responded, "Ninety-five, Coach."

He turned his attention back to Wendy, gestured for her to come to home plate and said, "Bring it in, miss. I need to talk to you."

Wendy made her way from the pitcher's mound to home plate. There, Coach Morrison asked, "Why didn't I see your name on last year's roster? It says you tried out, but I don't see your name anywhere as part of the team?"

"They wouldn't accept a girl on the team," Wendy replied.

"I'm sorry. I think I misheard you. Did you say they wouldn't let a girl on the team?"

"That's right. Two years in a row. I've pitched the same way since my dad taught me. Both years. And they said I should try out for the softball team, as that was where girls play. But I can't throw underhand and they don't allow overhand pitching in that league."

Mrs. Susan Tate was standing next to the dugout behind the 8-foot chain-link fence. Coach turned his head over his right shoulder and asked, "Were you aware of this, Mrs. Tate?"

"Not at all," she replied, "this is my first year here. But that is preposterous. I just saw that young lady throw three straight, 90-plus-mile-per-hour pitches in the perfect strike zone. If she was like this last year and they still didn't accept her on the team because she is a female, then that policy changes today. Are you prepared to accept her on the Hornets?"

"Without hesitation, Mrs. Tate."

Wendy's smile widened even brighter than when her mom agreed to sign the permission slip. She brought her hands to heart center, folded them together, and looked nervously up at Coach Morrison. Coach Morrison returned his attention to Wendy and asked, "So what about it, Miss Richards? Do you want to be the Hornets' new pitcher?" Wendy let out a shriek of enthusiastic celebration and nodded her head with great affirmation. "Congratulations, Miss Richards, you're a Hornet."

"Don't you want to see me bat?" Wendy asked.

"If your batting is anything like your pitching, young lady," Coach replied, "I have no reservations in believing that I will also have a strong batter."

"Oh, thank you, Coach, thank you!!!! I promise I will not let you down. I am dedicating my performance to my dad. I hope that's all right."

"I wouldn't have it any other way, Miss Richards." Coach Morrison extended his right hand to shake Wendy's right hand, while she still had the pitcher's glove on her left hand. "You're welcome to stay if you'd like, but I imagine your mother will want to hear this news as soon as possible. We will be calling the team together in the next couple days. Congratulations, and welcome aboard."

Wendy turned to her left and darted from home plate to the visitor's dugout. She raced through the opening in the fence, went around the bleachers to where she'd parked her bicycle, and took off her pitcher's glove and slid it over the right handlebar through the opening on the back of the glove. She kicked up the kickstand with such force that the back tire lifted off the ground about an inch before it fell back to the earth. She then mounted the black bicycle seat and began pedaling as fast as she could.

Daniel Richards was Wendy's 13-year-old cousin and lived three doors down from the Richards'. Daniel's father, George Richards' brother, was a farmer who worked with Old Man Miller on his property, tending to the fields, the livestock, and the general upkeep of the grounds.

Old Man Miller was at risk of defaulting on his mortgage, so Daniel's dad dug into a portion of his investments and entered into a partnering agreement with Old Man Miller. He would cover the outstanding payments and agreed to work on the farm for an equal percentage of the profits. Joseph Richards (Daniel's dad) retired early from a marketing company in Pittsburgh and brought this knowledge to the new partnership with Old Man Miller. It wasn't long before some of the surrounding towns (and some of the Pittsburgh small businesses, as well) contracted with Old Man Miller and Richards to supply them with all the feed, dairy, meats, and chicken from their farm. This resulted in soaring revenues as well as popularity.

It wasn't too much later that Daniel's mother, Cathy, joined her husband and Old Man Miller by creating a massive garden where she grew vegetables. Miller and Joseph also planted a grove of various species of apples that, with Cathy's gardening efforts, allowed them to include fresh produce along with their original products. This only increased the revenue even more.

It wasn't long before Joseph, Cathy, and Miller were the town's richest residents. Although their work hours were lofty, their days long, and their bodies sore, they still managed to be involved in Daniel's life whenever he needed it. Parent/Teacher meetings, Cub Scouts, soccer, talent shows, and school music concerts. As Wendy was Joseph's only niece, he spoiled her with

exquisite gifts and generosity. When George died, Joseph became more of a

father than a favorite uncle. Joseph also helped his brother's widow in those

dark times when money management fell by the wayside. George had been

Joseph's kid brother and, as a result, he felt the responsibility that his sister-in-

law's, as well as his niece's, well-being should be continued through him. It

wasn't an act of charity, but rather one of endless commitment to the memory

of his kid brother.

During the summer and after school, Daniel would ride his bike to Old Man

Miller's farm and would help around wherever his mom or dad needed. His

favorite task was to feed the cows, as well as milk them. The farm didn't have

horses, but that didn't stop a vivacious, energetic, adventurous boy from

hopping atop one of the cattle and pretending he was a cowboy . . . literally. He

gave names to each of the cows and looked forward to these particular tasks

when he helped out. His father gave him a generous weekly allowance for his

labor, which Daniel would use to buy trading cards, comics, and clothes. Cathy

would constantly tell Daniel not to buy clothes because that was her and his

father's responsibility, but Daniel would do so anyway. It made him feel

independent, as well as gave him the spirit of being an adult.

Daniel had a pituitary gland dysfunction that slowed his physical maturing process. Although he was 13 years of age, he had the physique, height, weight, and features of a 9-year-old boy. He stood 4 feet 5 inches, weighed 61 pounds, and had the sweetest complexion. His two front teeth were a little bigger than an average 9-year-old boy's, but that was also attributed to the growth affliction he had. He had jet-black, shoulder-length hair and his eyes were a deep brown. His smile was so hypnotically radiant that he rivaled most child models. He had a single piercing in his left ear and enjoyed wearing gemstones that represented all his family's birthstones, including his uncle's, aunt's, and cousin's. His eyes were narrow, which made him look like he was constantly squinting or straining to read something in small print. The bridge of his nose was as perfectly curved as a Winter Olympics ski jump ramp that led to a set of small nostrils.

He was very insecure about his form, which would cause great anxiety when it came to sports, but that didn't stop him from joining the Parks and Rec soccer team. He was a speedy little devil and would whip around that soccer field like a fly would zip from one picnic plate to the next. Daniel was very flexible and nimble, and that gave him an advantage on the soccer field. He was given the position of forward on the team and played his part flawlessly. His sportsmanlike conduct was one of sheer reverence which, combined with his athletic abilities, found him receiving MVP awards his first two years on the team. His dad was the farmer, but his uncle was the sportsman, and while

George coached Wendy in her baseball interests, he coached Daniel with his

soccer skills.

Daniel attended Wendy's tryouts and was just as giddy as Wendy was when she

was accepted onto the Hornets as their new pitcher. He and Wendy were

extremely close, and had been since they were kids. Daniel knew that this was

a dream of hers since he could remember. Much like his aunt, Daniel was very

concerned over what would happen if Wendy tried out for the third time and

was not offered a position on the baseball team.

When he overheard the discussion between Coach Morrison and Wendy, he,

too, was overwhelmed with relief and celebration. He was waiting for Wendy

to come off the field so he could give her a congratulatory hug but she was so

excited, she just passed him by and ran straight to her bike with the goal of

getting home as quickly as she could to proclaim the wonderful news to her

mom. Daniel took no offense to this, but instead ran right behind Wendy,

grabbed his small bicycle's handles, kicked up the kickstand with as much

intensity as his older cousin, and kept up with Wendy as she spun those pedals

with feverish force and raced towards her house. Daniel didn't have to be at

Old Man Miller's farm for another few hours, so he wanted to be part of the

festivities of Wendy sharing the glorious news with her mom.

Sadly, Wendy and Daniel never made it home to share the magnificent revelation of Wendy's achievement.

CHAPTER 16: LABYRINTH OF LAMENTATIONS

Celine Holden was a former forensics director for the State of New Hampshire

and an individual with an immeasurable heart when it came to the comfort and

counsel of others. Her caring rivaled that of most clerical counselors. Her field

of choice was the result of a childhood experience when her older sister was

found murdered in an open pasture during the winter. There was very little

evidence that could be traced back to any usual suspect. Due to the cold leads

and exhausting efforts to apprehend her sister's killer the investigation was

terminated, leaving the murderer to be unknown and free from the inarguable

incarceration that he (or she) should serve.

The unknown and unresolved closure that Celine and her family needed was

never experienced due to the forensic capabilities at that time. Celine's goal in

life was to never allow survivors of victims that degree of uncertainty and lack

of resolution. She majored in criminal justice at Temple University, graduating

magna cum laude in her class, then went on to earn a Master's of Forensic

Science at Penn State University. She had her dissertation accepted for her PhD

at the University of Pennsylvania. Celine submitted her application for the FBI

Academy and was immediately approved based on her educational achievements and unwavering perseverance when it came to working hard towards goals she wanted to accomplish.

After graduating from the academy, Celine relocated to New Hampshire, where she worked for the state's local FBI branch as a senior forensic science officer, which included forensic technical analysis and crime scene investigations. Her methods were meticulous, her efforts fueled by the memory of her sister. Her resoluteness was nourished by the pain she endured over never knowing who her sister's killer was.

When her mother's Alzheimer's had progressively worsened and her neighbor could no longer provide full-time assistance, Celine retired early from the FBI, and she and her husband relocated to Marianna, Pennsylvania, in 1981 to care for her mother, as her children were adults and had families of their own.

Sheriff Langdon knew of Celine's experiences and abilities after working together on a crime scene back in 1982, not long after she had moved in with her mother and was called upon to assist in the apprehension of a drunk driver who had killed two teenagers who were walking home from school. It was for this reason that he reached out to Celine now.

"Hello," Celine answered as she picked up the phone receiver.

"Good evening, Dr. Holden," Langdon replied. "This is Sheriff Bud Langdon down here in Clarksville. I'm not sure if you remember me, but—"

"Yes, Sheriff," Celine said, cutting Langdon's introduction short. "I worked with you on the Benoit case. How can I help you tonight?"

"We are in kind of a pickle here, as we are investigating the disappearance of two teenagers. It is a very long story, and one that would be unimaginable to the rational mind of a professional like you, but we only have 14 hours to solve a case before we are delivered the dead bodies of two assailants."

"I'm sorry, Sheriff, but I don't understand what you're talking about. Do you have two dead bodies and no suspects?"

"I'm afraid it is more gruesome than that, Doctor. Is there any chance you could meet up with me and my officers in Clarksville this evening? I know it's late and this is very inconvenient of me to ask, but I would like to utilize your expertise. I will explain in more detail when you arrive."

"This is most unorthodox, Sheriff. As you know, my mother is very ill. She is my primary responsibility. I'm retired from that line of work. I was able to assist

you with the Benoit case, but I wasn't expecting that to be a usual calling. Can

you give me just a little more information?"

"All I can tell you is this: in the past 72 hours, there have been two mutilated

bodies discovered by the streetlight at the corners of Chartiers Road and

Summit Street. The murderer has told us that if we do not locate the suspects

that committed acts of violence on two innocent teenagers, he would invoke a

capital level of street justice and deliver the two criminals to that same

streetlight location by one o'clock tomorrow afternoon."

"Have you found the bodies of the two teenagers?"

"I'm afraid it's worse than that; we found the two teenagers alive, but

unresponsive and horribly violated. They are up at Brownsville now, but the

doctors have not been able to revive them. I do not want to find the two

culprits subject to vigilante retaliation, so I am pleading for your assistance at

this late hour. Would you be willing to drive over to Clarksville?"

"I would. Give me a half-hour and I'll be there."

"Thank you, Doctor. I sincerely appreciate this and genuinely apologize for the late hour."

"No problem, Sheriff. I'll see you in a half-hour."

Langdon returned the portable police phone receiver to its cradle on the dash of his cruiser. He had been sitting inside on the driver's seat with his feet on the pavement through the open car door. He grabbed his hat, put it on, then gracefully stepped out of the cruiser and headed over to where Officers Middleton and Jackson were standing at the beginning of the wooded area that separated Center Street and Angler's Point. He looked up at Middleton and said, "Doc's on her way. Are you two all right?"

Middleton, though exceptionally professional and leaving all emotions out of his responsibilities, stood with his head hung down, fists clenched, and the remnants of a tear stream branded on his right cheek. Jackson had his left hand on Middleton's right shoulder and then Langdon put his right hand on Middleton's left shoulder, patted it a few times and said, "All right, Jay, let's get all those emotions out before Doc gets here. I appreciate your pain and sympathize with you, but we need to put on our professional faces. Doc will be here within the half-hour."

Four officers were walking through different sections of that specific area, looking for any possible clue as to where the culprits or victims had been.

Jackson took the west side of the train trestle, McCormick the north side,

Langdon the south shore of the creek, and Middleton took the east section of

the woods. The scanning flashlights flooded the tree trunks, broke through the

jostling leaves in the wind, bounced off the water's surface, danced over acres

of ground vegetation, and pounded against bare sections of earth.

The Clarksville Police Department had a custom when they were doing these

kinds of searches, and they kept to that practice on that evening. They would

set a perimeter, take to their assigned segments, and would call out the

number of linear yardage they covered and say either "clear" or "yo." They

wouldn't say these notifications through a police scanner, but aloud, with a

stronger decibel level than in casual conversation. This gave each of them a

proximity level as to where each of them stood within that perimeter. They

were not concerned about alerting a suspect to their presence, as in that

section of the state, a woodchuck could flinch in the woods on the dead leaves

and you could hear it from a hundred yards away. At night, the atmosphere

was much like you would feel in an empty cathedral church: a deafening silence

of vast space. If an assailant was cowering behind a large rock or behind a tree,

he or she would only have to move their foot and the searchers would be able

to identify the proximity where they were hiding. Middleton was the first one

to reach Angler's Point.

"Twenty yards! Clear!" yelled Jackson.

"Fifteen yards! Clear!" shouted McCormick.

"Twenty-five yards! Clear!" Langdon exclaimed.

"Thirty yards. Cle—" Middleton stopped mid-word. It was almost as if someone snuck up behind him, put a gun to his head, and with a hushed tone said, "Freeze."

"Middleton, repeat that please!" Langdon demanded.

There was not a sound. No movement. No rustling. And seemingly no breathing. All the other officers stopped dead in their tracks and waited for a response from Officer Middleton.

"Middleton, please repeat. Are you clear or did you find something?" Langdon repeated.

Again, nothing. Langdon waited about 10 more seconds and then his tone became a little more authoritative: "Jay, clear or yo???"

With a labored and shaking voice, Middleton called out, "Yo!"

There was a ballet of lights illuminating the woods from three directions. The random, hasty dances of light cast a strobe-like effect on the wooded area while the song of dead leaves being kicked over played as heavy footsteps blew threw them like a tornado through the plains. Their pace was frantic, and the sounds of branches being pushed away filled the area as McCormick, Jackson, and Langdon sprinted through the woods to meet up to where Middleton was standing. It seemed like each of the officers, save Middleton, emerged from the tree line at the same time and from different directions.

They reached Middleton, and Langdon flashed his light on Middleton's face, which showed an expression as if he'd seen a ghost. "What is it, Jay? What is going on? What did you find?"

Middleton didn't speak a word, but instead slowly lowered his flashlight in the direction of a small section of Angler's Point beach, stopping at the sight that had caused all his senses to paralyze immediately. When the light reached a baseball glove, with blood on the thumb and forefinger slots, Middleton looked up at Langdon and said, "This."

Langdon met Middleton's spotlight with his own flashlight. It wasn't just a

baseball glove, though. Less than a foot from the glove was a circle trenched

into the sand about one-quarter inch deep and a little over a foot in diameter.

There was a straight line drawn in the sand that ran from one top right curve of

the circle to the lower left curve. The engraved shape had a deep red tinge to it

and appeared to have once been filled with some kind of red fluid, illustrated

by the wet soil within the etched circle and lines. In the middle of the line was a

giant, dead hornet about three inches in length. The hornet was depressed into

the sand with the red line lying over its body's center. Langdon shone his light

back up at Middleton's face, whose expression never changed, then returned

the light's focus to the glove and symbol. He moved the light a little further

beyond the symbol and found a pair of baseball cleats sticking upright in the

sand, toes first. Less than a yard from that was a pair of red, denim sneakers

about the size a 9- or 10-year-old would wear. The heels of the sneakers were

laced with dried blood, but they were lined up perfectly next to each other;

almost if somebody just snatched the wearer's body from the sneakers with a

quick jerk, too fast to topple the sneakers on their sides.

Langdon continued to survey the area with his light, looking for footsteps in the

sand. He didn't find any, but rather discovered a brush-stroke effect as though

one had taken a push broom to the beach to sweep away any evidence or

direction that would lead investigators to the incriminating scene.

"All right, gentlemen," Langdon began, "I want us to walk from this point into

the east woods with 10 yards between each of us. We need to find any other

evidence that would lead to the owners of that glove, the cleats, and the

sneakers; and I mean *now.*"

The officers spread out in a line with McCormick at the top, Jackson 10 yards to

McCormick's right, Middleton 10 yards from Jackson's right, and Langdon

taking the creek's bank. They moved with great caution and keen eyes, shining

their flashlights back and forth across the earth in a back-and-forth manner.

Not but 10 yards in, Middleton exclaimed, "Yo. Jesus Christ. **YO!!!!**"

McCormick, Jackson, and Langdon bolted to Middleton's location. When they

all reached where Middleton was standing, they all became nearer as white as

ghosts. The ground was covered with broken shards of glass, sharp nails and

spikes pressed into the ground with the points exposed upward, and three

paper-like oblong objects that looked like wasps' nests. There was splattered

blood on different sections of this pile of lethal objects. It was set up in the

same manner a foam mat would be under a gymnasts' parallel or uneven bars.

When they all looked up, they saw the two bodies: one was a girl with a blonde

ponytail, the other was a smaller boy with a ball cap on. They were suspended

15 feet in the air by roped restraints tied around each one of their limbs, and

fastened to a group of surrounding trees with the boy's and girl's ankles bound

together with rope. Both of the children's heads were dangling backwards with

the lack of any support for their necks as they hung there unconscious and

motionless. A baseball bat had been lashed with rope onto the right wrist of

the girl and a baseball adhered to the boy's right palm by some kind of

adhesive. The back of the boy's shirt had been slit in half by some very sharp

instrument and had pierced his skin in a few sections of his spine. The girl's

baseball jersey was cut halfway off her body and draped over her outstretched

legs. The girl's left cheek had been sliced and was still slowly dripping blood.

There were bruised impact points on both the girl's and boy's face and arms.

It was Jackson who first noticed two sets of rope lines leading away from the

children up in trees towards Center Street. Jackson and McCormick followed

the ropes that ended at the train trestle. They had been tied around one of the

train tracks. There were no footprints or any other pieces of evidence to see

with the naked eye. The two of them double-timed it back to where Middleton

and Langdon were standing, still under the two children flagged up in the air.

When Jackson and McCormick reached Langdon and Middleton, they shone

their flashlights up to where the ropes were secured around the tree trunks.

Their initial assessment wasn't quite accurate. They believed the teenagers

were bound to the trees by closed knots, but they weren't. The force of the

stretched rope line anchored to the train track was the thing that was keeping them suspended in the air. It appeared that the assailants had set up a device that would instantly loosen the kids' bodies when the train ran over the ropes, severing them under the massive weight of the train's wheels. The bodies would them plummet downward, landing on the shards of glass, the bed of spikes, and the wasps' nests below, releasing a swarm of angered wasps to attack the objects that disrupted and shattered their homes. The children were left alive to experience this brutal torture, but their weakness had caused them to lose consciousness. The contraption of egregious martyrdom was crafted by psychologically imbalanced rage. This was premeditation *in sua pessima*.

"SHERIFF!!!! SHERIFF!!!! You **have** to see this. You need to come now!"

Langdon looked at Jackson while he was gesturing his hand to join him and was beginning to walk back to the tracks. "What is it, Jackson? Why are you so panicky and rushed?"

"Do you hear that, Sheriff? That's the westbound freight steaming down those tracks." Jackson shone his light up at the two rope lines that stretched off into the blackness of the night towards Center Street and the train tracks. "You see those ropes, Sheriff? The ends of those two lines are tied around one of the train tracks. If we don't get to those ropes and release them with equal balanced weight, those two kids are going to drop onto all that glass, those nails, and those hornets' nests with all their weight increased by the gravitational pull. They will be sliced up, pierced, and stung like no adult could ever endure, let alone two children. We need to go **NOW**!!!"

Langdon looked at Jackson with an expression of severe dread, then yelled out, "Hustle, boys. Double-time! That freight is going to hit those tracks in less than two minutes judging from where that whistle just came from!"

The four men wasted no time in darting off towards the train tracks that lined Center Street. It was if the starting gun went off and they only had a few seconds to get to the finish line after jumping hurdles. As they ran through evergreen limbs, not having time to move them out of their way, they were developing branch-shaped welts on their necks, faces, and arms. Although their flashlights were illuminating the ground and the wooded metropolis, they paid no mind to where they were stepping and were operating on pure adrenaline.

One of the branches caught Langdon in the head so hard that it snapped his sheriff's hat clean off the top of his head. However, Langdon didn't stop, nor did he even seem to notice it was gone. There was only one objective at this point in time: untie the ropes fastened to the tracks and slowly make their way back to where the kids' bodies were suspended, maintaining a firm grasp on the rope and with enough tension to keep from the kids slowly falling on top of the pool of macabre intentions.

Middleton was the first one to reach the train track as he broke through the tree line with much frenzy and determination. Next to follow was McCormick, then Jackson, then Langdon. Middleton dropped his flashlight on the ground and ran over to where one of the ropes was fastened. He grabbed the knife from his first aid fanny pack, knelt down on his right knee (against a bed of trap rock), grabbed the rope line with his left hand, and began sawing at the rope tightly knotted around the rail. He knew that if he cut the line too quickly, he wouldn't have time to react and the kids would fall. McCormick grabbed hold of the line that Middleton was cutting with both hands, his back to Middleton, and provided extra support by leaning back a little, much like you would see in a tug-of-war team.

As Middleton was cutting through the line like a lumberjack, Langdon knelt down next to the second rope line, produced *his* pocket knife from the first aid fanny pack he was wearing, grabbed the rope line with his left hand, and began sawing on the part of the line that was on the top of the railroad track. Jackson followed suit with how McCormick was positioned and braced for the snap of the rope as it got to the point where it was too thin to hold the weight of the children on the other end.

There was an echoing *snap*, and Middleton's line broke free from the track. McCormick had braced himself solidly enough so the rope didn't even move a single inch. McCormick was holding the rope that was suspending Wendy up in place, while Jackson was holding the rope that held Daniel suspended.

"Mick, you got it?" Middleton frantically asked.

"Got it, Jay," McCormick responded.

Middleton dropped his knife and was on both feet in a flash. He pounced towards the 3-foot rope tail that was produced between McCormick's grasp and what had been lashed around the railroad track.

"All right, Jackson, I'm almost through," Langdon informed.
"Just . . . a . . . little . . . mo—"

Another loud *snap*, and the end of the line frayed loose from the railroad track. Jackson had the rope in his grasp, but when the rope severed from the track, Langdon fell backwards and caught Jackson in the back of both knees, causing Jackson to buckle and the line to go free from his clutches. There was the sound of rope being pulled through tree branches and with looks of stunned horror, the four men waited to hear the boy crash against the ground and on top of the bed of pain. But they didn't hear any *thump*. They didn't hear any

screams of a boy being brought back to consciousness with shards of broken

glass being impaled into his flesh, swords of nails puncturing his skin, muscles,

tissues, and bone, and a furious, stinging army of hornets defending their

crushed homes. There was nothing. Nothing. Each of them were holding their

breath and preparing for the inevitable, which didn't seem to happen.

McCormick and Middleton slowly began taking small steps towards where the

kids were hung, moving their grip up on the rope about a few inches with every

step they took. Langdon got to his feet with Jackson's assistance, and the two

of them shot over to the kids' location and were there before either one of

them knew it.

Jackson, arriving at the site first, let out a very audible sigh, bent down, planted

both of his palms on his knees, and lowered his head. Langdon appeared only

seconds behind him. Despite the gruesome sight, a smile appeared on his face.

He walked up behind Jackson, rested his left hand on his back, and patted it a

few times. They saw the boy dangling in the air, suspended by the rope bound

around his and Wendy's ankles, arms hanging down over his head and body

swaying back and forth, without one single millimeter of flesh damaged, and

the hornets' nests hadn't budged a single bit. Between Wendy's strong, athletic

legs and the force of tension that Middleton and McCormick were providing, as well as Daniel's abnormally small frame, there was not enough gravitational pull to release Daniel upon the bed of torture.

Langdon walked over to where Daniel was pendulously rocking back and forth, grabbed hold of the boy's head with one hand and his nape with the other, pushing them up ever so delicately and providing a means of support for that part of the body.

"Sheriff. Sheriff? How's everything there?" McCormick bellowed as he and Middleton continued their cautious approach, keeping tension on the rope.

"He's fine, Jack. He's unharmed. Just take it slow, concern yourselves only with keeping that girl where she is."

McCormick broke into the light generated from the two flashlights that were on the ground and pointing in his direction. He was clutching the rope with the strength of a wrestler. His steps were narrow, as if he were trying to stealthily sneak up on someone. Not but a step behind him, Middleton appeared into the lit area. The two of those officers provided enough strength to maintain the tension, allowing Wendy's body to never shift even an inch downward. When they were both directly under Wendy, they began to carefully release the tension, inch by inch. Jackson was now next to Langdon, his hands under the small of Daniel's back, with his left forearm and the right forearm straight out

under Daniel's knees so when he was lowered far enough down, there would

be something there to support his legs and feet from touching the ground.

As Langdon and Jackson moved around the area, they heard glass breaking

apart under their feet and creating a muffled snapping sound, like someone

walking over a carpet of Rice Krispies. McCormick and Middleton had released

the tension far enough to where Daniel's body was completely under the

support of both Langdon's and Jackson's strategically positioned supports.

"You got it, Mick?" Middleton asked.

"Go," McCormick replied.

Middleton released his part of the rope, now that Daniel's body wasn't adding

weight to Wendy's body, and headed over next to Jackson on his right.

"Jackson, you got your aid blade?" Middleton asked.

"Yes. Right there, just under the zipper of my first aid pack."

Middleton reached down to Jackson' first aid fanny pack on his right hip. He

pulled the zipper open, produced the knife from the pack, opened it up, and moved towards Daniel's ankles. He began cutting the rope as carefully as a surgeon making his first incision in a patient's chest. After a minute of delicate strokes of the blade across the rope, he finally broke through and removed the line from around his right ankle. He then bent down and moved under Daniel's body like he was going through a small cave, stood up on the other side, grabbed hold of the rope around Daniel's left ankle, and began cutting. It took the same amount of graceful sawing to get through that rope before Daniel was released from his bound connection with Wendy's ankles. Langdon and Jackson carried the boy far enough away from the sharp debris and gently rested him onto the earth.

Jackson got back up and headed over to Middleton's side. Middleton grabbed Wendy's ankles while Jackson maneuvered his arms to be in the position to support Wendy's back, neck, and head. McCormick continued releasing the rope inch by inch. When Jackson and Middleton had the full weight of Wendy's body on their arms, they began walking her over out from above the dangerous debris while McCormick maintained a watchful grip on the rope, but allowing it to be pulled from between his hands as the girl's arms pulled the line the more she was moved away from the area.

Jackson and Middleton gingerly lowered Wendy to the earth, slowly pulled their arms out from under her, then Middleton went and got Jackson's knife he'd dropped when he'd finished cutting Daniel's roped restraints. He returned to Wendy, grabbed both of her wrists, and slowly moved the knife under the rope with the sharp edge of the blade facing up, carefully beginning to cut the rope. When he had split the line in half, the dissected rope fell to the ground and Middleton lowered her arms to the earth.

He then stood up and walked over to where Daniel was laying, with Langdon and Jackson still kneeling next to him. In the same manner as he had done with Wendy, Middleton knelt down on his right knee, grabbed both Daniel's wrists with his left hand, and began cutting the rope with the sharp edge of the blade facing upwards. When both kids were completely free from their ropes, Langdon and Middleton stood up, while Jackson and McCormick maintained physical contact with Wendy and Daniel, respectively.

Langdon turned to Middleton and said, "I think I'm going to have to call Dr. Celine Holden and get her help. I don't think we can find those two sick criminals in the time span we've been given. We need her extensive experience and expertise to solve this horribly despairing puzzle before that menacing phantasm takes the law into its own hands."

Langdon began turning away when he felt a strong hand grab a hold of his right arm, right at the elbow. Then Middleton said, "You know, boss, I never thought I'd ever say this in my entire life, and certainly never in my professional career, but maybe, just maybe, those two culprits deserve a dose of street justice . . . from **anyone**. I wouldn't mind just calling the paramedics, getting these kids to the hospital, and then heading back to the station and let karma have its way with those two hellish demons."

Langdon looked up at Middleton's face; a tear had made its way down Middleton's right cheek, and with a dismayed expression, responded, "Jay, I would be prepared to do the same after seeing what I have tonight. Unfortunately, street justice was not part of our oath to uphold the law. We have to proceed with proper protocol. But if I was planning on retiring tomorrow, I would do exactly what you suggested, except I would stop for a case of beer to acknowledge the heroism and selflessness of my men."

Middleton released his grip on Langdon's arm. Langdon turned in the direction of Center Road and began walking. He paused when he heard the deafening sound of the train whistle signaling its passing, then continued until he reached his car. He opened the door, turned with his back facing the inside of the car, and sat down on the seat. He reached for the portable police phone on the dash, removed it, pressed seven digits, and waited two rings before a person answered on the other end.

"Hello," Celine answered as she picked up the phone receiver.

"Good evening, Dr. Holden," Langdon replied. "This is Sheriff Bud Langdon down here in Clarksville. I'm not sure if you remember me, but . . ."

CHAPTER 17: IT TAKES ALL KINDS

Terrence Blake was an educated, highly skilled 35-year-old man from Litchfield,

New Hampshire. He was the ideal neighbor, the token church-goer, and one of

the most successful pioneers in information technology since the Neolithic

invention of the hammer. What began as a curiosity with kitchen gadgets and

appliances had progressively flourished into a fascination with blooming

technology. By the age of 24, and after years of schooling though various

educational institutes, Terrence had positioned himself as one of the leading

technological innovators in the northeastern United States. His field of

expertise was computer systems and infrastructure.

Devoted to the evolution of technology, Terrence had secured patents on a

number of different technologies that would be adopted by corporate giants

and government programs alike, and change the face of systemic architecture

for years to follow. He prided himself on attention to detail, flawlessness, and

profound meticulousness. Terrence was also the iconic father; attending all his

son's athletic competitions, attending all of his daughter's ballet and theater

performances, hosting birthday parties and inviting half the zip code, selfless

hours of charity work, and greatly involved in both his children's scholastic

successes.

Terrence was a textbook specimen of health, standing 6 feet 1 inch, weighing 195 pounds, and muscularly chiseled like the statue of David. His black hair was always kept neat, his face never showing a single sign of stubble. His clothes were never wrinkled, his hygiene was impeccable, his thin-framed, gold-rimmed glasses always polished, his fingernails professionally manicured, and his skin was smooth as silk. Terrence was known to all he met as the good-natured soul of angelic measure who didn't have even the slightest trace of malice.

Yet Terrence harbored a soul black with avarice and tyranny, masked by an external shell of charm and charismatic hypnotism. His expectation for perfection and professional ethics shone through his submissive subordinates whose financial lives and well-being were held in the balance of his hands. He had such influential power that even the slightest hiccup of one of his underlings could give him ammunition to dismiss those whom he objected to. He had informants scattered about several departments to keep a stealthy watch over others who were not in his immediate sight.

Terrence's authoritative tentacles spread across his inferiors' chain of command like a vine of poison ivy growing over a garden trellis, suffocating blossoming flower petals. His lackeys' absence of a $70,000 piece of paper (also known as a college degree) was used as cannon fodder when it best served his needs and opinions. He would often use it as a means to dismiss an applicant or inhibit an employee's chance for promotion. He was a "best of the best" advocate, discounting the incontestable fact that all humans are flawed, even if his dictatorship mind convinced him otherwise.

Terrence was also one to spotlight another's random shortcomings and closet all the other successes and accomplishments his peons achieved. He was a man with power, and he trumped that card as often as he could, but maintained compliance to federal statutes when it came to labor laws. Terrence was tactfully skillful in discovering any loopholes he could use to get what he wanted and to get his way, and he used them without any regard to his servants' livelihood.

Yet to the unknowing eye, his debonair appearance, gleaming-white smile, and entrancing hazel eyes would lead one to believe that he was the kindest and most compassionate boss to ever exist.

Mark Devlin was a temporary consultant working a few tiers under Terrence Blake. His immediate bosses had gained a trust and reliability of Mark's skills, knowledge, commitment, and ingenuity when it came to processes and

efficiency. Mark didn't possess a multi-thousand-dollar piece of paper, but

rather brought years of practical experience with him, a valuable asset to any

typical employer. Entering the information technology field after years of

accrued experience and comprehension for the industry, as well as a few years

of being unemployed, Mark intertwined his previous business experience with

this newfound organization. Mark's first three and a half years were without

any detrimental incidents that would cast a gray shadow over his name. He was

the ideal temp: punctual, able to meet customer deliverables, professional,

personable, honest, and dedicated. While other peers in his organization who

held the same role and responsibilities were entering and leaving the same

area, he remained with steadfast hope for advancement.

It was not too soon after his 3.5-year stint that Mark began to have a small

handful of occurrences that neither had any impact on the organization's

integrity, nor did it lead to any degree of maleficence of the reputation of the

department. They were simply slip-ups that were unfortunately performed.

Through his busybody, intrusive informants, Terrence learned of these

shortcomings just as Mark was being primed for full-time employment, which

would provide a stable income (as stable as the job market was in the '80s) and

grant him access to many corporate benefits not commonly offered to

temporary consultants.

Terrence's penchant for perfection caused him to re-evaluate Mark's candidacy based solely on that handful of innocuous blunders, and not the years of emblematic dedication and expectations that his role demanded. Mark had entered into a realm he found detestable: micro-managing and extensive scrutiny. The poison of those few innocuous transgressions began to bleed into outside parties, giving them the necessary armaments to squelch Mark's reputation he'd so vigilantly built.

Believing that his advancement would be sabotaged by persons of influence, Mark headed over to the State of New Hampshire's Department of Labor to research whether he would have any legal protection from such an egregious act of deflation, looking out for his own wellbeing.

Mark returned to work the next day prepared to present his defense as sanctioned by state and federal law. Mark picked up the receiver of the phone, pressed 10 digits on the keypad on the face of the base, and waited three rings before someone answered.

"This is Blake," Terrance responded with an imperious tone.

"Yes, Mr. Blake. This is Mark Devlin. Do you have a few minutes to spare for a quick conversation?"

"Make it quick, I have a brunch date with some of the board of directors."

"Well, it is regarding my candidacy for full-time employment with this company."

"What about it?"

"It is my understanding that you would like to bar me from that opportunity. I would be appreciative if you would give me some reasons behind that."

"First off, I owe you nothing. You are paid to come in here and work, and that's it. You temporary consultants are meant to be expendable after your purpose has been served. You should be grateful I kept you on this long."

"I don't think that's very fair, Mr. Blake, to treat any kind of worker as lesser than another because of their origin."

"What do you mean by 'origin'? Are you insinuating that I am a bigot? That I am a racist? That I am discriminatory?"

"No. Not at all. I meant a person's measure of worth shouldn't be based on how they came to be under your management, but rather the degree that their work has progressively shown."

"So now you're telling me how I should do **my** job? If memory serves, *I* am the one with two college degrees and *I* am the one who has worked hard to get where I am. If you did the same, you could have as many opportunities for advancement as any other model employee. What makes you think you're better than anyone else who's been here longer?"

"I don't think I'm better or worse than anyone else, I just know that I have accomplished a great deal of successful achievements, and this is something that is typically rewarded with opportunities. Would you disagree?"

"No, I don't disagree with that theory. What I **DO** disagree with is a temp telling me how I should do my job."

"That is not my intent, and I apologize if it came across that way. I just want to know what happened between three months ago and now that would change your perceptions about my value to this organization."

"Like I told you before, I am the decision maker around here, and you're skating on thin ice."

Mark watched the images in his mind of the deterioration of all he'd worked for and achieved. No, Mark **didn't** have a fancy degree (or two, for that matter), but what he DID have was practical experience acquired from that very company; a skillset that most companies would do anything to protect and retain. "I'm not trying to be argumentative or combative, but according to the New Hampshire State Department of Labor, I am entitled to understand the actions of superiors to either better my performance or understand the situation I find myself in. That's all."

"Wait, you went down to the Department of Labor? When? Why? Are you trying to threaten us?"

"Absolutely not, Mr. Blake, I'm trying to protect myself."

"Protect yourself from **what**?" Terrence's tone introduced a hint of impatience and uneasiness.

"All workers have rights. It is important to know these rights. If I believe my rights are being infringed upon, I have the right to use those tools as a basis of getting more information. That's all I went down there to find out: what my rights are."

"What would possess you to do something like that? That is very unprofessional and very slanderous against this company."

"Slanderous, Mr. Blake? No. Not at all."

"You know, your rebellious insubordination is going to get you in trouble one day. I **don't** appreciate having my judgment questioned. Who the hell do you think you are, anyway?"

"I am a worker who is engaging his rights to know what the purpose is behind a decision."

"Did you tell the Department of Labor who you work for?"

"No. I had no intention of bringing the company's name into my research. The information was solely for my benefit, and not to cast an unsightly shadow over a company with such a great reputation and client base."

"Good. That would've been a very unwise thing to do. Well, Mark, I have to get going to the brunch. I'll be gone for the remainder of the day, but we can certainly catch up tomorrow if you'd like."

"That would be great. Thank you. Enjoy your lunch."

"Well, thanks for your permission."

There was a *click* on the other end of the line. Mark kept the speaker up to his left ear in a daze. He was awakened from that daze when the dial tone sounded through the speaker on the handset of the phone. Mark gently rested the phone's receiver back on its cradle in the phone's base, then turned to look down at the pamphlet he was given by one of the Department of Labor's representatives. He fanned through some of the pages until he landed on the section that talked about the rights he was speaking to Terrence about. With his left elbow braced on the desktop, his left hand supporting his head as it leaned slightly to the left, he held the pamphlet open with his right hand and began reading more about what the State had to say about the predicament he was in.

Sitting at his desk, working on the daily newspaper's crossword puzzle (that he breezes through with very little effort), Terrance's phone began to ring. "Hello," he answered.

"Good morning. Am I speaking with Terrance Blake at Innovative IT?"

"This is he. May I ask who is calling?"

"My name is Janet Mancini. I am calling from the New Hampshire Department of Labor."

Terrance dropped his gold-plated ballpoint pen on his executive desk. His hand gripped the phone's receiver with brute strength and his eyes narrowed with nervous frustration. Getting a call from the State's DoL was like getting a call from the IRS to let citizens know that they owe an exorbitant amount of back taxes that they were not aware of. Being an executive and receiving calls from the DoL always incites a grave feeling of intrusion and threatening. After all, the DoL rarely calls an employer to let them know they're doing an exceptional job with how they treat their employees. In fact, Terrance couldn't recall a time when he'd heard of ANY employers receiving such a call. "Yes, Ms. Mancini. How can I help you today?"

Janet Mancini was the mother of two children and the wife of a devoted husband who had his own company. She was very familiar with both ends of the managerial spectrum through her years of service at the DoL. She was also very knowledgeable about the different kinds of conduct that employees

exhibited. Janet's husband had to deal with many an employee who had acted

in an unprofessional manner, but he also gave credit where credit was earned

and always showed appreciation for the accomplishments and contributions his

employees achieved.

Janet's two daughters had personalities that were polar opposites of each

other. Her oldest daughter was a seemingly uncontrollable rebellious and

defiant girl who challenged Janet and her husband's tolerance and boundaries,

while their younger daughter was composed, obedient, and respectful. Despite

the stressful life that her oldest daughter caused her parents, Janet never let it

impact her work or how she approached these types of behaviors in a

workplace. Her experiences with her daughters helped mold a level of balance

with any reports of employer/employee grievances.

Janet answered, "We were contacted by a couple of your employees alerting us

to some unprofessional operations from unidentified managers in your

company."

"Excuse me, Ms. Mancini? This is the first I am hearing about any maleficence

in my business. Did the complaints come from managers or workers?"

"Unfortunately, Mr. Blake, I am not at liberty to disclose that information, as the DoL is under federal mandate to maintain anonymity for anyone who files any allegations."

"I believe I'm entitled to know who is spreading misconceived rumors about my company. It is my responsibility to handle any unprofessional behavior among my employees. Would you disagree?"

"I would completely agree, Mr. Blake. However, when the allegations are with the individual who **is** responsible for carrying out such resolution, such as a person of the highest seniority, employees generally find it intimidating and concerning to do so."

"Hold on, Ms. Mancini. Are you saying that an employee filed a complaint about **me**? My reports know they are free to talk to me about any wrongdoings occurring in my company. Did the employee provide examples of these wrongdoings?"

"Again, Mr. Blake, I am not at liberty to disclose that information. This is just a courtesy call to let you know that we will be sending over an investigator from the DoL to interview random employees to determine if the allegations are genuine."

"Ms. Mancini, we are a very busy company with proprietary products that are covered under the Information Protection Act. I cannot afford, nor risk, any of those items being compromised by outside persons."

"Mr. Blake, that is not the intention of the investigation, nor is it a practice we condone here. We are not out to engage in proprietary espionage. We are there to corroborate the allegations that have been brought to our attention. You shouldn't feel threatened or infringed upon; this is a standard response to any complaints filed with the DoL."

"Very well, Ms. Mancini. Are you able to provide a time when the DoL investigator will be here? I do a lot of business travel and outside meetings with prospective clients. In fact, I have one in Concord tomorrow afternoon."

"That is something I cannot do, Mr. Blake. I will let you know that you do not have to be physically present when these interviews are being conducted. In fact, any of these interviews need to be done without your immediate presence. In other words, if you were onsite, there would need to be an area where there are no surveillance devices present. We pride ourselves on complete privacy and protection of speech when it comes to responding to complaints."

"I can completely understand that. Shall I let my employees know that a representative of the DoL will be visiting the company, and the activities he or she will be performing?"

"No, Mr. Blake. In fact, we would appreciate you not saying anything to any of your employees, and comply with the DoL's regulations regarding matters such as these."

"Sounds fair. I have always advocated the right to privacy. I will comply with the DoL's rules and regulations. Thanks for your call today, Ms. Mancini. I will look forward to the findings of the interviewer."

"We will only provide the outcome of the interviews if there is sufficient evidence to corroborate the allegations. You have a good day, Mr. Blake."

"You do the same, Ms. Mancini. Good-bye."

Terrance slammed the receiver back onto its base after hearing the *click* on the other end of the line. His face filled with blood from rage and fury, and his temper began to build like a volcano about to erupt. He felt threatened and angry at his employees and began going through the list of employees in his mind. He had a new mission: find the worker who had gone over his head to a government organization that could create a black mark against his reputation. When his mind reached Mark's name, a lightbulb went off in his mind and the clouds began to clear. "That pompous sonofabitch. What right does **he** have to spill spiteful rumors to the Department of Labor? If I find out that that uneducated weasel went crying to the DoL, he is going to regret the day he ever set foot in this building."

Terrance began patrolling the grounds and different areas of the building, trying to overhear any conversations that may have involved Mark going to the Department of Labor. It didn't take long before he came upon the programmers' department where Vernon Boylston, Debra Morrison, and Lisa O'Donnell were sitting. Each of them were facing their respective computers and typing code for the latest application that Innovative IT was scheduled to release at the beginning of the year. They were gabbing about life, and not paying any attention to those who may have been passing by or hovering by the coffee stand. Terrance listened intently to their conversation while standing behind the high divider that separated the programmers' area from the coffee and snack station.

"Do you believe the balls on that guy?" Vernon said.

"Who are you talking about, Vern?" Lisa asked.

"Mark Devlin. That contractor over in research and logistics," Debra answered.

"What about him?" Lisa inquired.

"You didn't hear?" Vernon replied. "Oh, wait until you hear this. Deb, do you want to tell her or shall I?"

"It's better if you tell it, Vern. After all, you were there to see it firsthand," Deb responded.

Lisa knew that Vernon's wife, Margery, worked at the New Hampshire Department of Labor as an investigator for complaints with construction organizations. He had gone to pick her up after work, as her car was at the mechanic's getting a tune-up and repairing a busted taillight resulting from her negligence while backing out of their garage. He was walking through the department when he noticed Mark Devlin sitting at Janet Mancini's cubicle, who sat three cubicles over from where Vernon's wife sat. Margery was finishing up a report she was typing, so Vernon sat in the available chair that was on the other side of Margery's desk. He had overheard all of the conversation between Janet and Mark. He began telling Lisa what was said during that conversation and the accusations Mark was disclosing about Terrance. When he was done recalling the overheard discussion, he said, "That man better pray Mr. Blake doesn't find out about that visit."

"I don't think we should be interfering with any of that, and I don't believe it is proper to be gossiping about the conversation between the DoL and Mark. Those conversations are meant to be private and kept within the person's right to confidentiality," Lisa added.

"It wasn't like I was spying," Vernon continued. "I was just waiting for Margery to finish her report, and those cubicle walls are not necessarily soundproof."

"Nevertheless, Vern, it is not your place to be sharing that information with anyone; especially your peers and people who know Mark. From what I heard, he had every right to seek counsel so he would know his rights in the event that he was being mistreated by anyone here. I think you should stop saying anything further to anyone else here," Lisa suggested.

"I didn't say anything to Mr. Blake. Lord knows what that Pontius Pilate would do to Mark."

Terrance slunk away from where Vernon, Deb, and Lisa were sitting; exercising extreme stealth so as not to be discovered. He walked down the hallway, past

the coffee and snack station, and into the research and logistics department.

There, he saw Mark sitting in his cubicle with his back to the doorway. Terrance

stared at him and said in his mind, *All right, you lowlife peasant; you want to*

play dirty, I can play dirty.

***

Celine Holden was called to the scene where they found Mark Devlin's body.

He was discovered by a little kid, Joey vanBrunt, who was riding his black-and-

red BMX mountain bike on the biking trail at Bear Brook State Park in

Allenstown, New Hampshire. Joey noticed a figure about 10 yards in the woods

that looked like a man. He skidded his bike to a hold by squeezing the brake

levers on the handlebar with as much pressure as a 12-year-old can apply. Joey

was wearing a Van Halen ball cap, sunglasses, white biking gloves, and a t-shirt

with a Voltron character on its center. In those days, kids rarely wore bicycle

helmets because there wasn't as much of a hysteria with parents about their

kids weighed down with protective gear.

Joey stared off into the woods for a minute, dismounted his mountain bike, let

it drop on its side to the dusty earth that made up the biking trail, and slowly

began to walk towards the figure. As he neared, he noticed that it was a man

without a shirt on, and there were some plastic squares covering his torso. The

316

man had been tied to a tree with some type of restraints that were not rope,

but some kind of wire. Joey stopped about 15 feet away from the body and

gasped with shock as he noticed what the plastic squares were impaled into

the man's chest and stomach. They were letter keys from a keyboard that

spelled out four words: "Learn your place, Proletarian." The keys were of

different colors: black with white lettering; white with black lettering, and grey

with black lettering. There were outlines of dried blood around each key that

resulted from the keys being burrowed into the man's flesh. There were

puncture wounds and ripped skin, fat, and frayed muscles pulled out from the

man's shoulders, arms, bare legs, and face. Hungry crows perched above in the

trees, squawking in protest, waiting for the invading boy to return to his bike so

they could swoop back down and continue their feast on the man's rotting

corpse.

Joey turned to his right and began to sprint towards where he'd dropped his

bike. He picked the bike up off the ground and raced like a bat out of hell

towards the pond. As he emerged from the woods and onto the beach area he

began yelling, "HELP!!!! HELP!!! HELP!!!"

This caught the attention of the lifeguards and some of the fathers who were

resting in their beach chairs while watching their kids splash around in the

roped-off swimming section of the water. One of the lifeguards jumped off the raised guard chair and began running over to where Joey was riding from, and

two of the fathers darted up out of their chairs and began tromping through

the soft sand of the beach. When they reached Joey, he informed them of what

he saw, which prompted the lifeguard to race back to his guard chair, climb up,

and grab the radio from the pocket tied to the armrest. The fathers stood on

both sides of the boy with their arms around his shoulders and shoulder blades,

and waited for authorities to arrive.

Celine arrived at Bear Brook State Park, where she was met by two of the

town's officers who escorted her towards the beach, then turned right to

where the biking trail began. They hiked in about 200 yards to where Joey had

pointed out the location of the dead man. Celine hiked through the small

section of trees until she reached the body. The police had already cordoned

off the area with bright-yellow tape that had black words that read "Police Line,

Do Not Cross." The first thing she noticed were the keyboard keys embedded in

the man's torso. The different-color keys were taken from a number of

keyboards, as there are no repeated letters on a single keyboard, and repeated

letters were needed to make up the words on the man's chest and stomach.

Celine set her case of forensic tools down on the earth, opened it, and

produced a device that had a transparent blue cylinder connected to a black,

flashlight-type handle. She switched on the power and the device produced a

bluish/purplish glow. She positioned the light over the keys and began to slowly run it over them from the first line of the words to the last line. She was looking

for any fingerprints that were left on them and noticed, right away, that there

were many different prints. Celine believed that's what she would find, as the

various keyboards used to create this message must have been used by a

number of different people who once owned them. She then moved the

device's light on the restraints that she recognized as computer wires, looking

for any noticeable prints. Finding none, she deduced that the culprit was

wearing gloves, thus preventing any fingerprints from appearing on the wires.

She turned off the device's light, bent down, and returned it to the case.

Next, Celine produced a small canister and a small brush that looked like the

brush a lady would use to apply blush to her cheeks. She unscrewed the lid of

the canister, dipped the brush into the top, and when she removed it, she

began painting over the keys, producing a translucent black dust over the

keyboard keys. When she was done, she bent down and placed the brush

inside the case, screwed the lid back on the canister, returned it to the inside of

the case, and then took out a block of individual strips strapped together, like a

group of paint swatches one would find in a paint store.

Celine tore off one of the strips and began picking at one of the corners with

her right index finger, removing the protective covering of the strip. Next, she

gently pressed it against the keys, rubbed over them lightly with her left index finger, then slowly peeled them off of the keys. She repeated this process until she had collected all the fingerprints from each key.

She then turned to the coroner, who had arrived moments after she did. She looked at both him and one of the paramedics who were there and said, "All right. You can cut him down now, and take him to the morgue. I'm going back to the station to run these prints."

Celine returned to police headquarters and placed the sheaths of clear strips onto a machine that looked like a photocopier. She pressed a button and the machine began to whirl, and shortly spit out four sheets of paper with images of the fingerprints on them. She grabbed the sheets of paper and headed down the hall to the forensics department, which took the prints and ran them through a scanning machine.

After a couple hours, one of the forensic specialists printed out a list of names from a dot matrix printer and handed them to Celine, who took them and returned to an office. Celine visited each of the persons on that list to see if they had any alibis or knew who Mark Devlin was. When she arrived at the Blake residence, she was greeted at the door by a gentleman who was known throughout the state.

Celine began asking him questions about his whereabouts at the beginning of the week, as her years of experience of examining dead bodies indicated that Mark Devlin had been tied to that tree for about a week. Terrance recalled all the places he had been at the beginning of the week, and each place had an alibi; which included his wife. Like the other suspects she'd visited, she delivered a piece of paper to Terrance that was a court order to permit her to search the premises. With subtle trepidation, Terrance welcomed Celine into his home to allow her to look around. After searching all around the house— paying more attention to Terrance's home office, where he had a computer, monitor, and keyboard on his desk—she couldn't find any evidence that would link him to Mark's untimely demise.

As she was leaving the house, she noticed Terrance's son sitting on the grass, Indian-style, near the tree line, with his back to Celine. His fingers were pressing up and down on a rectangular device rested on the ground in front of him. She slowly began to walk towards him, trying to avoid startling the young boy, and when she reached where he was sitting, she saw that he was typing against a keyboard that had grey keys with black letters on them, and it was missing a number of letters. Celine said to the young boy, being cautious to maintain a neutral tone so as not to scare the kid, "Hey, Scotty, whatcha doing there?"

Scott Blake stopped typing, turned his head to the right, and looked up at

Celine. "I'm writing a letter to my dad."

"Is that so," Celine asked. "What happened to the keyboard? You have some

keys missing?"

"I don't know. I just grabbed this out of the trash," Scotty said as he pointed to

his left.

Celine followed the direction of his finger over to two large, brown trash cans

and began walking towards them. When she reached them, she looked back at

Scotty and asked, "You mean these, here?"

Scotty replied, "No, the one in the shed, over there."

There was a brown, wooden shed to Celine's right. The shed's door was slightly

ajar. She walked over to the shed, grabbed the side of the door, and opened it

up. Inside was a third large, brown trash can with the lid pulled off and laying

on the wooden floor beside the trash can. She stepped inside the doorway and

looked into the trash can and saw a collection of keyboards with missing keys

on them and experienced a passing bolt of terror. Shortly after seeing what was

inside, she heard footsteps quickly approaching, as if someone was running towards her. When she turned around to see where they were coming from,

she saw Terrance charging at her with a butcher's knife he'd grabbed from the

kitchen. Celine sidestepped as Terrance lunged forward with the knife gripped

in his raised right hand, causing Terrance to nearly stab the knife into Celine's

flesh, and then crashing into the trash can inside the shed and falling to the

floor. Celine quickly looked around for some object to use for defense and

came upon a wide medal spade attached to a long wooden handle. She

grabbed the garden tool from where it rested against the shed's inside wall,

pulled it behind her, and with a mighty force, she slammed the back of the

metal spade into Terrance's skull, knocking him out. She dropped the tool,

knelt down, and rested both of her knees against Terrance's back. Producing

the police radio from her left hip, she pressed the call button and said, "Dr.

Holden to Sheriff, come in."

"This is Sheriff. Go ahead, Doc."

"I'm here at the Blake residence. You need to send over some officers and

paramedics. I think we've found our man."

CHAPTER 18: THE MORTAL DEADLINE APPROACHETH

Through the vicissitudes of her career, Dr. Holden had been exposed to a

plethora of horrors and the diminishing fiber of humanity. Responding to calls

of ravaged, dismembered bodies, remnants of humans brutally maimed and

left for a crows' banquet, heaps of crimson-stained shaved flesh scattered

around, and other morbid sights, Celine had developed a strong stomach for

the ultimate sins of man. Her ventures into the very narrows of the minds of

hedonistic souls evolved a degree of forensic clairvoyance the more she

witnessed the mutilated spray of victims left behind by the pinnacle of human

sludge. Rapists. Child abusers. Murderers. Corrupt political figures. Gang

violence. Drunkards. Drifters. Pyromaniacs. Extremists. Vulgar fetishes. The

victims who were left alive to live a life of torturous, post-traumatic existence,

rife with emotional and mental anguish, were the ones that impacted Celine

the most.

It wasn't that she was apathetic to those victims who perished as a result of the

criminal escapade, but when she had to look into the eyes of a living soul who

had survived the greatest violation to their bodies, she saw the pain and fear

that the individual would have to live with for the rest of their life. Dr. Holden's

line of work was not for the faint of heart, nor was it for those who were overly sensitive. Again, this is not to imply that Celine was heartless; quite the

contrary. Her passion for the forensic sciences stemmed from her experience

with her sister's untimely demise and the culprit who got away with what he

did. Her solemn oath to her late sister was to do everything in her power to

ensure that there were no vicious acts that were left unpunished.

Even with brutal scenes of rage and malice, such as the Mark Devlin case,

nothing could have prepared Celine for the diabolical stage where Wendy and

Daniel Richards nearly endured a heinous and excruciating death. By the time

Celine arrived at Center Street, the sheriff's department had acquired three

battery-operated halogen spotlights capable of producing enough light to equal

that of a theater's center spotlight. A few of the officers had positioned the

lights in a fashion that illuminated the entire area in the woods where they'd

found Wendy and Daniel Richards, and angled them at such a degree that they

lit up the scene like the bright afternoon sun would've produced.

Langdon met Celine at her car when she pulled up. He shook her hand as she

exited the car and said, "Good evening, Doctor Holden. A few of my men have

set up bright spotlights at the scene of the crime to hopefully provide enough

light for you to conduct your investigation and collection of evidence." As

Langdon said this, he pointed his right index finger out into the woods, where

Celine could see the bright lights created by the halogens that were set up.

"Will you come with me?"

Langdon began walking towards the tree line and Celine followed closely behind. They walked through the uneven terrain, rich with various ground vegetation and remnants of collections of leaves dispensed by the towering trees over the years. They had to push aside low-hanging branches that blocked their path, being mindful of each other's whereabouts so as not to strike each other with the released tension of the branches.

Not but a couple minutes into their hike, they appeared in the open area, where they were met by a flood of light and three officers: Middleton, Jackson, and McCormick. At first, Celine didn't think too much of the layout and spread of shattered glass, reflective steel nails, and the hornets' nests. But when she raised her head and eyes up into the trees and saw the dangling ropes, her heart nearly stopped as she could only imagine the horrid apparatuses the ropes originally made up. Langdon had not had time to prepare Celine about the scenario or what she'd find when she was brought into the scene of the crime. All she knew was that there were two unconscious, injured children at the hospital and that they only had until 1:00 p.m. the next day to find the culprits to a crime.

Celine immediately pieced the puzzle together between what she was seeing

and what Langdon had told her over the phone, and had to suppress her

terrified tears of what those innocent children had to experience at the hands

of criminally disturbed individuals.

Taking a few deep breaths to compose herself back to a professional

demeanor, she said, "OK, Sheriff, tell me what you found."

Langdon proceeded to describe the scene that they first saw when they

reached the area. He told her how the two teens were suspended 15 feet in the

air by ropes over the splay of broken glass, planted nails, and three hornets'

nests. He continued to describe how they were fastened together and how the

ropes that restrained them had leads that led over to the train tracks. How the

ropes were fastened around one of the tracks, and when the train ran over the

ropes tied around the tracks it would sever the lines, triggering the lethal

contraption to cause the kids to plummet into the deadly pile of debris below

them. Langdon further went on to describe how he and the other officers

proceeded to release the unconscious teens from their restraints without

causing them to fall onto the glass, nails, and nests.

When Langdon finished describing the events up to when Celine arrived, she

looked over at the three officers, then back at Langdon. "Tell me a little more about this deadline."

Langdon looked up at the other officers, then looked back at Celine and asked, "First, tell me how you feel about the supernatural."

Celine's eyelids involuntarily squinted a little. Her eyebrows lowered, causing the skin on her forehead to stretch down and the left side of her mouth to shift slightly, exposing the dimple on her left cheek. "Supernatural?" she asked. "What do you mean by supernatural? Ghosts? Spirits? Grim, floating apparitions? Those kinds of things?"

"Exactly," Langdon replied. "Do you believe in any of that?"

"To be honest, Sheriff, I don't believe in any of that."

Langdon looked over at the officers again, then back at Celine. "Well then, none of this is going to make any sense, and I believe you will think I'm crazy and going senile. But I'll tell you the truth, everything I am about to tell you happened, and I have witnesses who can corroborate my story."

"All right, Sheriff, lay it on me."

Langdon told Celine of the discoveries of both Noah Callahan's and Billy

Donnelly's bodies at two different times. He described the conditions of their

bodies when they were discovered, and the mysterious way in which the boys

were adhered to the Summit Street/Chartiers Road intersection's streetlight.

Langdon spoke of a shadowy entity that lurked up and behind the streetlight

post and described all the features the shadowy apparition possessed. He

talked of how this specter had the ability to move objects, break objects, and

talk through electronic devices. He told her of young Jasper, and the eerie

events that transpired when he went over to the Callahans' and looked in on

Jasper sleeping, only to see him, moments later, in his upstairs bedroom

window wearing a different set of pajamas than he had on when Langdon was

in his bedroom. Langdon told Celine about Ralph Dubain and his recounts of

the events before the police were on the scene, how this ghostly shadow

talked to him through his telephone with Jasper's childlike voice and how it

communicated similarly through his police radio.

Langdon informed Celine of the spirit's temperamental disposition and

felonious intentions. He provided all the riddles that the "Jasper voice"

presented, and how it became physically violent when he answered a question

incorrectly. The last thing he said before allowing Celine to respond was the

last riddle asked of him by the Jasper voice: "Look at the numbers on my face,

you won't find 13 any place. What am I?" He told her that Jasper was going to "leave a little gift" for them if they didn't apprehend the two culprits before 1:00 p.m. tomorrow.

"Well, Sheriff, that is quite some tale. I would say you were trying to pull one over on me, but I know someone of your stature and reputation wouldn't go that far and be that detailed with such supernatural phenomenon. Do you have any leads at all?"

"Not a one. After we securely got both the teens to safe ground and comfortable, we began to rack our brains trying to come up with someone, or multiple people, who had the ingenuity and strength to rig such a contraption together and hoist two bodies 15 feet in the air. Obviously, it would take someone of barbaric strength to do that alone. So the individual or individuals would need to have a strong build, and definitely be someone who knows both Wendy and Daniel; those are the names of the two teen victims we discovered here."

"Let me take a look around and see if I can find anything," Celine suggested. She turned and looked at Officer Middleton and asked, "Sir, could you retrieve the case from the trunk of my car, please?"

"With pleasure, Dr. Holden," Middleton replied.

As Officer Middleton turned in the direction of Center Street and began making his way through the trees and low-hanging branches, Celine walked around the perimeter of the crime scene with short steps and paced very slow. Her eyes moved back and forth as she scouted for any evidence that could be seen by the naked eye. She would pause here and there, looking around intently at the ground, then continue walking in slow, short steps. Langdon looked down at his watch: 12:30 a.m. They had just over 12 hours to apprehend the two assailants before Jasper's ghost took it upon itself to inflict street justice on them.

Langdon then looked over at Jackson and McCormick, who were both intently following Celine's every footstep, waiting for her to discover something. Jackson felt Langdon looking at him and lifted his head to make eye contact with Langdon's face. Langdon lifted his arm slightly from his side and lightly tapped on his watch with his other index finger so as not to alert Celine to his gesture, indicating they were running out of time.

"Do you want me to do this the right way or the quick way, which would probably cause an incorrect identification of the evidence?" Celine asked, still looking down and surveying the ground.

Langdon was shocked by this because even **he** didn't hear the tapping of his finger against the glass front of his watch. "Of course I want this to be done the

right way, but I am just being very cautious of time here. Whoever did this

deserves criminal justice, not an abrupt death from a menacing spirit."

"I understand that," Celine said, still looking back and forth on the ground, "but

this kind of work fails with haste and succeeds with patience."

"You're right, Dr. Holden. I guess I'm just anxious to get to those individuals

before anyone else does," Langdon responded.

"I can certainly sympathize with you, Sheriff, but patience is a ve—" Celine

stopped mid-sentence as she noticed something on the ground, peeking out

from under one of the ferns in front of her and four feet from the pile of glass,

nails, and nests. She knelt down next to it, produced a pen from her breast

pocket, and used it to move the fern branch away from where it hung over the

object. What she'd discovered was a fingernail. A fingernail that had red nail

polish on it. It was about 1.5 inches long and half an inch wide. This definitely

came from someone of slim physique, and most likely a female. There were

little spots of blood underneath the nail, as well as a dark-brown, fibrous

substance. Some of the red nail polish was scratched as well.

Celine released the fern branch she had moved aside with her pen, then began

moving some of the other fern branches around to see if she could discover

anything in addition to the fingernail. With no success, she stood upright,

returned the pen to her breast pocket, and walked up to the tree that was right

next to the fern where she found the fingernail. She began to examine the tree

bark to see if she could find any scratch marks that might identify the

substance on the underside of the fingernail. Celine was still waiting for Officer

Middleton to return with her evidence case before disturbing the fingernail. As

she was running her right hand up and down the lower areas of the tree trunk,

Officer Middleton appeared into the lit area with Celine's case. He brought it

over and sat it down on the ground next to her.

"Here you go, Dr. Holden," Middleton said.

"Thank you, dear," Celine replied.

Celine knelt down onto the earth again, reached her right hand to the zipper at

the top of the case, and slowly began to unzip the case. She paused, turned her

head to her left to look at Langdon, and asked, "Do you want to take any

pictures of this before I move the fingernail?"

"Quite frankly, Dr. Holden, at this point in time, proper investigative protocol is out the window. Go ahead and do whatever you need to do," Langdon

responded.

Celine took a pair of surgical gloves out from the bag and proceeded to put

them on. She stood upright, walked a few paces over to the fern and knelt

down, pushing the fern branch aside and reached down to pick up the

fingernail. Being very careful not to disrupt the condition of the fingernail, she

pinched the fingernail between her right thumb and index finger, stood up, and

went over to the oak tree she was earlier looking for scratches on. She held up

the fingernail's nail-polished front facing the tree, so the back of the fingernail

was visible. She compared the color and fibrous substance that was under the

fingernail to that of the bark on the oak. An exact match. She bent down and

reached into her evidence collection case, pulled out a small bag, opened it up,

and placed the fingernail inside. Using her right middle finger and her left

thumb, she pinched the top of the bag and ran her thumb and middle finger

down along the top of the bag, sealing it closed. Although the fiber under the

fingernail and the oak tree's bark color and texture matched up, there were no

scratch marks on the tree she was standing in front of. She turned around to

see Langdon, McCormick, Jackson, and Middleton standing together about nine

feet behind her.

"I need you boys to start looking over all these trees and see if you can find any kind of scratch marks. Start with the ones around this area," she said as she

raised her left hand, extended her index finger, and gestured to the trees

behind her. "Let me know as soon as you find anything."

Jackson, Middleton, and McCormick walked towards Celine, being very careful

to not disturb too much of the crime scene more than they had when they

were on a time limit to rescue Wendy and Daniel. They each began looking at

the different oak trees near the fern, walking around them and using their

flashlights on the sections of the tree trunk that were not illuminated by the

halogen lights. Langdon stood in place and watched as Celine continued to

move around the perimeter of the crime scene, searching for more clues.

When she reached the pile of glass, she saw a trace of dirt that was foreign

compared with the earth around it. It had more of a sandy grain to it and not

the same texture as the soil in the rest of the scene.

"Sheriff, can you come here for a moment?" Celine beckoned.

Langdon began walking towards Celine and when he reached where she was

standing, she asked, "Is there a beach around here?"

Langdon replied, "Yes. About 40 yards in that direction." He lifted his right

index finger and pointed towards Skin Beach.

"Would you mind accompanying me to that location?" she asked.

"Not at all," Langdon replied. He produced the flashlight that was in its holder, which was fastened to his belt. He moved in front of Celine and then said, "This way" as he gestured with his hand. They moved cautiously through the trees and over the earth as they had when they were heading to the crime scene from Center Street.

It wasn't long before they emerged from the tree line behind Skin Beach and walked out onto the soft, sandy floor. "Oh, there is something I want to show you over here, Dr. Holden." Langdon pointed his light over at the circular symbol with a line through its center and an oversized, dead hornet in its center. He made sure to point out the dark-crimson substance that coated the inside of the lines. "What do you make of this, Doc?"

"Hmmm," Celine responded. "This appears to be some message, but it doesn't make sense to me. Is there some significance to a hornet in this town?"

"Actually," Langdon replied, "our Parks and Recreation sports teams are called the Hornets."

"Curious. This symbol usually implies 'No' or 'Don't' when it is posted on signs.

Like two silhouette figures posed in walking stance with a red circle around it

and a red line going through the image means 'No Walking.' Or a picture of a

black silhouette dog with the same red circle and red line crossed over it means

'No Dogs Allowed.' This could've been created by a rival league or someone

who really didn't like some players on that league. Was there anything unusual

about the clothing that either Wendy or Daniel were wearing?"

"Well, the back of the boy's shirt was slit in half and the girl's baseball uniform

was cut off and draped over her legs. She was just wearing a sports bra and

white girl's underwear with pink hearts all over it," Langdon answered.

"A baseball uniform? Was she on the Hornets ball team?"

"Not that I'm aware of," Langdon replied. "Wendy's father ran a sporting goods

store and I know he was teaching her to perfect her pitching skills. I know that

she tried out for the baseball team a few times but was never offered a

position because she was a female and the league's regulations stated that

females were not allowed on the baseball team, only the softball team."

"Why would Wendy continue to try out for the baseball team then?" Celine

inquired.

"It had something to do with her style of pitching. That's about as much as I know," Langdon replied.

"Interesting. Were there any events today that involved the Parks and Rec athletic league?"

"Yes. Today was tryouts for all the different sports the town offers."

"Were there baseball tryouts as well?"

"Most certainly, Doc."

"Do you happen to know if Wendy tried out for the baseball team again today?"

"Sadly, I don't know that."

A voice shot through the tree line, slowly followed by Jackson appearing out onto the sand of Skin Beach. "Yes, Dr. Holden, Wendy tried out for the team today. I was there because my son, Zachary, was last year's MVP and, per league rules, is automatically invited back to the team the next season."

"Officer Jackson," Celine began, "was Wendy offered a position on the baseball team this year?"

"Yes, Doc, she is the first female to have been invited to play on a boy's baseball league, ever," Jackson responded.

"Do you know of anyone who protested this invitation? Like someone who didn't want to have a girl playing baseball on an all-boys team?" Celine asked.

Jackson thought for a moment, opened his mouth to say something, paused, and then closed his mouth. He waited another few seconds, then began to answer Celine's question: "Actually, I don't know of *anyone* who would put up such a fuss over having a girl on an all-boys baseball team. I always thought that policy was sexist, to be honest."

Celine's brow lowered and an expression of curiosity appeared on her face. "What were you going to say just before you told me your answer? You were starting to say something, paused, and then responded. What stopped you from saying what first came to your mind?"

Langdon turned his focus to Jackson. He, too, wore an expression of curiousness and perplexity. Jackson spoke up, "I was going to say maybe one of the girls on the softball team, but Wendy knew all of those girls and they were all close friends. I didn't think any of them were angry enough, let alone capable, to do something like this to Wendy."

"In the future, Officer Jackson, I'd prefer if you said exactly what comes to mind first."

"I understand. I will do that." But what Jackson told Celine wasn't true. His **first** thought was that his son, Zachary, had objected to Wendy's previous tryouts citing that "girls are supposed to play softball, and only boys are supposed to play baseball." Jackson had a flashing, terrorizing thought that his son might have been involved in this somehow, and he didn't want to bring any suspicions into the situation. So he thought of the next viable answer to give Celine that would placate her suspicions about what he was originally thinking.

Celine turned her attention back to Langdon and asked, "This is definitely a sign of extreme hatred and furious wrath brought on by some kind of objection to Wendy making the baseball team. What about Daniel? What could be the reason he was one of the victims here? Was it just because he was with Wendy when she was abducted, or could there be another reason?"

"Daniel made the soccer team," Langdon responded, "but that team has always been coed, so there wouldn't be any objections to girls playing there. I am at a loss to explain why Daniel would be subjected to this kind of torture, though. I can't think of any person who would have any ill feelings towards him."

"It might be a case of his presence when the abductors wanted to force Wendy here and not want Daniel to be a witness to Wendy's abduction," Celine proposed.

Celine turned back to Jackson and asked, "Do you think I can have a word with your son?"

Jackson hesitated for a moment, then said, "I don't see why not. I know he's sleeping right now, but that won't matter. If he has any information that can lead us to the teens' assailants, then I will make sure he is up and alert enough to answer any questions you ask of him."

McCormick burst out from the tree line and ran out onto the beach. "Dr. Holden, you have to come see this, right now!"

Celine and Langdon immediately began to jog towards McCormick while Jackson stood in place, looking over at the symbol etched into the sand, and dazed with the thought that his son could possess even the slightest ounce of behavior that led to the torture of the two teens.

McCormick disappeared into the darkened woods, closely followed by Celine. As Langdon approached the tree line he stopped, turned his head around to the left, and saw Jackson just standing there in a daze. "Jackson, let's go!!!"

Jackson snapped out of the trance he was in, turned toward Langdon, and jogged over to the bank, following Langdon into the woods. Soon, the four of them stepped out into the lit crime scene and saw Middleton standing over by one of the trees. He was pointing at a spot about three feet up from the base of one of the oaks.

Celine stepped closer and saw that there were some scratch marks in the bark of the tree. But there was something else: there was a used condom just below those scratches.

Celine walked over to her evidence collection case, knelt down, and pulled out two more surgical gloves. She reached into the top of the evidence collection case and pulled out some tweezers, a plastic bag, and a small vial of liquid with a rubber top with an eyedropper on its lid.

As she was walking over to where the condom laid, Jackson began to feel his heart rate climbing to paramount levels. He began to fear the worst and, even though he didn't want to believe it, believed that his son could very well be one of the culprits.

Right next to the used condom was a deeply compressed shoe mark. It had a pattern that consisted of a number of wiggly lines, six holes punctured into the earth, and a backwards symbol of a "J." He couldn't recall a shoe brand that had that kind of symbol and they were the only family, in that area, whose last name began with a "J"; he remembered picking up a custom pair of cleats for Zachary that **did** have an embossed letter "J" on the heel of both shoes. Jackson knew very well that the fluid contained in that condom would produce strong DNA evidence of the culprit, and that could be his only son.

Celine knelt down next to the condom, then reached the swab into the condom all the way to the tip where the pool of semen had collected. She twisted the end of the swab around the viscous fluid and, with the hands of a surgeon, removed the swab from inside the prophylactic so as not to touch the insides of the tubular sheath. Holding the swab in her right hand, being extra careful not to let it touch the ground, she used her left hand to twist open the top of the

343

vial. She then squeezed the rubber bulb at the top of the vial's cover, then

released it. She slowly removed the glass tube attached to the rubber bulb,

positioned it over the swab, and slowly squeezed out two drops of the liquid

onto the tip of the swab. Within seconds, the chalky white fluid on the tip of

swab turned a purplish color. "Well, it's semen, all right," Celine concluded.

"What was that stuff you put on it, Doc?" McCormick asked.

"Acid phosphatase. It is used to determine if a substance contains sperm, and

reacts to the strong enzymes in semen," Celine answered.

"So if the color changes to purple, that means that there is sperm and seminal

enzymes present," McCormick expounded.

"Correct. One of the perpetrators did ejaculate into this condom, but that's

about all we know. Were there any signs of sexual assault on either one of the

teens, Sheriff?"

"No. And I've seen victims of sexual assault before, so I knew what to look for,"

Langdon replied.

"True as that might be, did you also examine the boy?"

"No. I didn't. The thought never crossed my mind," Langdon said with a tone of shameful embarrassment.

"Can we head back to the beach?" Celine asked as she reached down and picked up the used condom with the tweezers.

"Certainly," McCormick responded.

"All right. Give me second." Celine grabbed the plastic bag and opened the top. She lowered the used condom into the bag with the tweezers and sealed both of them in the bag in the same manner as she had with the fingernail. Twisting the eyedropper lid back onto the small vial, she returned it to the evidence collection case. She then removed both surgical gloves inside out and placed them in another empty bag. She grabbed the handles of the evidence collection bag, and stood upright. "Lead the way," she ordered McCormick.

McCormick escorted Celine back to Skin Beach, followed closely by Langdon, but Jackson stood at the scene where the condom was discovered. He didn't know if any of the others saw the shoe print in the earth next to the condom. He cautiously walked over to it, bent down, snapped one of the fern branches off, and began sweeping over the shoe print in a back-and-forth brushing manner. He swept enough of the loose soil to fill the holes that the cleats had made and continued to brush over it to smooth it out and make it appear as undisturbed as the surrounding soil. After that he stood up straight and began walking towards Skin Beach to catch up with the others.

When he was halfway there, he threw the fern branch into the woods to his right, then continued until he stepped out onto the beach. To his right he saw Langdon, McCormick, and Middleton standing next to Celine, who had knelt down on both knees next to the dark-crimson etched symbol in the sand. She was putting on a fresh pair of surgical gloves and had two small vials sitting on the sand to her right, along with a 4-ounce brown bottle that Jackson recognized as hydrogen peroxide, as this is something that was in all of the first aid pouches every officer carried.

After Celine had put the new pair of surgical gloves on, she reached over and grabbed one of the vials that had the same pipette-designed lid as the previous vial she'd used to test for semen just moments before. McCormick then asked, "Is that acid phosphatase again?"

Celine replied, "No. This is something different. I want to see if that dark-crimson substance is blood." Celine squeezed the rubber bulb of the pipette, then removed it from the vial, positioned it over a section of the circular symbol, and squeezed a few drops on it. She returned the pipette back to the

vial, fastened it back onto the vial, then grabbed the other bottle with a

different pipette top. She unscrewed its cap, squeezed the pipette's rubber

bulb, removed the pipette from the vial, positioned it over the same area she'd

dropped the other chemical on, then squeezed out three drops. She held the

pipette over the section she applied both chemicals to and watched for a

moment. McCormick was flashing his light over the symbol, producing enough

light to help her see a chemical reaction. The color didn't change. She returned

the pipette back into the vial, tightened the cap back on, retrieved the 4-ounce

brown bottle of hydrogen peroxide, unscrewed the cap, then poured a

thimbleful of peroxide into its cap. She positioned it over the same area she

had applied the first two chemicals, and then sparingly applied the hydrogen

peroxide to the mix. Not but a second after, the color of the dark crimson

began to turn green. "Yup, that's blood, all right."

"What was that stuff you were dripping onto the line there?" McCormick

asked. He seemed to be genuinely interested in the scientific methods she was

using to determine certain substances.

Holding up one of the vials, she said, "This is leucomalachite green, or LMG."

She set that vial down and picked up the other vial and said, "This is ethanol.

You apply both to a sample of blood and if it doesn't change color, then a little

347

hydrogen peroxide is applied. If the color turns from red to green, then the

enzymes from blood reacted to the agents, changing the color of the sample."

"Fascinating," McCormick admired.

"You're getting warrrrrrrmer."

All five of them froze in place as they heard this child's voice speak those

words. It startled each and every one of them. McCormick was the first to react

and spun his light around to the direction that the voice was coming from. In a

flood of eeriness, McCormick's light settled on young Jasper Callahan. Jasper

was wearing his shape-shifting robot cartoon pajamas and was standing eight

feet behind the group. His hands were down by his side, his head slightly

bowed down, his ghostly eyes raised and staring at the group, and he wore an

ominously unsettling smile on his face.

Jasper began to giggle before turning and bolting through the tree line and out

of sight into the darkness of the towering covering of oaks, pines, birches, and

maples. "Get that boy, McCormick!" Langdon hollered.

McCormick wasted no time and sprinted off into the same direction that Jasper

disappeared to. McCormick raced through the trees, ignoring the need to push the low-hanging branches from in front of his face, causing them to create

small red welts on his head and neck. He leaped over natural objects in his path

like he was jumping over hurdles. He was trying to follow the giggling from

young Jasper as a means of location and direction. McCormick emerged out

onto Center Street and stopped. He looked to his left, then to his right, and

didn't see young Jasper running anywhere, but he could still hear Jasper's

boyish giggling in the distance.

Back at Skin Beach, Celine stood up from where she was kneeling in the sand.

She brushed the sand off her knees with her hands, looked over at Langdon

and asked, "Who the hell was **that**???"

Langdon looked back at Celine, who had a mix of confusion and shock on her

face. "That was young Jasper, the little boy I was telling you about. The one

who was seen under the streetlight when we discovered the body of Billy

Donnelly. The one with the parasitic shadow."

"Why the heck is he out this late? And down here so deep in the woods with

just pajamas on? And why was he looking at us like that?"

"Well, the first thing that comes to mind, Doc," Langdon responded, "is that

the evil entity was checking up on us. I know that sounds outlandish, but that's the only reason I can think of for a little boy being out here at 12:45 a.m. with just his shape-shifting robot cartoon pajamas on."

"Are you going to send one of the officers over to his house to see if he's there and awake?"

"To be quite honest," Langdon said, "we've already disrupted Mr. Callahan a couple times this evening. I have Rogers stationed at the streetlight, and he'll let us know if anything odd happens."

"*Odd*??? What do you call a young boy being in the woods at 12:45 a.m. in his nightclothes? Normal???"

"Doc, you haven't seen anything yet."

Celine had seen more than she wanted to see already. Nothing in her entire career had ever measured up to this. Even the Devlin case paled in comparison to everything she had witnessed so far that evening. "This is absolutely puzzling. But we are racing against the clock, and now we have a 10-year-old boy wandering around the town in the cold November air with nothing but his pajamas on." Celine turned her head to her right and looked directly at Jackson. "I think it's time we went over to your place and had a chat with your son."

Jackson truly didn't want anyone talking to his boy, especially when he could be implicated in such a heinous crime as this one. He didn't want to believe that his stunningly accomplished son possessed any degree of malice that would lead to a severe act of rage. However, if he began to object to the request of Celine talking to his son, then that might incite suspicion and probing questions Jackson wasn't prepared to answer.

Jackson looked back at Celine and with a compliant tone replied, "Of course. We can head over there now. Should I radio ahead to my wife and have her wake up Zachary?"

"No," Celine responded. "It would be best if I was there to see him awakened."

Langdon looked over at Middleton. "Jay, you stay behind and make sure no one comes near the crime scene." Langdon switched his focus from Middleton to Jackson. "Jackson, you and I will escort Dr. Holden to your home." Langdon looked over at McCormick. "Mick, I want you to go up to the Callahans' and park yourself down the road enough so you can keep watch on the house, but far enough away so as to not arouse suspicion."

Langdon and Jackson began walking up the beach towards Angler's Point, with

Celine following closely behind. They walked along the tree line until they reached Center Street. "Doc, why don't you follow Jackson and me to his house. I want to have a squad car with us in the event we have to leave suddenly."

Celine headed over to her car, opened the door, sat inside, placed the evidence collection kit on the seat next to her, and started her car. Langdon and Jackson headed over to their respective vehicles, got inside, and started their cars. Langdon was the first to pull out, then Jackson pulled out behind Langdon, and Celine pulled out to follow them.

They headed up Center Street, turned onto South Street, then onto Clarksville Road. They took a right onto A Street and when they reached the third house on the left, they pulled over to the side of the road and parked their cars. The house on the right was behind the Jackson residence and was bordered by hedges all the way around. There was a small opening in the hedges halfway between each of the corners that led to the back of the house. Langdon didn't want their motorcade to be sighted by anyone who might still be awake in the Jackson house.

Langdon, Jackson, and Celine all turned their vehicles off, got out of their respective cars, and met up at the opening in the hedges. Jackson's pulse began to rise as he noticed Zachary's bedroom light on.

Langdon was the first one to enter through the opening in the hedges, followed by Celine, then trailed by Jackson. They all stopped at the back door and Jackson went up, took his house key out from his right pants pocket, put it into the deadbolt lock, and turned the key, producing a slight clicking sound. He opened the door and allowed Langdon to enter first, and then Celine. They walked into a small mud room and Celine spotted a pair of baseball cleats on the floor, neatly placed next to each other, and next to a pair of rain boots, a pair of white Adidas sneakers, and a smaller pair of pink-and-white girl's sneakers. She knelt down in front of the baseball cleats, grabbed a hold of both of them with her left hand, then twisted them around to look at the bottom of the shoes. She noticed three different types of dirt dried around the spiked cleats and a raised "J" on the heel of the shoes. There was grainy sand particles, thicker soil, and dusty dirt. She began to think that most athletes would remove their special sport shoes and pull on some sneakers to go home with so as not to dull down the spiked cleats. She set one of the shoes back down where they were sitting and kept one in her hand. She stood upright, looked over at Jackson and asked, "Where is Zachary's room?"

Jackson walked ahead of Celine and Langdon until they reached the hallway

and the bottom of the stairwell. He turned right and began to ascend the stairs.

Langdon followed next, and Celine held the rear.

Reaching the top of the stairs, Jackson turned left and stopped at the first door

on the right: Zachary's room. He reached his right hand out to the polished

brass doorknob, paused for a moment, took a deep breath, then slowly twisted

the doorknob to the right. He softly opened the door and saw Zachary sitting

on his bed with only his boxer shorts on. His arms were crossed across his

chest, he was slightly bent down, his head hanging low, and he was rocking

himself back and forth, sobbing.

Jackson raced over until he was standing in front of Zachary. He knelt down in

front of his son, rested his hands on both of Zach's knees and asked in a

panicky voice, "Son, what is it? What's the matter?"

Zach didn't respond. He continued to rock himself back and forth, lightly

sobbing as he did. Langdon went into the room next and Celine entered last.

They both just stared down at this teenage boy, nearly naked, hunched over,

and steadily rocking back and forth as he sat at the edge of his bed.

"Zach," Jackson repeated. "What is going on? You have to answer me."

Zachary looked up at his father's worried face, tears staining his cheeks, then turned his head to the right and saw Langdon and Celine standing just inside the doorway of his bedroom. He saw that Celine had one of his baseball cleats in her left hand. His sobbing intensified; he turned his head back to the left and lowered his head down, all the while maintaining his back and forth cadence.

Langdon saw an immense amount of fear in his eyes when he had looked over at Celine and himself. He walked over until he was in front of Zachary, knelt down next to Jackson, and looked up at Zach's lowered face. "Son, what is going on? Why are you so upset?"

With his head still hanging down, Zach began to speak with broken words, "It's not fair. It's not fair."

"What isn't fair, son?" Langdon responded. Langdon turned his head slightly to his right and caught a few tears flowing down Jackson's left cheek.

Zachary slowly lifted his head until his red, tear-filled eyes met Langdon's. "Girls are not supposed to play baseball."

CHAPTER 19: AN OVERTURE OF ABOMINATION

Langdon turned to Zach's bedroom window and walked over to it. He pulled one of the red translucent curtains aside to the right with his right hand and peered out. He looked out at the overgrown tree in the front yard and out to the road. With no streetlights there, he couldn't see very much of anything, nor did he know what he was looking for. He was about to release the bedroom curtain when he looked down at the front yard and saw Jasper standing there, still in those shape-shifting robot cartoon pajamas, and standing with his hands down by his side. His head was bent down. His hair was all scruffy, with his bangs hanging over his head like an umbrella, covering his forehead and face.

Langdon maintained his fixed gaze on Jasper when all of a sudden, Jasper nonchalantly began raising his head up towards Zach's bedroom window. His eyes seemed black and he had a devilish grin. He caught Langdon looking down at him and maintained that ominous smirk as he stared at Langdon. Langdon's eyes widened as Jasper began to raise his right arm up towards the window. Jasper's hand was clenched, and he held it there for a few seconds. Jasper then casually raised his right index finger and held it there for about 10 seconds. Then he lowered his index finger, returning to the clenched fist, and lowered his right arm back by his side.

While still holding the curtain open with his right hand, Langdon reached down to the police radio clipped to the belt and resting against his left hip. Langdon jerked the radio up, continuing his focus on Jasper standing in the darkened front yard, pressed the call button, and said in a sharp tone, "Sheriff to McCormick."

There was slight delay before a boyish voice came through the speaker of the radio: "Uh-uh-uh. No fair cheating."

Langdon was looking straight down at Jasper's face the whole time, with Jasper staring hauntingly back up at Langdon. When that voice came over the radio, he noticed that Jasper's mouth never moved. It maintained that sinister smile. Celine was spooked by the voice and sharply looked up from her focus on Zachary to Langdon. "Who the hell was **that**?"

Langdon ignored Celine's question. Instead, he pressed the call button again and asked, "What do you mean, cheating?"

The sweet, childish voice came back through the speaker of the police radio: "You're trying to get that prick, McCormick, to go into the Callahan home, aren't you?"

Langdon paused for a moment, then pressed the call button on the side of the police radio and began to reply: "Not necessarily."

"Not necessarily, old man? What do you take me for? A naive fool? You should know better, by now, that I'm the furthest thing from naive. Now play fair."

"Sheriff to McCormick," Langdon repeated, still keeping his focus on Jasper's face.

The voice that came through the speaker of the radio was a chilling tone that Langdon had heard earlier that evening when he had tested Jasper's patience while playing his game. It was a satanic voice one might identify with Linda Blair's demon-possessed body in *The Exorcist*: deep, guttural, threatening, and demanding. Jasper's expression morphed from his sinister smirk to one that was scarily filled with wrath: "Play . . . **FAIR!!!!!**" Jasper's lips still remained closed when the voice came back through the radio.

Langdon lowered the police radio down to his left hip and held it there for a moment. He remembered the repercussions he'd experienced the last time he'd tested Jasper's patience, and decided he wasn't going to run the risk of having any of the others in the room be the victims of his negligence. Without raising the radio back in front of his mouth, Langdon whispered, "All right, you little brat, I'll play along . . . for now."

Jasper's expression returned to the malevolent smile and playful eyes. He then slowly raised his right arm again with a clenched fist in the air, turned his wrist to the right, and calmly raised his thumb. Then Jasper lowered his thumb back down and gracefully lowered his arm. He turned around to his right and began walking out into the darkness of E Street. Langdon watched him until he could no longer see the little boy when a dim light from across the street and to the right caught his eye. The light was coming from inside Clarksville Missionary Church across the street from the Jackson residence. Langdon snapped around to his left, releasing the curtain back over the glass bedroom window, and swiftly marched towards the doorway. "Doc, come with me. We've got to hurry. Jackson, you stay here with your son; and don't even think about leaving this room."

Langdon and Celine darted out the bedroom, turned left, then turned right and raced down the stairs. When they reached the bottom, they ran towards the front door. Langdon reached for the door handle, pushed it down, then pulled at the door. He failed to acknowledge that the deadbolt was still engaged, so he twisted the polished brass switch to the right until they heard a clicking sound, and Langdon whipped the front door open. They both shot out from inside the house and Celine followed behind Langdon as he was jogging

diagonally across the front lawn towards the driveway.

Reaching the roadway of E Street, he turned right and ran about 80 yards down

until he was standing on the property of Clarksville Missionary Church, just

outside the side door of the building. The dim light was casting a soft glow on

the side steps, which he and Celine walked up.

Langdon reached out, grabbed hold of the doorknob, and turned it to the right.

To his surprise, the door was unlocked and he pushed it open with such force

that it collided with the inside wall behind it, creating a hole in the sheetrock

wall.

Entering through the doorway, he turned right and headed into a large, open

room. There were pews set up underneath a lofty ceiling, facing the pulpit that

was resting on an elevated platform. There were 12 folding chairs set up

behind and to the right of the pulpit. An enormous gold cross with oak

bordering hung securely on the back wall behind the pulpit.

Langdon noticed a young girl sitting in the front pew. Her wavy, brunette hair hung down over her back. She was wearing a white collared blouse and staring motionlessly up at the oversized cross on the wall.

Langdon began down the middle aisle, between the oak pews lining both sides of the red-carpeted aisle. Celine stayed at the back of the room as she watched Langdon slowly nearing where the girl was sitting. Langdon walked a little beyond the front pew, keeping his gaze on the girl's head, and then turned to face the girl. Her face was pale. Her eyes were bloodshot. Her hands were folded neatly on her lap. She was wearing a denim skirt that had spatters of dried blood on it. Langdon noticed a gold, heart-shaped locket attached to a thin gold chain peeking out through the girl's folded hands. When Langdon looked at the girl's blank expression, eyes fixated on the behemoth cross on the wall, he recognized her as Allison Rogers, Officer Rogers' oldest daughter and Zachary Jackson's girlfriend.

"Allie," Langdon said, breaking the deadening silence in the room. "What are you doing here?"

There were a few moments that passed before she finally replied: "It isn't fair. Girls are not supposed to play baseball." Her eyes never swayed from her stare on the cross. Her only acknowledgement of Langdon's presence was that soft-spoken response.

"I was just over at the Jacksons', talking with Zach, and he said the same exact thing. What do you mean, girls are not supposed to play baseball? Why would **you** object to something like that?" Langdon asked.

Celine began to make her way towards Langdon and Allison and stopped when she reached them. She stood to Allison's left and listened intently, awaiting the young girl's response.

With her eyes still focused on the cross, she began to speak in her soft, hushed tone again: "Girls are not supposed to play baseball."

Celine chimed in and asked, "But why, dear? Why do you think girls shouldn't play baseball? Do you think it is improper and unorthodox?"

Allison's tone never changed. The only movement she made was with her mouth when she spoke. The rest of her body was stationary and frozen still. She opened her mouth again and responded to Celine's inquiry: "Girls are not supposed to play baseball."

Celine moved her attention from Allison up to Langdon. "This girl is obviously in shock from something, Sheriff. I don't think we're going to get anything else out of her at this juncture. We need to take her somewhere where she can receive medical attention." Celine looked back towards Allison and said, "Let's go, child. We're going to get you to someplace safe."

Celine went to caress Allison's shoulder as a sign of comfort and reassurance. When she made contact, Allison's folded hands separated and she flung her left fist up towards Celine. The gold, heart-shaped locket launched through the air like a set of bolas whipped at an enemy. The pointed end of the heart caught Celine in her left cheek, instantly producing a small slice on her face. Celine's reflexes found her catching Allison's left wrist with her right hand, stopping it from connecting with Celine's face. Langdon lunged forward and restrained Allison by putting his right hand on her sternum and his left hand on her right shoulder, pinning her to the pew. With Allison's left wrist clutched by Celine's grasp, Celine noticed that Allison's left middle fingernail was missing. The rest of her fingernails were painted with glossy red nail polish, and there were dark-brown, fibrous substances under the other fingernails. Celine immediately recognized this substance as the same fibrous material that she saw under the fingernail in the woods at the crime scene. Allison was squirming around in the pew, protesting the human restraints administered from both Langdon and Celine. Allison began to let off deafening shrieks of anger and venomous, obscene words poured out from her mouth.

"LET GO OF ME, YOU FUCKING CUNT!!! LET GO OF ME BEFORE I PUNCH OUT SOME OF THOSE PEARLY WHITES YOU HAVE BEHIND THOSE GERIATRIC LIPS OF YOURS!!!!"

Celine smiled with amusement and let out a slight chuckle. "Go ahead, my child, go ahead and try."

Allison continued to writhe around in defiant rage and whipped her right leg up, swiftly landing between Langdon's slightly open legs. Langdon instantly gasped for air as the wind was knocked out of him from the hammering kick to his groin. "How did you like that? I bet that's the only action your drooping, wrinkled balls have seen in years, you miserable pervert!"

Langdon's strength was lowered as he tried to regain composure from the strike to his most sensitive body parts, giving Allison the ability to move out from under his restraining hands. She then made a fist with her right hand and swung it towards Celine's face. This wasn't the first time someone had taken a swing at Celine and she was fully alert and prepared this time. Celine caught Allison's right hook with her left hand, now having control over both of Allison's arms. Allison struggled to free her wrists from Celine's superhuman grasp, with no success. Langdon was doubled over, with both his hands resting on his knees, still trying to recover from the shock his groin had taken from Allison's slingshot leg. "Sheriff, your cuffs!" Celine ordered.

Langdon was still working on getting some of the strength and air back in his body. **"SHERIFF, YOUR CUFFS!!!! NOW!!!!!"**

When Langdon was finally able to muster up some semblance of strength, he reached his right hand around his back, flipped open the secured strap that held this handcuffs in place, grabbed hold of the heavy metal restraints, and stood upright. He began walking towards Celine when Allison's right leg kicked up in the air again.

Much like Celine, Langdon was prepared this time. He turned to his right to dodge Allison's ankle, but she caught him on his left butt cheek. This had less of an impact than the shot to his groin and didn't faze Langdon in the least. He moved towards the elevated stage to steer clear of Allison's lethally flailing leg and made his way around to Celine's back. While Celine held a strong grasp on Allison's wrists, Langdon reached over Celine's left forearm and fastened one of the handcuff's loops on Allison's exposed left wrist, then followed by attaching the other end of the handcuffs to Allison's right wrist. Allison shot up onto her feet and began wrestling away from both Celine and Langdon, but with no luck. Celine's trained grasp on Allison's wrists showed no sign of weakening.

Throughout her physical attempts to free herself from Celine's grasp, she kept

yelling the same thing over and over: "Girls are not supposed to play

baseball!!!!! Girls are not supposed to play baseball!!!!! **GIRLS ARE NOT**

SUPPOSED TO PLAY BASEBALL!!!!!"

Allison continued to kick her right leg through the air, hoping to find it connect

with Langdon or Celine, but the short pew wall created a shield between

Langdon, Celine, and Allison. At one point, Allison's foot wailed the side of the

pew, sending a surge of pain up through her leg, and she lost her balance. This

allowed Celine to tackle Allison onto the red-carpeted floor and kneel her

knees on top of Allison's forearms. Langdon reached around his back with his

left hand and produced the backup pair of handcuffs from their holder. He

moved around to Allison's legs, which were now flailing around, making it look

like she was swimming on the carpeted floor. Langdon found the momentary

opportunity to collapse down on Allison's legs with his knees, just below her

hips. He wrapped his right arm around both of Allison's shins and proceeded to

attach both sides of the handcuffs around her thin ankles.

Langdon got up to his feet and moved a few feet up until he reached the top of

Allison's head. He reached his right hand into a small pouch attached to the

right side of his belt and pulled out a key. Langdon proceeded to insert the key

into the small keyhole of the cuff around Allison's right wrist, disconnecting it and allowing the now empty cuff to dangle down. He reached over to Allison's

left wrist, inserted the key into the keyhole on that cuff, and removed the cuff

from her left wrist. He grabbed hold of Allison's right wrist and forced it around

to her back. Celine pushed Allison's left wrist down and behind her back.

Langdon attached both cuffs to Allison's wrists and when he was done, Celine

released her grasp from Allison's left wrist and both she and Langdon stood

upright.

"Now **THAT'S** one hell of a strong girl," Celine sighed.

"You can say that again, Doc," Langdon chuckled.

Allison continued to squirm and fight to free herself from the handcuff

restraints, but inside she knew she had absolutely zero chance of succeeding.

Allison settled down, resting her face against the red carpet, and began to

speak muffled, sobbing words: "Girls are not supposed to play baseball. Girls

are not supposed to play baseball!"

Langdon lifted his head up to the ceiling. He held it up there for about 10

seconds and began to lower it. When his head was halfway back down, he felt a

sharp feeling, like someone was staring at him. He turned to one of the glass

windows on his left and saw Jasper peeking through the window. His small legs were barely tall enough for Jasper to look into the window, but standing on his

tippy-toes gave him the ability to stare through to the dimly lit chapel, enough

so that his entire head could be seen.

Jasper wore the same sinister expression as all of the other times Langdon had

seen him throughout the course of that evening. Langdon gently elbowed

Celine, who was standing on his right, and then raised his right arm straight

out, pointing at the window where Jasper stood outside, peering in. Celine

followed Langdon's pointed finger until she caught Jasper looking through the

window. Celine's heart began to feel two times heavier, and her chest felt like

there was a swarm of butterflies racing around just behind her rib cage.

The next thing they saw was Jasper's right hand stealthily rising up in the air

with his fist clenched. Jasper gracefully raised his right index finger, held it

there for a few seconds, then slowly raised his middle finger and moved them

apart from each other. After about half a minute, Jasper lowered both fingers

and returned his hand back to a clenched fist. He began dropping his right arm

down when he jerked forward, let out a loud yelp, and then disappeared from

the window.

Langdon raced towards the window and peeked out to find Jackson lying on his back and applying a bear hug around Jasper's body. Jasper was writhing around in protest, but the strength of the 10-year-old boy was no match for the muscular Jackson. Langdon turned to his right and raced down the right side of the pews towards the door at the back of the chapel. Going through the doorway and out into the small hallway that he and Celine entered from, he turned left and bolted out through the doorway. He jumped off the right side of the concrete steps and continued running towards where Jackson was clutching young Jasper. Reaching the two, Langdon saw two shadowy hands appear from behind Jackson's neck. They wrapped around Jackson's throat with such force that he began to choke and fight for air. Jackson wasn't about to release his grasp around Jasper, as he didn't want the boy to flee. Langdon fell to his knees right next to where Jackson was laying and reached out to grab hold of the shadowy hands that were choking Jackson. When he went to grab them, he discovered that there was no tangible flesh to grab hold of as the shadow maintained its clutch around Jackson's throat. Langdon noticed that Jackson's throat was compressed and his skin pressed in towards his windpipe. Langdon believed that the only way to release those ghostly hands was to have Jackson release Jasper so he could run away. As much as he didn't want to do that, Langdon turned his attention towards Jackson's arms and proceeded to yell, "**JACKSON!!!! JACKSON!!!! LET HIM GO!!! LET HIM GO!!!!**"

Jackson paid no attention to the order his superior was giving, but instead squeezed the boy a little bit harder. Langdon wrapped his hands around Jackson's wrists and used all his strength to try and pry his hands apart. It felt like he was trying to loosen a rusty, frozen vise grip, to no avail.

Jasper's boyish shrieks changed to that low, villainous, satanic tone and began yelling out, "Let him go. Let the boy go. I will choke this sonofabitch and crush his windpipe if you don't release the boy. You better do something to this motherfucker before his life comes to an untimely end!"

Langdon could think of only one way to loosen Jackson's clutches, but hesitated. He watched as Jackson continued to fight for air, all the while never loosening his restraint around the boy. Langdon reached his right arm around to his right hip, took his night stick out from its holder, raised it up in the air, and slammed it down onto Jackson's arms with a mighty force. The solid wooden rod produced a massive shock of pain, causing Jackson to momentarily lose the strength in his arms. Jasper broke free from Jackson's restraints, rolled over to his right and off of Jackson's stomach, stood up, spit in Jackson's face, then turned towards Clarksville Road and ran off into the blackness of the night.

The shadowy hands disappeared from around Jackson's neck and Jackson began to cough violently as he fought to get air back into his lungs. Langdon's mighty blow had created a hairline fracture on Jackson's left ulna. Jackson reached his right hand over to his left arm and grappled onto his forearm, over the fractured bone. His face was red with pain that radiated up from his arm and he was rolling back and forth on his back.

"I'm sorry about that, Jackson," Langdon said. "It was the only way for you to free Jasper and have that shadowy apparition release its choking grasp from around your neck."

With tightly closed eyes and an expression of anguish, Jackson nodded his head in agreement, acknowledging his boss's reasoning for breaking his arm.

"Can you move at all? Do you think you can stand up?" Langdon asked.

Jackson's expression of sheer pain changed to one of affirmation. He nodded again, and Langdon reached his right hand under Jackson's left armpit and proceeded to guide Jackson back up to his feet. During the whole ordeal, neither Jackson nor Langdon was aware that Celine had made it out to where they were and witnessed the entire thing. Langdon felt her presence and turned his head to face Celine while he maintained a balancing support under

Jackson's armpit. Celine wore a puzzled expression. It was more than 10 seconds before she could mutter any words. When she did, she looked up at Langdon and said, "If I wasn't here, I would never have believed you, Sheriff. What the hell have we gotten ourselves into?"

Langdon responded in an agreeable tone, "Exactly, Doc . . . what have we gotten ourselves into."

"Sheriff to Rogers."

"Go for Rogers."

"Son, you need to get over here to Clarksville Missionary Church as soon as you can," Langdon ordered.

"Why's that, boss?" Rogers asked.

"We have Allison in custody and need you to come here right away. We believe she was involved in the events that transpired yesterday."

There was a long pause before a shocked voice came over the radio: "MY Allison, boss?"

"Yes, son, *your* Allison. We found her sitting in the chapel of the church. When we went to escort her out of the building, she became violent and struck both myself and Dr. Holden. We're both all right, but I think it best if you come over here and take your daughter into custody and bring her back to the station."

"Ummm," Rogers replied, "OK. I'll be right over."

Langdon looked over at Celine. "This is not good. Two of my finest officers' children performing such evil acts on two innocent kids. This is beyond any comprehension and reasoning."

Langdon looked over at Jackson, who was standing up with his head bowed down in disbelief as he heard Langdon speaking these words to Celine. Jackson raised his right hand to his face, covering his eyes, and began crying. "How could this be? How could my son possess such violent rage over something so petty? I didn't raise him to be a monster!"

Langdon looked over at Jackson, moved his head until his mouth was directly next to Jackson's left ear and said, "You didn't do anything to cause this. You are a great father and a wonderful role model. Sometimes, kids go astray. Unfortunately, in Zach's case, 'astray' doesn't even begin to describe his actions tonight. But none of this is **your** fault, son, you have to begin

acknowledging that." But Jackson only continue to weep uncontrollably.

Jackson picked his head up and looked into Langdon's eyes. "Do you know what

they do to child abusers in prison, boss? Do you have any idea what my son is

going to be facing when he is locked up? It might be the last time I see my son

alive." Jackson's tears began to flow over his face like the water over Niagara

Falls. "Do you have *any* idea of how that feels? My boy's entire future is

nonexistent! His fate waits for him behind those prison walls. He has

completely ruined his life, and I didn't do anything to stop it."

"How could you have stopped what you had absolutely no idea was

happening? All you knew was that your boy was a star athlete and a

respectable scholar. He never showed any signs of such wrath. If he did, we

would've picked up on it and made sure he got the help he needed. You *have*

to recognize that, son. You cannot blame yourself for any of this."

"I've lost my only boy, boss. Can't you understand that, boss? I've lost my only

boy!"

CHAPTER 20: JASPER'S LIBERATION

It was now 5:30 a.m. Standing outside of 113 Emerald Street and facing Ralph

Dubain's porch, Jasper sat dead center of the intersection of Emerald Street,

Chartiers Road, and Summit Street. Ralph was inside heating up some water in

the kettle on his stove. He was taking the coffee canister out from its place in

the cupboard over the kitchen sink when he caught a flickering light from out

of the corner of his right eye. With his arms still reached up to the shelf of the

cupboard, he turned his head to the right and paused there for a moment.

Ralph dropped the glass jar, which hit the hard, porcelain sink basin and

instantly shattered, sending granules of dry coffee grounds in the air like the

geyser at Yellowstone National Park. Ralph raced over to his broken living room

window, now covered with plastic drop cloth, crushing small shards of glass

scattered around the floor that was the result of Jasper's phantom's fury. There

he saw the streetlight flickering, and instantly noticed Jasper sitting in the

middle of the road. Jasper's head was hung down and the bangs of his blonde

hair hung over his face. Ralph concentrated on the streetlight's illuminated

message as it flickered more and more:

.-. . .--. . -. - / --- .-. / -.. .. . (pause) .-. . .--. . -. - / --- .-. / -.. .. . (pause) .-. . .--. . -. - /

--- .-. / -.. .. . The same message kept repeating. Ralph watched as this message flashed in a never-ending loop:

"Repent or die" (pause) "Repent or die" (pause) "Repent or die"

Recalling his conversation with Jasper and Jasper's haunting friend, Ralph

remembered the grimacing expression on the Mrs. Davis-Carpenter shadowy

figure (from behind the lamppost) and the authoritative tone blaming Ralph for

its unspeakable peril.

Ralph turned to his left, headed towards the front door, stepped outside, and

began approaching Jasper. The streetlight maintained its repeating sequence of

flashes, but rapidly increased the closer he got to the little boy sitting in the

center of the intersection. Upon reaching Jasper, Ralph knelt down in front of

the boy and asked, "What do you mean by repent or die? Are you suggesting

that *I* repent or I'll be faced with my own demise?"

Jasper sat there, motionless, and didn't respond to Ralph's inquiry. Ralph asked

again, "Jasper, what do you mean by repent or die?"

Jasper reached his right hand down, wedged it under his right thigh, and

retrieved a sharp butterfly knife that was hidden beneath his leg. He twisted

and spun the knife around in his hand until the blade was exposed and he was

clenching the handle that had holes bored out of it. He lifted his left hand in front of his face with the palm facing his eyes, brought the blade up to the tip of his index finger, and with a sharp downward motion, sliced through the flesh, instantly creating a waterfall of bright-crimson blood.

He lowered the knife down to his right side, dropped it to the ground, then positioned his left finger over the pavement. He began to draw out words using the blood as ink and his index finger as the pen. When he was done, he moved his left arm to his side and became motionless once again. Ralph looked down at what Jasper had scribed on the road with his own blood: "Blood for blood."

"Blood for blood? Whose blood for whose blood?" Ralph asked in a state of horror at what he'd just witnessed. This 10-year-old boy had just gashed his own tiny finger open with a lethal blade without showing any signs of pain or reaction to the self-inflicted wound.

Jasper didn't move. He didn't speak. He just sat on the ground with the back of his left hand resting on the pavement and blood pouring out from the cut he'd made on his left index finger. A pool of viscous, red blood began to form around his left hand. Ralph looked at the boy and said, "You'd better let me look at that. You cut yourself very deep. Here . . ." As Ralph went to grab the boy's left arm, Jasper whipped his left arm up, pulled his left index finger down from the top of its fingernail with his left thumb, then released the index finger, causing it to snap up and send blood flying through the air. The blood flew through the air like horizontal rain in a hurricane, splattering Ralph's face with crimson spots. Jasper's head remained hung down, with only his left arm, hand, and fingers moving that created this splattering action.

Jasper lowered his arm back down and rested the back of his left hand into the pool of blood that had formed from the deep gash that he'd created with his butterfly knife. Ralph jerked back when the blood hit him in the face, surprised at what the boy had just done. "What was that for?" Ralph asked. Still, the boy remained motionless and unresponsive. "Boy, you're going to bleed to death if you don't allow me to control that bleeding. Is that what you want?"

Jasper raised his left arm again, turned his wrist clockwise, extended his index finger, then lowered it to the pavement until he reached the last word in his message. He drew a straight, vertical line with his finger and bodily ink, lifted it up, held it there to allow more blood to collect on the tip of his finger, then moved it a couple inches down. He proceeded to press his finger down onto the pavement just below the vertical line he had just made. He lifted his hand up in the air and held his finger up in front of Ralph's face for a few seconds, then moved his left arm back, spun his left wrist counterclockwise, and rested the back of his left hand into the pool of blood, which was growing larger from the volume of blood flowing out from his index finger.

Ralph looked back down at the message which now read: "Blood for blood!" It was no longer a message of warning; it was now a message that had a strong emphasis assigned to it by Jasper creating the exclamation point at the end. The boy's body and head never moved during any of these actions. It was as if the boy was a human marionette being controlled by some disturbed wraith.

"But *who* has to repent? Me? I didn't do anything to cause this. I had no part in what they did over at Danvers. I wasn't even in the same state when that happened. How can you blame *me* for any of that?"

The streetlight stopped flashing its message it had been cycling through over and over again, and then the light went out. Ralph sat there in the cloak of night, anxiously waiting for a response from the streetlight. Moments later, the streetlight gave off a blinding burst of light that made Ralph close his eyes and turn his head to the right, down and away from the streetlight. There was blackness again for a little more than a minute before a new message began to flicker, then shut off after it delivered its message:

-.. . .- - .... / -... -.-- / .- ... ... --- -.-. .. .- - .. --- -.

"Death by association? What does that even mean?" Ralph asked inquisitively.

There was a long 2-minute gap before the streetlight produced another burst of blinding light. It went dark again for half a minute, then began to deliver a new flashing message before shutting off again:

.- ..- -. - / -.-. .-.. .- .. .-. .

Ralph sat and thought for a moment before speaking out into the night air, his breath crystallizing as he did: "What about my Aunt Claire? She's dead. How can she repent if she's dead?"

There was an eerie stillness in the atmosphere. Ralph began to hear the whistling of the tea kettle coming from inside of his kitchen and radiating through the shattered living room window. That was the only sound that filled the bitter November air. The streetlight began to flicker another message; this time, it was brighter and more powerful than any of the other times he'd seen previous messages delivered:

.-. . .--. . -. - / --- .-. / -.. .. .

"But how? How can Aunt Claire repent or die? She's not been alive for more than 50 years."

The biting-cold air began to penetrate through Ralph's skin and sink into his

aging bones. He began to feel a tightening discomfort as the chilled air took

hold of his sensations as his bones were consumed with cold. Ralph winced a

little, then the streetlight flashed on. Again, after the flickered message was

presented, it shut off.

.- -- --- -. - .. .-.. .-.. .- -.. ---

"Amontillado? You keep bringing this up. I already told you, I had no idea what

you were trying to tell me all those years ago when we were at Danvers. I

always treated you with the utmost respect and compassion. Why are you

doing this?"

Ralph looked back and forth in the night's blanket of darkness, needing to see a

message of reassurance. The streetlight released another burst of blinding

light, but this time, it also produced a thunderous sonic boom. As it had before,

the light delivered its message, then shut off:

. -..- -.-. ..- ... . / . -..- -.-. ..- ... .

"But I'm *not* making up any excuses. I was only nine years old. What did I know

of classic American literature? I was reading comic books back then."

The streetlight began to create a dim illumination, enough for Ralph to see

Jasper again. He had stood up while it was dark and Ralph couldn't see two

inches in front of his face. Jasper's left arm was raised straight out, his left

index finger extended, blood dripping down off the tip of it, and pointing

towards a small brick shed to the left and a short way beyond Ralph's house.

This structure was used to house ash and debris from the fireplace inside the

house. It was 9 feet long, 4 feet wide, and 3 feet deep; about the same

dimensions as a coffin. Ralph turned his head to followed Jasper's direction and

saw that he was pointing out towards that brick structure. Ralph whipped his

head back towards Jasper and asked with a frightened tone, "What about the

ash bin?"

There was no response from either Jasper or the streetlight. Ralph turned his

head again and the side light on the left side of the house just beneath the

roof's edge turned on, casting a highlight on the ash bin. Ralph snapped his

head back at Jasper and repeated his question: "What *about* the ash bin?"

The streetlight produced another blinding burst of light, accompanied by

another deafening sonic boom.

-.-- --- ..- .-. / ..-. .- - .

"My fate?" Ralph asked. "How is the ash bin associated with my fate?"

There was a very soft, gentle flashing of the streetlight as it delivered another

message.

.- .-. . / -.-- --- ..- / --. --- .. -. --. / - --- / .-.. . .--. . -. -

"No, I'm not going to repent. I have nothing to repent *for*. I did nothing wrong. I

couldn't ask you to repent for World War II, now could I?"

The streetlight's next message carried with it a furious brilliance of light.

- .... . -. / -.-- --- ..- / -- ..- ... - / -.. ... .

"Hold on a minute. Why must *I* die? I shouldn't be punished for the savage acts

of others! Tell me how any of this is fair."

With the same intensity as its previous message, the streetlight let out a

sequence of flashes, bright enough to rival flashes of lightning.

..-. .- .. .-. / .-.. .. ..-. . / .. ... -. .----. - / ..-. .- .. .-.

"Well, life might not be fair, but I shouldn't be blamed for that."

The streetlight calmed its intensity upon its next message, and then went

completely dark:

- .. -- . / - --- / -- . . - / -.-- --- ..- .-. / -- .- -.- . .-.

"Time to meet my maker? Oh, I don't think so."

The next thing Ralph felt was Jasper's tiny hands around his neck. Ralph heard

the clacking of the butterfly knife swinging and spinning in Jasper's hand, in the

manner that a trained individual opens a butterfly knife. Ralph couldn't see a

single thing because the streetlight had shut itself off. The clacking of the knife

stopped, and Ralph felt the razor-sharp blade pierce the left side of his neck.

Ralph screamed in agony as Jasper slowly turned the blade while it was impaled

two inches into Ralph's neck.

Ralph lifted his hands and planted them on Jasper's chest. He gave a forceful

shove, knocking Jasper back to the ground, but the butterfly knife's blade

remained in Ralph's neck. Ralph got up to his feet, but he was still unable to see

where the boy was. His intention was to restrain the young boy, but he couldn't

see a single thing. Ralph then heard small shuffling footsteps run by his left-

hand side and around to his back. Ralph spun around, following the noise that

came to a halt. Ralph reached both arms out in front of him and moved them

around, hoping they would land on Jasper so he could keep the boy from

attacking him any further. Ralph's neck was rapidly pouring blood out through

the puncture of the blade that was still in his neck. He knew better than to take the knife out of his neck or it would open up the vein even further, causing

Ralph to have only seconds before he passed out.

He continued to search through the darkness with his hands and arms, looking

to catch the boy. Ralph began to hear those tiny footsteps again, shuffling to

his left and working their way behind him. Ralph spun around to his left, his

arms still extended and whipping through the night air, but not having any luck

with catching the boy. The shuffling of the boy's Lilliputian feet began to move

around to Ralph's left again until they stopped behind him. This time, Ralph

wasn't quick enough to spin around and he felt Jasper leap onto his back,

wrapping his bony right arm around the right side of Ralph's neck, and

returning his left hand around the handle of the butterfly knife. Jasper

continued to twist the blade clockwise while Ralph hollered in absolute pain

through Jasper's debilitating mutilation.

Ralph reached his left arm back and grabbed hold of the section of Jasper's

pajamas that covered his left chest. He grabbed a handful of fabric and with all

his might, launched the boy up over his head and threw him out about 10 feet

in front of where Ralph was standing. There was a blinding pain from his neck,

and when Jasper hit the pavement, there was a clinking sound of the butterfly

knife slamming onto the frozen asphalt. It bounced a few times before it came

to rest, thus ceasing the sound of metal hitting pavement.

Ralph collapsed to the ground, landing on his knees and stopping his fall with

his hands. When Ralph had opened his hands to brace his fall to avoid face

planting into the pavement, he heard a different clicking tone right beneath his

chest. Ralph hung his head down and used his left hand to survey the area

where he'd heard the second clinking sound. His hand fell upon an oblong,

cold, metallic object that had a thin rod in the back with some of the fabric

from Jasper's flannel pajamas. There was a sudden burst of light from the

streetlamp, followed by an explosion of glass that sent shards of broken glass

out and over a 14-foot radius. In that one moment when the light burst

brilliantly and the high-pitched splintering of glass shrieked through the night,

Ralph saw Jasper laying on his back, his right leg bent underneath his backside,

his left leg lying straight out on the ground, his right arm resting on the

pavement up over his head, and his left arm draped across his chest. Jasper's

eyes were closed and he wasn't moving an inch. Ralph grabbed the metal

object in his hand, which he deduced was the petunia brooch affixed to

Jasper's left chest pajama top, and threw it in the direction of the streetlight.

He heard it hit a couple tree trunks that produced an echoing sound through

the air.

Ralph began to feel dizzy and weak. He reached his left hand up and applied

pressure to the gaping hole on the left side of his neck and began crawling towards Jasper's unconscious body, using only his right arm to support his

torso and his legs to propel him forward. When he reached Jasper, Ralph could

no longer fight the spell of weakness that he was succumbing to, and he

collapsed to the cold ground and passed out. Blood continued to pour out of

his neck and flow down to his shoulders, then chest, progressively making its

way all the way down to his feet. It wasn't too long before Ralph was laying in

his own blood.

In the distance, there were flashing red-and-blue lights combined with loud

sirens piercing through the stale winter's night. Langdon's car was the first one

to round the corner of Chartiers Road coming from the direction of Clarksville

Road. He arrived at the intersection of Emerald, Summit, and Chartiers streets

and saw the gruesome aftermath of Ralph and Jasper's confrontation.

Langdon slammed the brakes on, flung open the driver's-side door of the

cruiser, got out, and ran over to where Jasper was laying. Ralph was lying

lifelessly at the left foot of Jasper's leg. Max raced out and laid next to his

dying master. Jasper was breathing laboriously, but was alive.

McCormick was the second to arrive at the scene, followed by Celine. Jackson

and Rogers had taken their respective teenage children to the station.

Middleton was the last to arrive, as he had been radioed to meet Langdon,

McCormick, and Celine at the intersection of Emerald, Summit, and Chartiers.

Bringing his cruiser to a halt, slamming the gearshift into park, and pushing the

driver's-side door open, McCormick raced towards Langdon with a thick

blanket, handed it to him, then went over and knelt beside Ralph.

The headlights of the cars provided enough illumination for all of them to see

what lay before them. Middleton brought his car to a stop and put the car into

park. When he stepped out and saw the bodies lying on the ground, he reached

for his police radio, brought it up in front of his mouth, pressed the call button

and said, "Sheriff's department to EMS."

A few seconds after, there was a voice that came through the speaker of the

radio: "EMS to sheriff's department, what's going on, Jay?"

"I need two ambulances here at the intersection of Emerald, Summit, and

Chartiers as quick as you can," Middleton continued.

"We'll be there in a couple minutes. Hang tight."

The daylight was slowly beginning to break the horizon and the sirens and

lights had hypnotized and drawn some of the residents out, like the Pied Piper

leading the rats to water. Middleton and McCormick had already cordoned the area off with the yellow police tape and were keeping the nosy crowd at bay while the paramedics worked on Jasper and tended to Ralph's dead body. More and more residents began to appear at the scene, with some even arriving in their cars and wearing their pajamas, bathrobes, and slippers.

Ricky Stanley, an 11-year-old boy who lived in the first house on the left up Summit Street from the intersection of Chartiers Road, raced from his home across the long spread of lawn towards the intersection. Just before reaching the road he saw a shiny, metal object that was reflecting the dim morning sun. He bent down, picked it up, and realized it was a piece of jewelry. He unhooked the pin on the back of it, pierced it through his blue-and-grey Rabbit pajama top, hooked it back into the latch, pulled down on his pajama top to straighten out the fabric, then continued out onto Chartiers Road. He stopped next to one of his classmates who was standing next to his parents. Ricky turned to his friend, grabbed the bottom of the gold piece of jewelry he was now wearing, showed it to his friend, and said, "Look at this pretty pink flower."

DEDICATION

Many years after his passing, my dad continues to inspire me to move forward, take risks, and try my best at goals I am passionate about. Both he and my mom were constant sources of encouragement, support, love, and nurturing. Both made extensive sacrifices for all five of their children; and no one was ever chosen as a favorite.

Both my mom and dad did not have college degrees or any trade certifications, but they were successful in making sure each one of us kids had a memorable childhood. There are many experiences I could share that exemplified my dad's love for everyone he encountered. His degree of philanthropy and charity (in every form) was immeasurable. His character and compassion are traits that I continue to try to carry on his legacy through my own actions; although I fall short at times.

If I were to recall a single instance of his selflessness and incalculable kindness for others, it would be this. In the late spring of 1988, we were all sitting around the house when the phone rang. It was my cousin, in tears, because her prom date's car broke down while he was en route from Massachusetts. She did not want to miss her junior prom, but at the same time, did not want to attend alone. She had no other individual to ask and was consumed with a great sense of anxiety and heartbreak. My dad never hesitated and instantly thought of a way to resolve my cousin's misfortune. He asked my oldest brother if he'd be willing to go up to New Hampshire (two states away from where we lived) to attend our cousin's prom. My brother agreed. My dad and brother quickly went to a tuxedo rental store, where my dad rented a tux for my brother and then, from there, began their 3-hour trip up to New Hampshire. Before arriving at my aunt's place, my dad stopped and purchased a corsage for my cousin. My brother and dad arrived in time to pick up my cousin and get her to her prom, on time, and she had a memorable experience because of it.

This was just who my dad was. He was ingenious, spirited, and honorable.